# MURDER IN TOULOUSE

THE MAGGIE NEWBERRY MYSTERIES
BOOK 25

SUSAN KIERNAN-LEWIS

SAN MARCO PRESS

*Murder in Toulouse. Book 25 of The Maggie Newberry Mysteries.*

Copyright © 2024 by Susan Kiernan-Lewis

All rights reserved.

No part of this book may be reproduced in any form or by any electronic or mechanical means, including information storage and retrieval systems, without written permission from the author, except for the use of brief quotations in a book review.

Revenge may be a dish best served cold,
   but vengeance is best when it sizzles.

When Laurent gets word that his friend Antoine Dubois, head chef at a top culinary bistro in Toulouse was brutally murdered on the opening day of the city's famous Merguez Sausage Festival, he drives to Toulouse, determined to find the killer.

As Laurent interrogates staff and rival chefs, it becomes clear that more than reputations are at stake. When Maggie joins her husband in Toulouse to help in any way she can, she quickly vanishes without a trace and Laurent is told to stop looking for his friend's killer or she will die.

Maggie's job now is to stay alive and try to leave a trail of breadcrumbs for Laurent to follow. Working with the Toulouse police, Laurent must find Maggie in the treacherous Pyrenees mountains before it's too late. To do that he will have to outwit two cunning killers--Antoine's killer and the ones who kidnapped Maggie and who will stop at nothing to keep their crimes buried—including killing her.

In this edge-of-your-seat mystery infused with the rich culture and cuisine of southern France, Maggie will once more risk everything during a pulse-pounding game of cat and mouse high in the French alps.

## Books by Susan Kiernan-Lewis
### The Maggie Newberry Mysteries
Murder in the South of France
Murder à la Carte
Murder in Provence
Murder in Paris
Murder in Aix
Murder in Nice

Murder in the Latin Quarter
Murder in the Abbey
Murder in the Bistro
Murder in Cannes
Murder in Grenoble
Murder in the Vineyard
Murder in Arles
Murder in Marseille
Murder in St-Rémy
Murder à la Mode
Murder in Avignon
Murder in the Lavender
Murder in Mont St-Michel
Murder in the Village
Murder in St-Tropez
Murder in Grasse
Murder in Monaco
Murder in the Villa
Murder in Montmartre
Murder in Toulouse
A Provençal Christmas: A Short Story
A Thanksgiving in Provence
Laurent's Kitchen

**The Claire Baskerville Mysteries**
Déjà Dead
Death by Cliché
Dying to be French
Ménage à Murder
Killing it in Paris
Murder Flambé
Deadly Faux Pas
Toujours Dead

Murder in the Christmas Market
Deadly Adieu
Murdering Madeleine
Murder Carte Blanche
Death à la Drumstick
Murder Mon Amour
A Killable Feast

### The Savannah Time Travel Mysteries
Killing Time in Georgia
Scarlett Must Die
The Cottonmouth Club
A Haunting on Forsyth Street
Savannah is Burning

### The Stranded in Provence Mysteries
Parlez-Vous Murder?
Crime and Croissants
Accent on Murder
A Bad Éclair Day
Croak, Monsieur!
Death du Jour
Murder Très Gauche
Wined and Died
Murder, Voila!
A French Country Christmas
Fromage to Eternity
Crepe Expectations

### The Irish End Games
Free Falling
Going Gone
Heading Home

Blind Sided
Rising Tides
Cold Comfort
Never Never
Wit's End
Dead On
White Out
Black Out
End Game

**The Mia Kazmaroff Mysteries**
Reckless
Shameless
Breathless
Heartless
Clueless
Ruthless

**Ella Out of Time**
Swept Away
Carried Away
Stolen Away

# 1

There was something about the idea of a life well-lived that had always bothered Laurent.

Mainly, it was the question of what decided the matter? And then there was the question of what defined *well-lived*? He imagined most people would hold that living in the South of France was the epitome of the good life. Great weather, good food, plentiful wine. He'd been mulling over the idea of a life well-lived ever since he left Aix-en-Provence on his way to Toulouse. Maybe it was the purr of the road—the radio in the car didn't work—or just the hum of his own overactive brain as he tried to decompress from a summer that had been more fizzle than sizzle.

It was three-and-a-half-hours to Toulouse from his home in St-Buvard. He'd been driving for a little over two hours, yet he felt as if he'd only been on the road a matter of minutes. He glanced at the highway sign up ahead. *Toulouse 12 kilometers*.

Before he left this morning, he'd attributed his malaise to the frustrating work on the vineyard this year. It hadn't occurred to him that some of it might be connected to the actual *place* he was driving away from. The thought was startling.

*Does it take your whole body unspooling with every mile you put behind you before you to see how much you needed this?*

Laurent shook his head in bemusement as he took the exit ramp toward Toulouse. He'd have to mention that to Maggie when he called her tonight. She'd tease him that he was becoming more American, like her. The thought made him smile. He rolled down his window to let the crisp mountain air fill his lungs as he took in the beauty of the Pyrenees Mountain range in the distance. She'd been right about this, too, he thought. He'd needed to get away.

Minutes later after he'd turned a corner off the access road from the highway Toulouse seemed to abruptly present itself. Known as "La Ville Rose" due to its distinctive terracotta-brick architecture, Toulouse always felt to Laurent like a combination of history and modern life. It was a hub of aerospace innovation, the home to one of the oldest universities in Europe, and renowned for its arts and culinary scene. Truly a Renaissance city, Laurent mused. He followed the Garonne River, its banks dotted with wide paved promenades and parks.

He tried to remember the last time he'd visited Toulouse. It wasn't a long drive. He should have brought Maggie and Amelie with him. He quickly amended that thought. Amelie didn't yet travel well, and Maggie intended this weekend to be one where Laurent truly relaxed. Amelie and relaxation didn't exist together in the same galaxy. He smiled at the thought of Maggie and her determination that he take some time for himself. Nobody worked harder than she did, but she was always ready to pick up a load that didn't belong to her.

Within moments, he found himself maneuvering through crowds packing the Place du Capitole, a sprawling square dominated by the majestic Capitole de Toulouse, the town's city hall and the epicenter this weekend for the opening day of Toulouse's famed Merguez sausage festival. The town was laid out in a series of streets emanating from the square and currently overflowing with a lively presentation of colors and energies as people of all nationalities milled about to celebrate the famous sausages or just to enjoy good food. Each street Laurent passed was decorated with bright banners and flags and lined with food stalls, themselves adorned with colorful signs and enticing displays of mouthwatering sausages. People swarmed the square holding plates piled high with sausages. Many were dressed in the colorful traditional Pyrenees costume with clogs and turbans or dressed in *vestido de flamenco* to honor Toulouse's proximity to Spain.

Laurent drove through the winding streets until he found the address of his bed and breakfast located just off the town center. He left his bags in the car, deciding he'd check in after he'd explored a bit first. Truth be told, the sizzling aroma of sausages, combined with the scent of frying garlic and onions had prompted a visceral reaction in Laurent as his stomach growled in anticipation. He'd already stopped for a snack on the way to Toulouse and had a table reserved at Antoine's award-winning restaurant tonight at eight 'o'clock, but he was still more than ready to eat.

The air was thick with the rich and spicy aroma of the famous Merguez sausages as he made his way to the center of the festival. He stopped at the first kiosk he came to and watched the flames from open grills licking the sausages and lamb roasts, their smoky aromas mingling with the scent of exotic sauces. Fat links of the famous Merguez sausage lined the large grill—which was nearly four meters wide. He ordered two. They came on fluffy buns that had been baked that morning. Eschewing mustard since he knew the nuance of the sausages would be lost under its overpowering coating, he ate the first sausage in a few bites—each one bursting with flavor, a perfect balance of spiciness and savory meat. He imagined that every vendor would be offering their own recipes to provide a unique twist on the traditional sausage.

He walked around the square, observing all the different kiosks and stands. Most were offering grilled sausages but there were also mulled wine stands, falafel kiosks, *crêperie* stalls, piroshki stands, and even steaming, fragrant paella sold by the individual pan.

Laurent finished his second sausage and bought another made of cured pork loin seasoned with cinnamon and garlic. He leaned against a stone pillar while he ate it. He looked around the square until he spotted a stand selling a selection of local artisan beers and headed in that direction. He had hours to kill before meeting up with Antoine at *L'Étoile Gourmande*—his friend's restaurant and Toulouse's crowning jewel in the city's culinary offerings.

He'd known Antoine Dubois from their days working the Côte d'Azur. They'd been close then but had lost touch in the intervening years. In the meantime, it was clear from what Laurent had read over the years that his old friend had done well for himself. It had been too long since the two of them had spoken. With his own work on the vineyard behind him for the year and only maintenance of the vines and an annoying melee of local politics to plague him for fall and winter, Laurent really needed to try to shake off his bad year. Normally, he would've refused the opportunity to walk away from his worries, but Maggie had been quite adamant that he take this weekend for himself. After all, they were raising his granddaughter, and Amelie wasn't an easy child. Maggie's insistence that he leave for the weekend was all the more generous because of that. But guilt aside for leaving her to deal with Amelie's shenanigans on her own, Laurent had to admit her plan seemed to be working. Ever since he'd been in town, he felt better. In fact, there was a distinct possibility that he'd begun to feel relaxed the moment he'd pointed his Citroen away from St-Buvard.

He wouldn't bother trying to decipher that phenomenon. For once, he was just going to sit back and enjoy what was happening all around him. And perhaps check out the *paella* stand.

# 2

Maggie shivered as she watched the trees that lined the long drive to their *mas* tremble in the breeze, shedding many of their leaves even though it was barely September. She turned back to her kitchen and wiped up luncheon spills from the counter while keeping an eye on Amelie who was attempting to brush one of their two dogs. The child was very intent on making a proper job of it and the dog—a Cavalier King Charles mix and a poodle blend—were patient and long-suffering.

From where Maggie stood a double set of French doors opened out onto a graveled courtyard with a heart-stopping view of the rolling vineyards beyond—over two hundred hectares of local grape and lovingly pruned and tended vines—and another fifteen hectares of sprawling lawn punctuated with olive, plum, fig, and cypress trees.

Laurent's vineyard was as neat and tidy as a hausfrau's linen closet, she thought with a smile. Every row was weeded, every mound raked, every stripped bough of grapes was now staked as meticulously as a careful line of stitches in the earth. Maggie wasn't surprised that Laurent gardened the way he cooked—with organized fervor. Their kitchen rarely had a spoon or sauce pan out of place.

She couldn't help but recall how she'd felt twenty-eight years ago about the vineyard and its surrounding grounds when she first moved to Domaine St-Buvard. The idea of moving in had been sold to her as a temporary situation until Laurent could sell the property he'd recently inherited. She and Laurent had only known each other barely a year and Maggie was eager to get back to the US to resume her career at one of Atlanta's top advertising agencies. Things hadn't quite worked out that way.

She'd hated Domaine St-Buvard in the beginning. Of course, that had been before Laurent renovated the kitchen and the bathrooms. Back then, it had all been very primitive. That first year in Provence had been an eye-opening education. As had living with Laurent. But they'd traversed the highs and the lows of an ex-pat marriage. They'd battled the elements and each other. The children had come—first Jemmy and then Mila and then Luc although he was the oldest of all of them. And throughout it all, Maggie had forced herself to see what Laurent saw when he looked at this land. And when she did, she realized that nothing else back home could compete with its beauty or its history. From the dusty village roads to the endless fields of lavender to the dramatic evidence of Roman architecture that seemed to materialize at the oddest moments. Had she ever had her breath snatched away shopping for plums in Atlanta? (Had she ever even shopped for plums in Atlanta?) That happened daily here.

After five years of living surrounded by all this natural beauty—not to mention what the Romans had brought to the table over a thousand years ago—Maggie had finally gotten to the point where she decided she was happy where she was. And all the losses she had tallied on her long list of *things she had left behind* seemed like nothing to her now when she saw all that she had.

And at the very top of *that* list of course was Laurent.

She stepped through the dining room and opened the French doors and both dogs immediately shot outside and raced for the fields, Amelie right behind them. Maggie saw Amelie hesitate for a moment and then turn to look back at Maggie. The child knew her boundaries. Of course, she did. Otherwise, how would she constantly be able to test them?

"They'll come back," Maggie told the child.

She turned her attention to the state of the courtyard. There had been a storm last night and she'd yet to pick up the debris from the terrace. She walked down the gravel path to where a large stone dining table sat underneath a canopy of tall plane trees bordered by a full bed of marigolds and geraniums. Maggie had long since given up trying to grow azaleas and gardenias, which for years she had planted every spring and watched die every summer. Now she tended to pots of lemon trees and bougainvillea bushes that were offset by the shrubs of lavender and rosemary that grew wild around the property. On the north side of the courtyard Laurent had established his herb garden tucked neatly into a side corner against the house.

Laurent was the cook in the family and his *potager* was lovingly tended and designed for easy access. It was an endless source of thyme, basil, lemon verbena, and several different kinds of rosemary. Amelie stood at the edge of the terrace and shielded her eyes, looking for the dogs. A strong breeze set her dark hair flying around her face. Their home, a one-hundred-year-old *mas,* was solidly constructed of stone and made to withstand the powerful *Mistral.*

Sometimes Maggie swore she could smell the *Mistral*, that icy-cold wind that came down the Rhône River Valley from the Alps to jolt the sun lovers of Provence back to their senses. As she sat on the stone knee wall that hemmed the terrace, she found herself pulling her cotton cardigan tighter around her shoulders. It was still warm these days. She wouldn't really feel the chill for another month at least. But still, it was coming. The little poodle mix *Fleur*, raced back from the vineyard and jumped into Maggie's lap. She had a few twigs and leaves in her fur which Maggie plucked out.

From where she sat, she could see the silhouette of grape vines and imagined seeing the form of her husband—always the tallest figure in any grouping—walking his vineyard which he did most mornings and evenings. The harvest was done for the year, and everyone was ready to breathe a sigh of relief. The grapes were in and off to be processed. Maggie always loved to watch Laurent when he was busy focused on his passions—the vineyard or cooking—especially during those moments when he was unaware of her.

She smiled at the thought his natural grace of movement which belied his size—at just a tad over six foot five. He was like a large cat who knew exactly how much space he took up. Silent as a panther and, depending on who he was dealing with, nearly as dangerous. Even as he aged—and she'd seen that, too—Laurent still appeared powerful to her. Or perhaps that was just his natural affect. A taciturn man, he embodied the principle of *speak less and do more*. One never really knew what he was thinking. Sometimes that drove her mad. Other times she found herself intrigued and seduced by it. After all these years.

Amelie came over and sat down next to her. She reached over to pet *Fleur*.

"When is *Opa* coming home?" she asked, a discontented tone in her voice.

"Tomorrow night," Maggie said. "I told you that."

Laurent's nights out were rare and his days away even rarer. Maggie hated to begrudge him the few he did take. Besides his monthly co-op meetings in Aix where all the *vignerons* collaborated and exchanged notes for the area's various grape harvests, and his one night a week at *Le Canard*, the local pub in St-Buvard, he almost never went out after dark.

She'd checked her cellphone an hour ago but there were no text messages from Laurent. Not that that was unusual. Laurent, although not exactly anti-technology, was resistant to it. Half the time he left his cellphone behind at restaurants, or in taxicabs and public restrooms.

"Can I swim, *Mami*?" Amelie asked.

Amelie's delicate features were framed by a cascade of chestnut brown hair, which fell in soft waves around her face. Her large, expressive eyes, the color of deep forest green, seemed to hold the weight of her thoughts, giving her a contemplative look that was unusual for someone so young.

"Are your chores done?" Maggie asked her.

Amelie energetically bobbed her head in the affirmative. Maggie knew she should check. Laurent would. Half the time Amelie fibbed. Perhaps more than half the time. The child claimed it was just easier, as if she were the sole arbitrator of proper behavior for any given situation and telling the truth was simply one tool in her arsenal with no moral judgement attached to it. Maggie understood the child's logic. Telling the truth took longer. And it often got Amelie into trouble. But they were having such a nice afternoon, Maggie decided to let it go.

She watched Amelie run into the house to get her swimsuit as if chasing the promise of childhood itself. And for that moment as she watched her go, Maggie couldn't help but feel that right at this moment in time, all was fairly perfect with her world.

# 3

The sun, still high in the sky, cast a soft, golden glow as Maggie sat half dozing in the pool chair. Looking up, she could see that golden glow infusing the surrounding vineyards with a radiant effect. She was nearly inspired to get her camera to photograph it. Instead, she watched Amelie race around the pool—regardless of how many times Maggie admonished her not to.

"Amelie, don't run!" Maggie said sharply. "We don't have time for an emergency room visit today."

Amelie turned to look at her and grin. She was never deliberately disobedient. But she had her own internal engine driving her, her own compass of moral direction. Maggie had no doubt the child loved her and Laurent—but that didn't mean she would mind them if minding them went counter to her plans. More than her own children, Maggie imagined that Amelie would either be a captain of industry or an artist. She didn't like rules and she loved to lead. Laurent was besotted with her.

Maggie often thought that if Laurent's own childhood hadn't been perverted in the way that it had with an abusive father and an absent mother then Amelie in boy form was who he might have been as a child. A male Amelie, intrigued by the world and not yet scarred by it, going forward led largely by his own compass, his own irrepressible confidence.

"Watch me, Mami!" Amelie called as she scampered over to the diving board.

Laurent had put the pool in eight years ago. It was surrounded by a mosaic tile terrace. Maggie was surprised to find that she used it nearly as much as the children. With their orderly rows of lush green vines, Laurent's vineyards were the perfect background for the backyard garden pool —an omnipresent reminder of the region's rich winemaking traditions, adding to the sense of timelessness and connection to the land.

Maggie frowned as she studied the vineyard and thought of how that very connection to the land had driven Laurent for so many years. Until now.

As she watched Amelie jump off the diving board, Maggie couldn't help but remember when Mila was her age and what a proud papa Laurent had been. To both his children, of course, but especially when they were small. As they grew, his trademark stubbornness couldn't withstand the preferences and individual dreams of his children. Jemmy was first, breaking Laurent's heart by dismissing out of hand the idea of working with Laurent in the vineyard or running Domaine St-Buvard with him. Instead, Jeremy had settled in Atlanta after college.

In some ways, it was Luc's rebellion that had been even harder for Laurent to accept. His nephew by blood, Luc had lived in foster homes and on the street until he was fourteen when he came to live with Maggie and Laurent. He and Laurent were close, and Luc's passion for the vineyard at St-

Buvard—something that Jemmy had never shown—had led Laurent to believe that Luc would come home after college to manage the vineyard with him. It had been seven years since Luc went to California for college. Afterward, he got an internship at a prominent American winery on the west coast, married the boss's daughter, and simply stayed.

That left Mila, the apple of Laurent's eye. When she left for college, she promised to come back to work the marketing and promotional side of the business. She'd since graduated college before going on to receive a degree as a *sommelier*. That was five years ago, and still there was no mention of returning to Domaine St-Buvard except for holidays and a few weeks in the summer.

Sometimes Maggie found herself marveling that the very man who had never expected or wanted children, had become so enrapt with his own that *his* case of empty nest syndrome had rivaled her own when they all finally left home. She knew how much Laurent missed them so that the opportunity to raise his granddaughter was more boon than burden. Yes, it was harder this time around—they were both older and they tired more easily. But they were also able to take it more slowly this time too. Instead of the frazzled balance of school and work with small children and their activities, this time there was more time to focus on Amelie. Which was good because Amelie needed more than the others had.

Just then Maggie's cellphone rang. She snatched it up, hoping it might be Laurent, but saw it was her best friend Grace who managed a *gite* a few miles away.

"Hey," Grace said when Maggie answered. "Any interest in coming over for a cookout in the garden tonight?"

"Sure," Maggie said. "Sounds like fun. What is Philippe up to?"

Philippe was Grace's thirteen-year-old grandson who she had raised from a toddler.

"He'll be here," Grace said. "Bring the dogs. In fact, pack a bag and spend the night why don't you?"

Maggie glanced at Amelie who was standing under one of the ancient yews in the back garden examining a chrysalis. Amelie had trouble making friends in school for various reasons, but Philippe was always patient with her—even when the result was less than pleasant for him. Maggie still remembered the black eye Philippe had sported for a week last spring after being in the middle of one of Amelie's not infrequent tantrums. But Maggie knew part of Amelie's problem was that she was lonely. As much as she was capable of amusing herself, what she really needed was more people in her life.

"That sounds like a great idea," Maggie said. "What can I bring?"

## 4

Laurent pushed open the door to *L'Étoile Gourmande*. The tantalizing scent of sautéed garlic and onions and cooking wine enveloped him, instantly drawing him in. Once inside he registered the cozy atmosphere, the warm lighting, and the murmur of animated conversations all around which instantly projected an ambiance that gave a feeling of refuge from the outside world.

*Well done, Antoine.*

The food would be good. Laurent knew that without doubt. But this feeling of safety, of respite from the crazy world outside the doors? T*his* was why *L'Étoile Gourmande* was packed every night, why it was the most popular restaurant in Toulouse. Laurent gave his name to the hostess and was immediately led through a sea of linen-covered dining tables to his table. Immediately he felt as if he'd been here before such was the undefinable feeling of comfort in familiar surroundings that couldn't really be familiar at all. Antoine's bistro felt like a sanctuary. That was quite a feat.

*Anyone can cook and some people can cook amazingly. But to make them feel at home? That is a gift.*

As he settled in at his table, Laurent turned his head to note that the restaurant was a melting pot of cultures, with locals and tourists intermingling, their conversations blending into a symphony of languages. All of it—the conversations blending harmoniously with the clinking of glasses and the melodious notes of soft jazz playing in the background, reminded Laurent of the simple pleasure of human connection. The bistro's reputation for exceptional cuisine had attracted a diverse clientele and not just tourists although there were plenty of them. Locals clearly reveled in the opportunity to savor innovative interpretations of classic regional dishes, while the tourists hungered to indulge in an authentic taste of Toulouse's gastronomic heritage.

Laurent's gaze wandered to the walls adorned with photographs that captured the spirit of Toulouse—its iconic landmarks, its festivals, as well as the faces of several of the city's residents.

The attentive staff, whether male or female, wore crisp white shirts and black aprons, and moved gracefully between tables, ensuring that every guest felt welcomed and attended to. Laurent himself felt a mix of gratitude and weariness. For a brief moment, he found himself forgetting the stresses and responsibilities of his life back in St-Buvard and found pleasure in the simple joy of anticipation and community within these walls.

As he glanced at the menu, Laurent was impressed with its simplicity but also its depth in describing the culinary journey that showcased the chef's creativity and mastery. Each dish was made with the finest local and seasonal ingredients, from delicate *amuse-bouches* to the more famous and meticulously plated main courses that made every bite a revelation. Antoine was a genius at this, Laurent realized. This was his *métier*, the thing he'd been born to do. The thought gave Laurent a sudden pinch of wistfulness.

Despite the constant buzz of activity all around. him, the restaurant managed to maintain an intimate and convivial atmosphere. Tables were arranged to allow for comfortable conversations and shared moments, fostering a sense of camaraderie among diners. It shouldn't have worked. But it did.

"Laurent, *mon ami*!" Antoine exclaimed as he made his way through the table groupings to Laurent's table. "You are here!"

As Antoine approached, Laurent caught the genuine warmth in his friend's eyes and felt viscerally moved. It had been too long—a decade at least—since they'd last seen each other. He returned Antoine's smile and the two men shook hands.

"Antoine, my friend," Laurent said. "You have done well. Your place is *extraordinaire*."

Antoine beamed at Laurent's praise. He'd aged since Laurent had known him, Laurent noted, but he'd done so gently. His dark hair was shot through with silver and his eyes sparkled amid the fine lines that told Laurent there had been much laughter in Antoine's life.

"Thank you, my friend. It was a labor of love, yes? A labor I enjoyed every minute of," Antoine said.

"It is the only kind to have. You have much to be proud of."

Antoine didn't sit and Laurent hadn't expected him to.

He knew the man had a busy night in front of him. There would be time later to fully visit.

"Order the veal, yes?" Antoine said. "And do not insist on the bill. I stand firm on this!"

Laurent laughed.

"Thank you, *mon vieux*," Laurent said. "I will order the veal."

"We will talk later, yes? It will be late."

"Late is fine," Laurent said.

# 5

The rustic wooden table, adorned with a vibrant floral tablecloth, was set at the center of the outdoor dining area in Grace's back garden. The area was surrounded by fragrant lavender bushes, and Maggie always thought it was a scene straight from a postcard. The air was infused with the sweet aromas of grilled vegetables and freshly baked bread.

Grace VanSant, pushing back an errant golden tendril from her face as she expertly tended the sizzling food on the grill. Philippe and Amelie, their laughter echoing through the air, played nearby with the dogs while Maggie and Danielle watched from their seats at the table. Maggie enjoyed seeing Amelie running around the yard carefree and happy. Grace's grandson Philippe was careful not to overstimulate or trigger the girl—so easy to do, Maggie knew—but neither did he act as if he preferred to escape indoors to play with his electronic devices as almost any other boy his age might.

Her silver hair catching the last rays of sunlight as she sat beside Maggie, Danielle Alexandre smiled as she watched the children play. In her seventies, Danielle was slim, elegant, and still very involved in helping Grace manage the property. She had come to live with Grace ten years earlier when Laurent first gave *Dormir* to Grace to run. When she arrived, Danielle had brought with her a strong sense of practicality and a level of stability that Grace's little family desperately needed at the time. Grace often said she had no idea how she'd managed before Danielle came to *Dormir*.

Grace turned off the grill and wiped her hands on a hand towel. Maggie always thought that Grace, who personified the elegance of her namesake Princess Grace of Monaco, was beautiful even when she was up to her elbows in one of the cottage toilets.

"Philippe! Amelie!" Grace called. "Wash your hands, please. Dinner's ready."

Both children raced into the house, the dogs at their heels. Maggie was pleased to see that for once Amelie didn't argue with an adult giving any kind of direction.

"Amelie has come a long way, *chérie*," Danielle said as she patted Maggie's hand.

Maggie knew it was true. Amelie was still half wild but when Maggie remembered how she'd been when she'd first come to live with them...in those moments, she was amazed at the power of love and regular meals.

In less than a minute, both Philippe and Amelie were at the table and taking their seats, their eyes wide with anticipation of the feast that lay before them. Danielle said grace and smiled dotingly on Philippe once she finished. That was hardly a surprise, Maggie thought with a smile. Childless herself, Danielle had helped raise Philippe since he was two years old.

"This looks *superbe!*" Philippe said to Grace. "I love lamb!"

An expressive, intelligent boy, Philippe's skin was light brown, heralding his mixed heritage. His eyes were large and expressive and his grin constant and infectious.

"I know you do, angel," Grace said. "You're half the reason I made it tonight."

Maggie glanced at Philippe as he put his napkin in his lap and helped Amelie with hers. The boy knew he was adored. Not just by Danielle and Grace but also by his aunt Zouzou who lived in Paris. He hadn't seen or heard from his mother, Grace's older daughter, since Taylor dropped him off with Grace ten years earlier. He'd never met his father either—a drunken one-night stand. Maggie knew that Grace watched him carefully, ready to help him understand his complicated history when he was ready to hear it and not pushing him in case he never was. She had to believe that the love they swamped him with at *Dormir* would someday protect him from the truth.

The dinner was noisy but full of laughter as they ate the grilled lamb and roasted vegetables. Maggie watched Amelie slip morsels under the table to the three dogs but forced herself not to scold her. Soon twilight descended, turning the sky into a tapestry of rich purples and oranges. Maggie eased back into her chair with her glass of wine. It was a beautiful garden and one that Grace had every right to be proud of.

Laurent had bought the house and property from Danielle ten years ago when she first became widowed and wanted a smaller place. He had it in mind to turn the land back into a viable vineyard—there were twenty-five acres of good grapes—and the house and its outbuildings into a working bed and breakfast. Renovated now to include three holiday mini-cottages in addition to the main cottage, its plumbing updated and new kitchen and swimming pool added, *Dormir* today was a profitable and popular bed and breakfast.

Grace was recently divorced when Laurent offered the property to her to run as a business. She had desperately needed the income along with a place to raise her then ten-year-old daughter, Zouzou. Up until Laurent gave her *Dormir* to run, Grace had never worked a day in her life. Maggie always found that astonishing since today Grace was the hardest working person she knew besides Laurent himself.

"Mami," Amelie said breathlessly standing next to Maggie with her empty plate in her hands. "Can I bring out the *tarte*?"

Maggie hesitated. Amelie had good intentions, but she did everything fast and often with little attention to care or detail. Danielle had made the lemon *tarte*—Grace didn't bake—and the last thing Maggie wanted was to ruin the evening by seeing Danielle's creation upside down on the slate terrace.

"Oh, let her," Grace said, nodding at Amelie who instantly ran to the kitchen. "If you don't let her drop a few pies, how is she ever going to learn?"

Maggie knew she was right but still, it had been many years since she'd had to worry about dropped pies. Before Amelie arrived, life had gotten very tidy.

"Besides, darling," Grace said with a laugh. "We always have ice cream if it ends up under the table."

"Good point," Maggie said.

Maggie admired Grace's ability to pivot and shake off

annoyances or sudden changes in plans. She and Grace were radically different people in that way. Maggie was the down-to-earth, practical one. She often paid little attention to her wardrobe, usually wearing the same clothes multiple days running. She barely noticed her hair, trusting it to do as it pleased. After living twenty-five years in a foreign country with villagers who always had an opinion and usually a negative one, she'd learned not to concern herself unduly with what other people thought of her.

Grace, on the other hand, was always perfectly coifed, and generally focused on appearances—both hers and anybody else's—including clothes, furnishings, her hair, and without doubt what people thought of her.

And yet the things that bound the two of them together —their love for their children, their mutual respect for each other and their very differences—connected them to each other closer than sisters. In the early years they used to talk about what they missed about life in the States, but as they grew into their roles in France they talked less and less about that.

Maggie watched as Amelie carefully walked out of the kitchen, her little face frowning with concentration as she carried the large *tarte* in her hands. Maggie revisited Grace's words and forced herself to smile. If Amelie dropped it, a look of horror or woe from Maggie would do nothing to help Amelie learn the lesson to be more careful. It would only underscore in Amelie's mind that she was not good enough.

Philippe ran to the table with his dog Kip beside him, nearly jostling Amelie as she concentrated on not dropping the *tarte*. By the time she deposited it safely in front of Danielle for cutting, the first thing Amelie did was look at

Maggie with pride. And Maggie was so glad she'd been smiling and not holding her breath when the child did.

"Well done, darling," Maggie said to her.

"Can Kip have a piece?" Philippe asked Grace.

Grace shook her head.

"Give him a piece of bread if you need to," she said. "I don't think dogs and citrus mix well."

Maggie remembered four years ago when Philippe had begged Grace for the puppy and Grace had finally relented not at all sure *she* wouldn't be taking care of Philippe, the bed and breakfast and a new puppy. But Philippe had risen to the task, taking full responsibility for the dog's care and surprising everyone by his maturity. She remembered Grace commenting at one point: *he's nothing like his mother.*

Maggie looked at Grace who sat at the head of the table gazing at her grandson as he fed his dog a piece of bread. It was a good life here in Provence, Maggie found herself thinking out of the blue. For all of us. While Grace and her ex-husband had tried not long ago for a second chance, it hadn't worked out. Since then, Windsor had gone on to marry again back in the states and was once more expecting another child. The first time he'd moved on after Grace, gotten remarried and had a baby with his new wife, Grace had hit rock bottom. But she'd come back to Provence where she and Maggie had first met. Then, when Laurent held out a hand for her to get back on her feet, she'd taken it.

These days, Maggie knew Grace dated men from time to time, but she also knew she'd never seen her friend as happy as these last months when she was clearly content just to run her business, raise her grandson and enjoy the wealth of her relationships with Maggie and Danielle.

Maggie took in a sigh to fully relax into the moment.

Danielle cut wedges of the *tarte*, chatting with the children as she fed bits of crust to the dogs, clearly happy to be surrounded by the people she loved. With the light fragrance of late-season lavender still drifting in the air and the scent of the dried rosemary branches Grace had used to grill the lamb, Maggie found herself thinking how marvelous it was that she and Grace had gotten so much more than they'd wished for all those years ago.

# 6

Antoine left Laurent's table to greet and mingle with the other tables surrounding him. Most of them were full of tourists, but Antoine knew it was all part of the game to shake hands and smile. They were there to see the magic they'd read about. Antoine knew it wasn't just what was on the plate.

Seeing Laurent again had been almost physically painful. Antoine wasn't surprised to see that Laurent looked and behaved much the same as he remembered him. But there was a difference. Subtle, but it was there. Laurent was a family man with a successful wine business. He wasn't running from the law, or disguising himself from his enemies, or worried for his family's safety. In fact, he looked as if he were a man at peace with the world.

As Antoine headed back to the kitchen, he felt a prickling on the back of his neck. By the time he reached the swinging doors of the kitchen and stepped inside, he realized that he'd honestly felt joy at seeing Laurent. As prosperous and content as Laurent appeared to be, Antoine knew he wasn't nearly as successful or famous as Antoine himself. That was something to hold close, to savor and enjoy.

He stood behind the swinging door for a moment, shielded from the curious eyes of the crowded dining room, and peered through the small round porthole, his eyes settling on Laurent who was focused on the menu. Yes, there were many years distance between them. Physically, Laurent looked much the same. There was no stoop to his shoulders with the added years, his face was tanned from working outdoors, his eyes as sharp as ever. Perhaps there were a few more lines around his eyes. That surprised Antoine. Did he remember Laurent laughing in the old days? He'd obviously laughed since then. Antoine shook his heard. To imagine Laurent domesticated like this, being allowed out for the weekend—by his American wife! of all things—was nearly as satisfying as anything else Antoine had observed tonight.

As he stood at the door with the bustle of his kitchen behind him, Antoine shifted his focus away from Laurent and found himself looking for someone else. There was that uncomfortable tingle again, like a feeling of misgiving or a premonition that someone was watching him. He scanned the dining area but saw only couples. Except for Laurent, everyone was with someone else. They were all laughing, drinking, talking, eating. Nobody was looking for him. Nobody was trying to find him. But how to explain this feeling of being watched?

His eyes swept the dining area again, his gaze lingering on anyone who seemed out of place. His mind raced, weaving intricate narratives of conspiracy and danger as he scanned and rescanned every diner, individually and in pairs. A bead of sweat trickled down his temple, and he felt his palms becoming clammy. His chest tightened.

There was a man standing by the hostess stand. Was he alone? Was that him? Antoine narrowed his eyes. Did he recognize him? Was he just asking for dinner times? Was he lingering? Except for the moustache, the man himself was nondescript.

*But he would be, wouldn't he?*

If Antoine were to step out of the kitchen, would the man's gaze redirect from the hostess to meet his own? Or would he slink into the shadows to avoid being caught watching?

*Am I losing my mind?*

∼

The man by the hostess stand scanned the room, his eyes lingering on the details—the arrangement of tables, the location of the kitchen, and the flow of the staff. A slight smile played across his lips. When it did, he felt the fake mustache on his top lip tickle and then itch. He resisted the urge to adjust it. He didn't expect to be recognized. The diners were focused on their Michelin Star meals in front of them; the runners and waiters were focused on getting the plates to the table still hot. It occurred to him that he could probably come undisguised, and no one would notice. Or remember him.

He'd seen Antoine stop at the table of a big man dining alone. The two had shook hands warmly which was surprising. He didn't recall Antoine having any real friends. He'd been tempted to move closer to get a better look at the mystery man. From just the size of him he was sure he wasn't from Toulouse. He'd have remembered him if the man was local.

He dragged his attention away from the big man and, feeling a strange unease tug at his instincts, looked in the direction of the kitchen where he knew the cooks and sous chefs were manically working to create Antoine's vision of his culinary masterpieces. His eyes narrowed as he imagined them working behind the scenes: chopping, dicing, spilling, burning, cooking, cursing. All of them intent on creating perfection. As impossible as that always was.

He could see the blurred image of Antoine's face looking through the small window in the kitchen door. He stood there staring out into the dining room. What was it he was hoping to see? Was he gazing with satisfaction at what *La Varenne Pratique* called the "Best Bistro in Toulouse"? Was he monitoring his wait staff to see if they could move faster, be more attentive, better?

*Is he looking for me?*

The man edged away from the hostess stand to slip quietly into the shadows of the foyer and the line of hungry diners with reservations waiting for their tables. As he stepped outside into the quickly dropping evening temperatures, he found himself wondering if Antoine had been staring out from the security of his kitchen because he could tell the air to his sanctuary had become a little colder.

Had Antoine felt that? The dropping temperature?

And the feeling that perhaps death was just a little bit nearer?

7
―――

Maggie watched as the sun sank below the horizon, painting the sky in shades of purple and orange while a final burst of golden light was shining through the trees to cast dappled shadows in the garden at *Dormir*. The flickering candles on the table added a cozy warmth to the scene while the glint of silver cutlery caught the last rays of light. The cool air carried the faint scent of autumn leaves and fresh herbs from the garden.

"Come inside, *mes crevettes*," Danielle called to the children. "Bring the dogs."

She stepped out of the kitchen, a pashmina wrapped around her shoulders. She turned to Grace and Maggie and motioned for them to remain seated.

"Don't worry about us," she said. "We will find something on TV to watch."

"Thanks, Danielle," Maggie said.

The gentle breeze brushed against her skin, carrying with it the insistent chill that signaled the coming of fall. "I have to say it's not until Laurent is gone that I realize how much he does with Amelie. I'm so ready for him to be home."

"You both have done wonders with the child," Danielle said with a reassuring smile. "When she first came, she was as wild as thistle."

As Maggie watched Danielle walk into the house with the two children and the dogs beside her, she realized with surprise that Danielle looked frailer than she remembered.

"Is everything okay with Danielle?" she asked Grace.

Grace turned to watch the group as they entered the house.

"She's fine," she said. "But you know she can't live forever, darling."

"But nothing on the horizon?"

Maggie remembered the terror of the health scare ten years earlier when Danielle was diagnosed with breast cancer. She'd been in remission since then and they'd all relaxed and gotten used to the idea that they weren't going to lose her.

"Nothing that I know of. You know how the old dear is though. If she had something dire, she'd never tell."

Maggie gazed out over the darkened garden. Mismatched wrought-iron furniture that Grace had found in *brocantes* and antique shops all over Provence were fitted with cushions and draped with vintage fabrics. The sound of trickling water from a nearby fountain lent a soothing soundtrack to the scene. Grace had done a marvelous job of furnishing and designing *Dormir*.

"The place looks great," Maggie said. "You had a busy season?"

Grace nodded.

"I'll say. We had all three cottages booked nearly all summer long. I can't wait for fall. I'm ready for a break."

Maggie laughed.

"Same. Every harvest seems to take more and more out of us. This one was agony from beginning to end."

"What's going on with Laurent? Did I hear he's selling his mini-houses?"

Years ago, Laurent had built four tiny cottages to house the seasonal workers for his annual harvest work. When she was little, Mila used to say the little cottages looked like playhouses, except these were equipped with kitchens, showers, toilets, and tiny pocket gardens filled with squash, tomatoes and flowers. In time, Laurent added another three cottages to help with the overflow of refugee families living at the nearby monastery.

"No, he's got some local government official in Aix who's giving him problems about the houses," Maggie said. "I think this guy is afraid that Laurent is going to flood the countryside with illegal immigrants or something."

Maggie knew that the politician, Mathieu Beaumont, was fairly new to the area. He had risen through the political ranks outside Provence and was known for his conservative ideas and policies, particularly in the areas of environmental sustainability and urban development. Maggie had never met him, but she'd heard he was ambitious, which of course didn't set him apart from any other politician she ever knew.

"What kind of problems specifically?" Grace asked.

"Oh, he's saying there are concerns about the legality of Laurent's houses. He is citing zoning regulations and safety standards."

"But you and Laurent own the land the houses are on, right?"

"Yes, but we still have to comply with certain regulations if we have housing that we're putting people into. Or at least that's the particular hoop this guy wants Laurent to jump through. Of course, he doesn't really care about overcrowding or anything having to do with these people's rights or comfort. He just wants Laurent to stop providing them a place to live."

"Horrid man. Will Laurent have to give up his mini-houses?"

"I don't know. He's working with the monastery on some options but honestly, they have space issues too."

It made Maggie angry to think of all the unnecessary work this politician was forcing Laurent to do. It seemed that every time he turned around, Laurent was being handed a demand for unnecessary changes or irrelevant permits.

"So this guy is basically a racist," Grace said.

"Well, he doesn't want undocumented people in France. You can imagine the uproar it's caused among Laurent's workers. The harvest was a nightmare this year largely because his workers were terrified that every day they went back to their homes, they'd find padlocks on the doors."

"I am sure Laurent will get it sorted. If anyone can, he will."

"I know. I just hate that he has to bother with it. The older we get, the more I want him to slow down a bit."

"That doesn't sound like Laurent."

"I know. Which is why I think I need to help him get there. I'm serious, Grace. I didn't see any joy in him this year working with the grapes. For the first time ever, it looked like he was going through the motions."

"I'm sorry, darling. I never noticed."

"No reason why you should."

"Except he's a dear friend and I should know when my friends aren't happy."

"Oh, don't listen to me. I'm sure he's fine," Maggie said. "Whenever I start to fuss over him, he suggests I find some kind of employment outside the home."

"That's very funny. Does he have any idea what that would look like? For an American? In a rural village? At your age?"

They both laughed.

"Thanks a lot," Maggie said in mock indignation. "I'll have you know that fifty is the new forty."

"Yes, well, darling, in France even forty is long in the tooth. Have you *seen* the crop tops that the young ones are wearing these days? I didn't expose that much skin when I gave birth."

As Maggie joined her friend in laughter, she was blessedly aware that in that moment, surrounded by the beauty of the garden and the warmth of their friendship, she had more blessings than anyone had a right to expect. She couldn't help but marvel at her enduring friendship with Grace and the bond they shared—whether they were watching each other's children being born—or watching them leave the nest—or just sitting together after a good meal and enjoying the night and each other.

It was a gift. And Maggie never forgot that fact.

# 8

Laurent leaned back in his chair and waited as his plate was cleared away. He'd quit smoking a decade earlier but for some reason felt the urge to light up. It was always an enjoyable moment to smoke after a meal, almost like dotting the i on a perfect repast. But Maggie and the children had long ago insisted he give it up. Now he glanced around the restaurant and noted that it had cleared out considerably.

He was to meet Antoine in the kitchen after the main rush and he imagined now was as good a time as any. Nodding his thanks to his server, he got up and made his way toward the kitchen. Once there, the clatter of dishes and the rhythmic sounds of cooking and cleaning greeted him. He paused at the entrance, his gaze sweeping the bustling space. Various white jacketed cooks and kitchen workers orchestrated their movements down the still busy line of grill tops and counters while waitstaff moved gracefully amidst the organized chaos. It was a well-oiled machine, Laurent noted, with each member playing their part to create the culinary magic that had made Antoine's bistro renowned.

Laurent leaned against the doorframe, his eyes wandering over the stainless steel counters. The kitchen was a world unto itself, as Laurent well knew. Here was the hidden realm where Antoine's culinary creations came to life.

As final orders were plated, he saw the kitchen gradually begin to wind down. Line chefs wiped their brows, their faces flushed with exertion and satisfaction. The waitstaff also seemed to slow and then just stand around, most of them exhaling with a mixture of relief and accomplishment. Laurent spotted Antoine emerging from his office, a warm smile on his face.

"Come, my friend," Antoine greeted him, his voice carrying a touch of weariness. "Let's find a quiet corner to talk."

Together, they made their way back to Antoine's office which was tucked away from the main part of the kitchen. In one corner of the office, Laurent saw a bookshelf with a collection of cookbooks, each one he imagined a valuable source of inspiration and reference for his friend. The worn spines bore testimony to the countless times the volumes had been consulted, their pages dog-eared and marked with handwritten notes.

Laurent imagined Antoine bent over these books at this desk, concocting menus and new dishes—each of which would add to his reputation and to the level of fame. In spite of that, Laurent didn't envy Antoine. His life as a vigneron was busy and satisfying. Or at least it always had been.

Antoine shut the door and gestured to the table in the corner of the room. It had been years since the two of them had last shared memories of that time when they had both made their criminal livings on the Côte d'Azur.

"Ah, Laurent, do you remember those days?" Antoine chuckled, a mischievous glint in his eyes as he poured a generous glass of brandy for Laurent. "We were quite the duo, *n'est-ce pas*? Weaving our web of illusions and charming our way into a fortune. More than a few as I recall."

"And losing a few along the way," Laurent added as he lifted his glass in a toast to Antoine.

Antoine laughed.

"Indeed, my friend," he replied, a playful smile tugging at his lips. "Our schemes were audacious, though, were they not? Do you never think of those times?"

It had been a long time since Laurent had thought about his time as a con man in the south of France. And when he did, it was rarely with pleasure. He was mildly surprised that Antoine remembered those days that way.

"Do you remember that one wealthy Canadian with the two hundred-thousand-euro diamonds around her neck?" Antoine asked as he poured his own brandy. "You were determined to relieve her of it. Do you remember?"

Laurent frowned slightly. Did he remember the woman? Her face? The jewels? The year? Whenever he thought back to those times, it was never the scores he remembered or the moments of jubilant celebration with his friends—Antoine and Roger and the others. It was always the anxiety, the constant fear, the guilt.

"Of course," he lied as he sipped his brandy. "One of the many highlights, *mon vieux*."

From there, as the evening wore on the two of them shared more memories of elaborate cons and daring escapades. They recalled the time they'd posed as wealthy aristocrats, attending extravagant parties and left with room keys, maps, account numbers—all the things that started with trust and led to late-night theft and betrayal and a seemingly endless stream of ill-gotten gains. The two drank and chuckled about the time they convinced an unsuspecting collector that they possessed a priceless artifact, only for them to disappear into the night with a hefty payment, leaving behind a worthless replica.

"But you know," Laurent said, his voice taking on a more contemplative tone, "there came a point when we tired of it all, yes? The lies, the dread, the uncertainty?"

Antoine nodded, his expression turning serious.

"And my arrest, of course," he said. "I'd call that a turning point. For me at least."

Laurent considered his friend. Had it been a turning point for the rest of them? But no. Antoine's arrest had been a shock, but in a way hadn't they all been expecting something like that to stop their forward movement? Roger Bentley never did stop conning. He just moved off the Cote d'Azur to Portugal and later Dubai and finally back to London where he began. And Laurent...well, Laurent had met Maggie.

Laurent wouldn't ask Antoine about his time in prison. They'd not been in much contact during that time. What was there to say? If he wanted to talk about it now, he would. But Laurent was sure he would not. Now that he was really seeing his old friend up close, Laurent thought he could detect a certain wariness in Antoine's eye that had always been there. It had been there in the heady, so-called carefree days on the Côte d'Azur, and it had likely deepened during his time inside. Odd that the guardedness was still there now—even when he was riding high at the top of his game.

"It wasn't an easy path to get where I am, my friend," Antoine said, his voice tinged with a mixture of pride and vulnerability. "I lost two wives in the process and am estranged from my only child. Plus, unlike yourself, I had a criminal record to surmount."

"No one cares about your past if you are a genius in the kitchen," Laurent said.

"That is true," Antoine said with a grin. "But getting here was a long hard slog. There were times I didn't believe it was worth it."

"But you kept on," Laurent said. "It must have been tempting to consider going back to the old ways."

"I thought of it," Antoine admitted. "I came close on more than a few occasions. But what about you? You walked away from it all too. When did you know you were destined to be a gentleman farmer and family man?"

Laurent caught the thinly disguised tenor of sarcasm in Antoine's voice. He didn't blame him for that. To imagine the person that Laurent had been when Antoine knew him in Cannes and St-Tropez now turned into the pillar of his local community, as Laurent now was, must seem nearly unbelievable to someone who knew him in the old days.

"That transformation I must lay at the feet of my wife," Laurent said.

"Ah, while I am sure she is an amazing woman," Antoine said, "nobody could have changed the man I knew if he hadn't wanted to change."

"I'm sure you're right," Laurent said.

"Shall we toast to the past?" Antoine said. "And to our many thrilling adventures?"

Laurent lifted his glass.

"And to the men we are today," Laurent said. "Better because of where we came from."

"À ta santé," Antoine said, a glint of watchfulness still evident in his blue eyes.

# 9

The kitchen outside Antoine's office was bathed in the soft glow of overhead lights, the space now radiating a sense of cleanliness and order, a testament to the frenzied efforts of the kitchen staff. Even through the closed door, Laurent could detect the lingering scent of spices and savory dishes mingling with the faint whiff of cleaning products and the sound of rushing water in the kitchen sinks.

He brought the glass of Remy Martin to his lips. From where he sat, he could see the kitchen workers through the large windowpane in Antoine's office as they moved around the kitchen.

"So you married an American," Antoine said with a laugh, his eyes twinkling. "When I heard that, I couldn't believe it. Was she a mark?"

Laurent shook his head.

"No, she was someone who needed help finding a missing person. Roger Bentley set it up."

Instantly Antoine's smile dropped from his face.

"Ah, Bentley. I was sorry to hear of his passing. He was a good man."

"He was."

Older and urbane in contrast to Laurent's rough Paris street ways, Roger Bentley worked the Côte d'Azur with Laurent for nearly five years. In that time, they'd gotten to the point where they could finish each other's thoughts. They were very different in their ways. Roger was English and never wanted a family. He was talkative and outgoing whereas Laurent was naturally taciturn. In spite of that, Laurent had never been closer to another man. Maggie had never liked Roger or trusted him. For years, it had been the one big bone of contention between them—until eventually things like that didn't matter anymore.

"And you have children?" Antoine asked.

"Two boys and a girl," Laurent said. "Although we are now raising my granddaughter."

"No rest for the wicked, eh?"

Laurent smiled. "It's not restful," he admitted.

"I didn't raise my boy," Antoine said. "His mother and I parted soon after he was born. I was sorry about that."

"Do you see him?"

"Not much. Martine allowed him to come to me in the summer holidays for a bit. At least we got to know each other. His name is Marco. He lives in London. Honestly, I don't know what he does for a living, but I am proud of him."

"Of course."

"So how goes things for the gentleman farmer?" Antoine asked. "You don't have staff or workers?"

"Not full time, no. In fact, it is the issue of my seasonal workers that is currently causing me problems."

"Tell me."

Laurent sighed. He knew that many people found comfort reciting their problems out loud, but he had never found it particularly helpful. Even Maggie liked to talk a problem to death. But Antoine seemed interested.

"There is a local politician in Aix," Laurent said, "who wants to disable the set-up I have with the migrants who come to live and work my land."

"To what purpose?"

"I am sure it is a political platform having to do with being tough on immigration," Laurent said.

"You are not worried about the migrants taking French jobs?"

Laurent laughed.

"Trust me, there are no born French men knocking down my door to pick my grapes."

"And I suppose pay is not the issue?'

"I'm not paying what a skilled artisan would ask," Laurent said with a shrug. "It's manual labor after all. The migrants want the work and I need the work done."

"As simple as that?"

"Not quite. I provide housing for my workers. And I work with the nearby monastery to employ them off season if they show an interest in staying in the area."

"I see. So you are an advocate for illegal aliens."

"I'm not sure what I am," Laurent said. "Except perhaps an advocate for the rights and wellbeing of all people even if they are not French. I am sure you do the same in your restaurant, no? Or do all your kitchen staff come with work papers?"

Antoine laughed.

"No, you are right, my friend. And I would also defend them against a petty bureaucrat."

There was something in the way that Antoine responded

that made Laurent believe that his friend didn't agree with Laurent's championing of his workers. That was fine. If he expected all his friends to universally accept everything he did, he would have no friends.

"What about you, Antoine?" Laurent asked. "How did you go from fleecing rich Americans in Nice to being lauded by *La Varenne Pratique* as the most inventive chef of your generation?"

Antoine beamed.

"A miracle, to be sure," Antoine said with a chuckle. "You and I both loved to cook I remember."

"Yes, but you turned your passion into fame and fortune."

"Not without greasing a few palms, being in the right place and generally doing whatever was necessary to succeed," Antoine said. "I cite my two divorces and the fact that I have only a nominal relationship with my one child as some of the payments I have had to make along the way."

"That is a significant price to pay," Laurent said.

"Yes, but worth it to me."

Laurent couldn't imagine giving up Maggie or his children or the love he had for Domaine St-Buvard for any measure of fame or success. To him, the things that Antoine had given up in order to make room for his success were the core of what made a good life. To have lost them, in Laurent's view, was nothing short of a tragedy. But he kept his expression neutral.

"You have competition in Toulouse, I assume?" Laurent asked.

"Of course. Remy Durand owns the *Café du Midi*. Do you know it?"

Laurent shrugged noncommittally. He knew it of course. French gastronomy was a major interest of his. But he also knew his old friend wouldn't enjoy hearing him praise a competitor's restaurant.

"He's actually attempted to sabotage *L'Étoile Gourmande*," Antoine said. "Can you believe it? And he regularly poaches my kitchen staff."

"Is that not to be expected in your business?" Laurent asked.

"Cutthroat kitchen wars, you mean?" Antoine laughed. "To a certain extent, I suppose, yes. But this is personal. I had a sous chef that I loved as a son. Lucas Moreau. He works for Durand now. May they both die violent, painful deaths."

Laurent tried to remember if Antoine had been this passionate when he'd known him in Cannes.

"It's personal with Durand too," Antoine said. "We are not competitors. We are enemies. There is a big difference."

"Was it something you did?" Laurent asked.

Antoine laughed.

"For some people, success is the worst crime you can commit," Antoine said. "Everyone who has made it to the top has enemies."

Laurent believed there was likely a lot of truth to that statement. But he also knew that there were many who made it to the top by stepping on the necks of friends and colleagues. He himself had made enemies—one in particular who'd nearly killed both him and Grace just last spring. But those instances were few and isolated cases. The more Antoine talked, the more Laurent began to think that Antoine's faction of enemies seemed unusually large.

"There's a food critic who wants to see me dead," Antoine said.

"Surely that is an exaggeration?" Laurent said.

"Perhaps," Antoine said with a shrug. "But still, to have a food critic who hates you?"

"What did you do to antagonize him?"

"Nothing! I can't remember having a single conversation with the man. Perhaps I resemble someone who hurt him as a child."

"Where does he publish his reviews?"

Antoine listed three national magazines and Laurent had to admit, if the man was writing critiques for those, he was probably well thought of. And negative reviews at that level would be damaging. Laurent's meal tonight was exceptional. But he wasn't sure it was worthy of the praise that he'd read from other culinary sources referencing *L'Étoile Gourmande*. Was it possible this food critic expected something more than just exceptional food? Laurent could see how Antoine might hold that against him.

Just then, Antoine's phone rang, and he fumbled in his pocket to retrieve it. As he glanced at the caller ID, a mixture of disgust and resignation washed over his face. Laurent leaned back slightly to give Antoine space to address the call. Antoine stood up and walked a few steps away, but not far enough in the small office for Laurent not to easily hear every word of Antoine's side of the conversation.

"Look, Claudine," Antoine said with a heavy sigh, "there's no point hounding me like this. Do not make me block your number."

From what Laurent could tell, the phone call was from Antoine's ex-girlfriend, a relationship that Laurent gathered had ended recently on less than amicable terms. Laurent watched his friend's face as Antoine's jaw tightened. It was evident that this Claudine wasn't completely out of Antoine's heart regardless of what he said to her now. Antoine spoke in measured tones as if attempting to find a balance between defending his own perspective and seeking common ground with her. Yet, beneath the surface, raw emotions threatened to spill over.

Just before Laurent made the move to stand up and leave the office all together, Antoine ended the call and turned to Laurent.

"I am sorry about that," he said. "Our breakup is fairly new."

"I'm sorry," Laurent said.

Antoine waved his words away.

"It is for the best. Now where were we? Ah! Neither of us is driving. So let me break open a bottle of Cordelier that I have reserved for a special occasion. We have yet to dissect how it is that two suave players such as ourselves ended up walking away from the million-euro playground in its heyday!"

Just then Laurent's phone rang and he saw that Maggie was calling him. He gave Antoine a thumbs up for the bottle of brandy and stepped outside the office to take the call. It was late now and all the kitchen workers and sous chefs had gone home for the night. As he closed the office door behind him, Laurent realized something he'd never noticed before.

He realized that every time he took a call from Maggie there was the faintest thread of anxiety that flashed though him. It was nearly imperceptible and gone as soon as he heard her voice and was reassured that all was well at home.

# 10

After tucking Amelie into bed and making sure the dogs were settled for the night, Maggie found her way to the guest room at Grace's place before collapsing in bed herself. She was about to turn the light out when she noticed she had a missed call an hour earlier from Laurent. She immediately called him back.

"Where are you?" he asked before he even said hello.

Maggie felt like laughing. Laurent was protective and on occasion even a tad overbearing in the way he demonstrated his love. These days, the pleasure she might have taken years ago at having a few days to herself was offset by the imbalance of being apart from him.

"I've shared my location on your phone," she reminded him. "You just have to go to the app and click on my name. If you had, you'd know that Amelie and I came to *Dormir* for the night."

"I prefer to get my information directly from my wife," Laurent said with a smile in his voice.

"So how was the dinner at your friend's fancy award-winning resto?" she asked.

Maggie knew that Laurent had been looking forward to eating at *L'Étoile Gourmande* almost as much as he'd been anticipating seeing his old pal.

"It was good," Laurent said.

Maggie wasn't surprised at the faint praise. Laurent was not one for superlatives. But in this case, it sounded like it was just possible he was a tad underwhelmed.

"And Antoine?" Maggie asked. "How was it seeing him again?"

"I am still with him," Laurent said. "He's older. As we both are. But otherwise much the same. It is good to see him again."

"Was he involved in your old business in those days?"

Maggie had already asked this question more than once before Laurent left for his weekend and had gotten his usual vague replies. In many ways, largely due to Laurent's taciturn tendencies, her husband's past still remained a mystery to her. Although Maggie had to admit that the practice of honesty, at least in the beginning, had not been a natural inclination for either of them. After decades of marriage, she and Laurent had both slowly, painfully, learned the benefits of not keeping secrets.

"Is Mademoiselle Amelie behaving?" Laurent asked.

Maggie sighed. When Laurent was uninterested in answering a question, he tended to redirect. This too, she was familiar with. But fortunately, she was usually no longer bothered by. She knew that Laurent didn't keep secrets about the important things. Not any longer. And she'd learned to be content with that.

"Well enough," she said. "Philippe is so good with her. But she keeps asking when you'll be home."

"I will be back by lunchtime tomorrow," he said.

Maggie heard the lilt in his voice when he answered.

Clearly Amelie wasn't the only one eager for him to be home.

~

The next morning, early, as most of Toulouse still slept, Pierre arrived at work as he usually did. As the first one into the restaurant it was his responsibility to note the manner and quality of the clean-up from the night before, to meet any early morning vendors—usually only meat as Antoine visited the produce markets himself—to inventory the existing vegetables, stir the *crème fraiche* on the pantry shelves, set a pot on the stove to begin the day's broth compilation and start chopping the mountain of onions and garlic necessary for just about every dish the restaurant offered.

Pierre had had one cup of coffee at home before he left his apartment and would have another midmorning when most of the other employees had arrived, and his morning tasks were finished. He walked into the kitchen, his worn apron tied tightly around his waist. He loved being the first one there. The familiar scents of the kitchen—an organic mélange mingled with the various cleaning products used last night—tickled his nose as he made his way first to the pantry where the jugs of *crème fraiche* sat in various stages. He gave them each a stir and then carried the ones that were ready to the refrigerator. Then he pulled out the bag of chicken and duck bones—this morning big enough to fill both arms—and carried it to the stove where he set it on the counter before extricating a large ten-liter pot from the bottom shelf and placing it in the sink to fill with water.

He glanced at his watch. He was expecting the lamb man and also the goat man in the next thirty minutes. He'd meet them in the back alley. He turned off the sink tap and carefully carried the heavy pot the six feet across the kitchen expanse to the stove where he set it on a burner. He turned the burner to medium and splashed the bag of bones into the pot.

Next came the vegetables—mostly peelings but some whole aromatics too. He went to the produce pantry for this. It wasn't refrigerated, but it was cold enough. He tugged down a wicker basket with a linen liner filled with onions and garlic bulbs and walked back to the stove. It occurred to him that since both meat vendors were coming at nearly the same time, he should make sure there was enough storage space for the meat in the walk-in freezer.

Checking to ensure the stock fire wasn't too high, he turned to the freezer, briefly bracing himself for the blast of cold when he opened the door. With a firm grip on the door handle, he pulled open the heavy freezer door. The sudden rush of frigid air raked across his skin, causing an involuntary shiver to razor down his spine. As his eyes adjusted to the dim lighting inside, he scanned the shelving, imagining the lamb and goat carcasses and how they might fit, when his eyes caught sight of a large object on the floor.

Was it the veal carcass? A spasm of annoyance shot through him as he took a step toward it when he stopped suddenly and sucked in a sharp intake of breath.

Not the veal carcass.

Sprawled on the cold floor amidst an upturned crate of fish heads.

A body.

## 11

Laurent woke to what the radio had promised would be a crisp fall day. Its colors were easily visible from the large window in his bedroom. He stretched his arms and yawned, feeling refreshed with no ill effects from the long night of drinking with Antoine. If he left for home after breakfast, he'd easily get back to Domaine St-Buvard by noon as he'd promised.

After showering and dressing, he grabbed his room key and stepped out into the bright morning. As soon as he squinted into the sunlight, he realized that he'd drunk more last night than he usually did. His head throbbed mildly but he dismissed the discomfort.

After all, how many times does one reconnect with an old friend? He was glad he'd come to Toulouse to see Antoine and to add his own accolades to what his old friend had achieved. As he made his way down the cobblestone street to the town center, he found himself registering that the day away from Domaine St-Buvard—especially after the less than satisfying harvest and the added annoyance of

Beaumont attempting to get his mini-houses dismantled—had actually been restorative.

He smiled as he thought again of Maggie's insistence that he get out of town for the weekend. She'd been right. As she so often was. As soon as he reached the spoke of streets jutting out from the town center, he looked around and then headed for one of the little street cafés he'd seen yesterday when he first drove into town. It looked like a good place to get a basic French breakfast. There was a *patisserie* next door that he'd noticed yesterday. The aroma of freshly brewed coffee and warm croissants wafted through the air, guiding his steps towards the café.

He was halfway down the street when his eyes widened in surprise. There, just across the square a small crowd had gathered in front of *L'Étoile Gourmande*. More than that, Laurent's gaze was drawn to the police presence that surrounded the gathering of people. Flashing lights and the unmistakable sight of a coroner's wagon sent a shudder through him, instantly filling him with a sense of unease.

He approached cautiously, his steps faltering as he took in the scene before him. Officers were conversing with each other in hushed voices, their expressions grave and focused. Yellow caution tape cordoned off the entrance to the restaurant.

Something terrible had happened. Laurent pushed past the clutch of onlookers until he reached one of the uniformed policemen standing guard by the front door.

"Excuse me," Laurent said to him. "What has happened?"

"Back away, Monsieur," the policeman said with a stony expression.

"I have a friend who works here," Laurent said.

It was clear that the policeman would tell him nothing.

Laurent stepped back from the front of the restaurant. He pulled out his phone and called Antoine. The call went to voicemail. He stood on the periphery, fear and worry churning inside him as he observed the activity around him. He spotted a young girl in the crowd, still wearing her kitchen cook's jacket with the name *L'Étoile Gourmande* stitched across the top pocket. Laurent edged his way through the crowd to her.

"Excuse me," he said. "You work with Antoine?"

The girl turned to him, her face white with worry. She nodded.

"I remember you from last night," she said. "You are Antoine's friend."

"What has happened?" Laurent asked. "I cannot reach Antoine."

The girl turned to look at him, and when she did, he saw her puffy, tearful eyes. She pulled out her phone and scrolled to a thread of text messages which she then turned to show to Laurent. Laurent took the phone and squinted at the list of comments at the top of the thread. Someone named Pierre had sent out a group text.

> Antoine dead in freezer! I called police! C'est horrible!

Laurent's gut twisted with nausea. For a moment he felt a wave of dizziness.

"He is sure it is Antoine?" he asked.

"Pierre opens up in the morning," she said. "He found him. It is definitely Antoine."

"How?" Laurent asked, handing her phone back to her.

She shrugged helplessly.

Laurent turned away, plowing mindlessly back through the crowd until he reached the sidewalk. He took in a deep breath as if the very confines of the crowd around him had hampered his ability to breathe. He tried to process the possibility that the man he'd just spent most of last night with was dead. He finally tore his gaze away from the scene. His appetite for breakfast was gone, eclipsed by the urgency to find out the truth.

He turned and headed in the direction of the city police station—an ardent prayer on his lips that the young cook was wrong.

# 12

The Toulouse police station was an imposing structure situated in the heart of the city. Just blocks from the busy town square, it had been easy to find. As Laurent entered, the scent of polished wood mingled with the faint aroma of freshly brewed coffee. The sound of ringing telephones and muted conversations added a sense of urgency to the atmosphere. The main lobby featured, incongruously, marble floors and ornate columns, and exuded an air of seriousness and elegance. A large, intricately carved wooden reception desk greeted visitors, while behind the desk a bulletin board displayed notices of wanted criminals and missing persons.

Past the desk, Laurent saw corridors stretching like arteries, branching off into various departments and offices. He approached the reception desk where a uniformed policewoman greeted him with a friendly yet businesslike demeanor.

"How may I assist you today, sir?" she asked.

"I'm here to speak with the chief inspector regarding a case," Laurent replied, his voice tinged with authority.

With practiced ease, the officer picked up her phone and spoke briefly, relaying the nature of Laurent's visit to someone on the other line. After concluding the call, the woman directed Laurent to the nearby waiting area. Minutes stretched into an hour as Laurent observed officers hurrying through the corridors, their purposeful strides a testament to the urgency of their duties. The distant sound of ringing phones and snippets of conversation filtered through the air. During his life Laurent had spent some time in various police headquarters throughout France—even in detention, although never prison. He'd been lucky. Undeservedly so. He felt a flinch as he remembered Antoine who had not been so lucky.

Finally, the receptionist stood and gestured for Laurent to follow her. She led him through a maze of corridors. The hallway walls were adorned with framed photographs of officers and emblems of valor, as well as official commendations and certificates, underscoring the station's commitment to upholding the principles of justice.

Passing through a set of heavy double doors, Laurent entered a more subdued and private section of the station, still following behind the receptionist who stopped at a door marked "Chief Inspector." Her knock on the door was firm and purposeful.

A voice from within granted permission to enter, and the receptionist opened the door, ushering Laurent inside. The room was lined with bookcases and was anchored by a large wooden desk. On it were neatly arranged files and a nameplate, that read *Maxine Rousseau*. Behind the desk sat a young plain-clothes officer, her short, dark hair neatly styled, her piercing blue eyes meeting Laurent's with a mix of curiosity and detachment. Laurent couldn't believe that she was the Chief Inspector. He imagined Detective Rousseau would still be at the crime scene.

The young woman stood up and shook hands with him.

"My name is Detective Eloise Burger," she said. "And you are?"

"Laurent Dernier."

"I am told you have information about Monsieur Dubois?" She reseated herself and pulled out a note pad.

"Is it definitely Antoine Dubois that was found in the freezer, then?" Laurent asked.

"How do you know Monsieur Dubois?"

Laurent sighed. He knew getting the information he needed would be a process of painstaking piecemeal as the police got what they wanted first.

"He is an old friend," he said. "We spent last night together."

"What time last night did you last see him?"

"We parted at just after three o'clock. What time was his body discovered?"

"Will you be staying in town long?"

Laurent felt a flutter of frustration as his questions were ignored.

"As long as you need me to," he said. "Can you tell me how he died?"

"It appears to be an unfortunate accident."

Laurent blinked at the woman in astonishment.

"In his own freezer?" he said. "That is hard to believe."

"Not if he was inebriated when he left you, Monsieur. Was Monsieur Dubois impaired at that time?"

"Not to the point where he would lock himself in a walk-in freezer," Laurent said pointedly. "When can I get an appointment with the Chief Inspector?"

Burger made a face.

"She is very busy at the moment," she said. "As you can imagine. Please leave your contact information at the front desk."

She stood up as if to indicate that the interview was over, but then hesitated and looked around the desk as if searching for something.

"If you're an old friend of the victim's," she said, "would you happen to know his next of kin?"

Laurent drew in a breath of discouragement and heard the strain in his voice as he answered her.

"He had a son. Marco Dubois. Living in London," he said.

"Do you have his contact information?"

"I do not."

She turned to her computer and typed something in before jotting a note down on a piece of paper and handing it to him. It was a phone number.

"Since you knew his father," Burger said, "would you call Monsieur Dubois *le fils* and inform him of his father's passing?"

Laurent left the Chief Inspector's office frustrated and even a little angry. He felt stunned by his meeting with the junior detective. The fact that they wanted *him*—a virtual stranger—to make the next-of-kin call was nothing less than astonishing. But he hadn't argued with the woman because in the end, he knew that Antoine would rather Laurent be the one to tell Marco the news rather than have the boy hear it from the police.

He made his way back dispiritedly to his bed and breakfast, his brain going over and over the words that he would tell the boy. The police had confirmed Antoine's death but that was all. He actually had very little to tell Marco except for the terrible news itself.

And of course how sorry he was for the boy's loss.

# 13

Maggie tossed a handful of flour onto her work surface in the kitchen and began rolling out the cold dough she'd taken from the refrigerator. Normally, she liked to freeze her tart dough already rolled out and fitted to her baking pans, but she'd had a bumper crop of strawberries in her garden this summer and she'd quickly used up all her pie pans weeks ago.

Making this pie crust from scratch, as she added the water and the cold butter to the dough, reminded her of how Zen and stress-relieving she usually found baking to be. Laurent tended to tackle the savory dishes at Domaine St-Buvard and left the cookies and tarts to Maggie. Anything more elaborate than that—*profiteroles, chouquettes or mille-feuille*—they both left to the professionals in their village *patisserie*.

She had just fitted the rolled-out dough into the tart pan when she saw that her phone on the counter was ringing. Quickly shaking the excess flour from her hands, she wiped the rest on a kitchen towel before picking up.

"Hey, you," she said. "This is a surprise. I wasn't

expecting to hear from you before you left town. Are you on the road?"

"*Allo, chérie,*" Laurent said wearily.

Instantly, Maggie stiffened at Laurent's tone.

*Something's happened.*

"I will be delayed," he said.

Maggie sat down on the kitchen chair. Amelie looked up from the puzzle she was doing at the dining table and gave her a questioning look, but Maggie smiled reassuringly at her. It hadn't taken the child long to be able to read the silences and expressions between Maggie and Laurent. In so many ways, Amelie was better at it than the other children had ever been. That was probably because the others, with the exception of Luc, hadn't known an insecure moment in their lives, whereas Amelie had only known chaos from the moment she was aware of the world around her. Plus, unlike the others, Amelie was essentially being raised as an only child. The rules were different.

"What's happened?" she asked.

"Antoine...has died. In his restaurant."

"Oh, Laurent," she said. "I'm so sorry. How?"

"The police think it is an accident."

Maggie felt a shiver down both arms.

"But you don't?" she asked.

"I don't know," he said. "He told me last night that he had enemies."

"You think it's murder?" she asked.

Amelie's head snapped up and she was fully concentrating on Maggie's side of the conversation now.

"I don't know," Laurent said. "I just spoke with Antoine's son in London. He is very upset of course."

"Naturally," Maggie said.

"He wanted to know how his father could've locked

himself in his own freezer and I had nothing to tell him. I think I must stay for a bit. Not for long. Just today perhaps."

"Do what you need to do," Maggie said.

Amelie was now at her elbow, a frown creasing her face.

"Is *Opa* not coming home today?" she asked.

"He might be later than he expected," Maggie said to her. "Go back to your puzzle."

"Put her on the phone," Laurent said.

Maggie handed the phone to Amelie who took it as if she were an equal adult in the equation.

"What's happened?" she asked Laurent.

Maggie marveled at the child who was seven years old going on thirty. She went to wipe down the kitchen counters and to give herself a moment to think. She could hear that Laurent was doing most of the talking—unusual for him—but Maggie imagined he was trying to reassure Amelie that he would be home soon. Finally, Amelie looked at Maggie.

"*Opa* said he'll call you tonight," she said and then hung up.

Amelie's small brow was furrowed in concentration and her lips were pressed together in a thoughtful line as if she were pondering a great mystery.

"Are you okay, sweetie?" Maggie asked.

"*Opa* thinks somebody hurt his friend."

Maggie hated for Amelie to get any further confirmation of the evil that existed in the world. Losing her mother to murder had been more than enough of an education for the child to expect boogie men to jump out from behind every bush and tree.

"He'll get to the bottom of it," Maggie said with a smile, determined not to make the issue as grim as she knew it was.

Amelie went back to her puzzle—although her face

showed that her brain was working overtime and not anything to do with the puzzle. Maggie picked up her phone and texted Laurent.

> I can come to Toulouse

"*Opa* said the police in Toulouse are incompetent," Amelie said as she studied her puzzle.

Maggie wondered if Laurent had in fact said that to the girl. Amelie was a master at providing trigger words to see if the adults around her could be tricked into divulging more than they intended. It was entirely possible that Laurent did indeed think that the Toulouse police were incompetent. And just as likely that without saying so, he'd communicated that opinion to Amelie. Or perhaps she just knew her grandfather so well that she was accurately filling in the gaps.

Maggie's phone dinged and she saw she'd gotten a text back from Laurent.

> no need

Maggie sighed. He was probably right. If for no other reason, than because someone needed to stay home with Amelie. But after so many years of marriage, Maggie was aware of a unique level of understanding that she and Laurent had developed. It was the ability to communicate without the need to verbalize every thought or feeling. They could often effectively convey their thoughts with just a glance or a touch.

As she arranged the apples that she'd sliced earlier in an overlapping pattern in the pastry pan, Maggie's mind would not rest. She thought back to Laurent's voice on the phone.

She was sure she could detect the signs of grief and frustration in his tone. She wasn't sure how much she could help by being there, but she was sure she could help some.

In truth, in the long years of their marriage Laurent had not always provided much emotional support for Maggie. Culturally they were just so very different. He wasn't just French, he was *Alpha French*. Some of that had to do with his size. At six foot five, he was used to towering over people and being listened to. And then there was his criminal past, something that made him intensely mysterious and enigmatic.

She sprinkled sugar and pats of butter on top of the apple slices and slid the tart into the hot oven. She set the timer for forty minutes and turned to see that Amelie appeared to be happily engrossed in her puzzle. Then Maggie walked to the French doors through the dining room that looked out over the back garden and the grape fields beyond.

However she and Laurent had started out, so many years ago, her bond with him had since grown to the point that whatever challenges they'd faced had been no match for the mutual reassurance and encouragement that had become second nature between them. Maggie tried to remember a single time when whatever was happening in their lives, she wasn't keenly aware of the fact that they were in it together.

It was how they worked. It was how they made their lives work.

And now, especially now, she couldn't help but think that what he said he needed and what he really needed were two different things.

## 14

Maggie spent the rest of the day in fitful activity, her mind busy churning out scenarios of Laurent and what he must be feeling. After a quick lunch of tuna salad sandwiches and tomato soup, she and Amelie sat down to slices of the warm apple tart with sweetened whipped cream. Amelie had begun to beg for a taste of coffee and Maggie had made her a very weak cup with extra cream and sugar.

After that, they went out to the kitchen garden—Laurent's *potager* and haven of earthy scents and colorful vegetables and spices—while Maggie tried not to worry about what Laurent was doing—or what she should be doing for him—and instead concentrate on her activity with Amelie. Maggie loved working in the garden with Amelie because it was one of the few times when the child was focused and not destructive. The girl's slim fingers were agile and quick, and she enjoyed the process of yanking out offending weeds and other invasive plants from Laurent's neat and tidy rows.

After several minutes of weeding, Maggie filled the

watering can so Amelie could shower the remaining plants—inevitably some non-weeds had gotten weeded.

"So is *Opa* coming home tonight or not?" Amelie asked. "You said we would make him a *tarte citron*."

"Yes, I did say that," Maggie said, privately scolding herself for getting ahead of herself with that promise. If you told Amelie something was going to happen, you needed to make sure it did. If you didn't, you'd never hear the end of it.

"Make sure you water all the vegetables," Maggie said, pointing where Amelie was mindlessly creating a mud puddle.

"I am," Amelie said stubbornly. "I thought *Opa* said the garden was finished for the year."

"Almost," Maggie said. "Look how many tomatoes we still have. And there's a last sweet potato."

Amelie put the watering can down.

"Can we have it for dinner tonight?" she asked.

"Absolutely," Maggie said as she felt her pocket vibrate with her phone. She saw it was Grace. "Hey, Grace. Can you hold on a moment?"

Maggie turned to Amelie who had just tugged the sweet potato out of the ground.

"Good job, sweetie," Maggie said. "Why don't you bring that into the kitchen?"

Amelie's eyes went to the phone in Maggie's hand and Maggie knew the child knew she was trying to get rid of her.

"And then you can watch some TV for a bit," Maggie added.

Amelie's face broke into a smile. She turned, dropping the sweet potato in the dirt, and ran into the house.

"Hey, Grace," Maggie said as she bent over to pick up the dropped potato. "you're not going to believe what happened."

"Oh? Tell me."

"The old friend who Laurent went to see in Toulouse? He ended up dead this morning."

Grace gasped. "No!" she said.

"Laurent is really thrown for a loop."

"What happened?"

"His friend was found in his restaurant's walk-in freezer. The cops think it was an accident."

"But Laurent doesn't?"

"I'm not sure. He had to tell his friend's son what happened. Pretty upsetting."

"Wow," Grace said. "That's terrible. You know I just read an article about Toulouse and the culinary scene down there. The article said there were rumors of syndicated crime operating in the area."

"Seriously? In what way?"

"The article wasn't too specific, but it did mention human trafficking. Maybe Laurent's chef friend had dangerous connections?"

"Maybe. I have to admit I don't love the idea of him staying on."

"He's staying on?"

"For a little bit, yeah. He said he wants to nose around a bit. He's pretty frustrated that the police appear to be sweeping this under the rug."

"Which of course they *would* do if they were under the thumb of the crime syndicate."

"We don't know that's what this is, Grace."

"We don't know that it isn't either, darling. So are you going to Toulouse?"

The afternoon sun began its descent, casting a golden glow over the garden, and Maggie stopped to gather her gardening tools and baskets.

"I offered but he said no."

"I think you should go," Grace said. "After all, you've done this sort of thing before. Laurent is not really one for puzzles, is he?"

"You have a point," Maggie said.

Honestly, ever since Laurent had called, Maggie had been feeling as if she should go to Toulouse. Laurent sounded so unmoored when she'd talked to him. She could only imagine how horrible it would be to connect with an old friend and then have him brutally snatched away just hours later.

"You know Amelie will be fine with us," Grace said. "Philippe has a couple days off school so he can help."

They talked a little longer, but the seed had been planted. That night as she put Amelie to bed, Maggie still hadn't made up her mind about what she should do, when Amelie narrowed her eyes at her.

"You're leaving to go be with *Opa*, aren't you?"

"If I do," Maggie said carefully, "I'll need you to stay with Aunt Grace and be very good for her."

Amelie snorted and Maggie forced herself not to smile. She'd heard that noise so many times coming from Laurent —and even from a few of the older French men in the village—but never from a little girl. It was just one more example of how Amelie was not like any other child she'd ever known.

By the time she'd snapped off the child's bedroom lamp, Maggie's mind was already buzzing with what she needed to pack for her trip to Toulouse.

## 15

From the outside, *Café du Midi* seemed to exude a vibrant charm to all passersby. Laurent thought its façade, which was adorned with elegant wrought-iron accents and stylish awnings, was a blend of modern chic and classic French architecture. Its large floor-to-ceiling windows allowed passersby to glimpse the mystery and magic within. He stared at the restaurant front, his mind filled with conflicting thoughts and emotions. The surge of frustration he'd felt over the police attitude about Antoine's death seemed to distill itself in a resolute determination to find out the truth for himself about what had happened to his friend.

And the start of that quest began here at the restaurant of Antoine's main rival and avowed enemy.

Beyond the fact that Antoine considered him a serious adversary, Laurent didn't know much about Remy Durand, the owner of *Café du Midi*. That was enough to be starting with. With a deep breath and a clenched jaw, he pushed his way through the throngs of people filling the narrow street —still crowded due to the ongoing sausage festival—and headed across the street toward the restaurant. He knew he should attempt to calm himself first and he'd hoped that the walk from his bed and breakfast would aid in that. But as his footsteps echoed on the pavement, his mind was filled with a simmering stew of frustration and anger.

Was he supposed to let the police just ignore what happened to Antoine?

He pushed open the door of the restaurant and entered, the clinking of cutlery and murmurs of conversation creating an ambience of bustling activity that immediately engulfed him. He scanned the dining room and the bar at the opposite end of the room. Immediately, he clocked Durand at the bar, recognizing him from a promotional brochure left at his bed and breakfast that advertised *Café du Midi*. Laurent's gaze locked onto the man.

Remy Durand was of average height but with a thick build. At first glance, he exuded a warm, persona but his sharp, hazel eyes constantly surveyed the flow of his establishment with a keen, almost predatory awareness. Laurent walked over to the bar. Durand turned to him, his face open and friendly.

"Monsieur Durand," Laurent said in a loud voice, "may I ask where you were this morning when Antoine Dubois was killed inside his own restaurant?"

The beneficent expression dropped from Durand's face as he faced Laurent.

"Who wants to know?" he said.

"Someone who wants the truth about what happened to Antoine Dubois."

Durand snorted.

"You mean the truth about a man who got drunk and locked himself in his own freezer?"

Durand looked around at the people standing at the bar

as if expecting an amused reaction. Laurent hadn't expected a confession from the man. He'd only wanted to put him on notice that even if the police weren't suspicious, other people were. What he *hadn't* expected was for this *putain* to mock the death of his old friend. Laurent ground his teeth and took a step closer to Durand, his voice edged with fury. He felt himself fighting to keep control.

"Repeat that, please," Laurent said in sinister tones. "I'm hard of hearing."

Durand's face flushed with a mixture of indignation and fear as he clenched his jaw. Laurent was at least six inches taller and broad in the shoulder. Without warning, he swung a fist towards Laurent.

Laurent raised a forearm to block the punch, his adrenaline surging as he then drove his fist into Durand's exposed midriff. The room immediately erupted into chaos as patrons gasped and jumped away from tables. Durand's face turned purple as he bent over, gasping as he brought down a nearby table as he started to fall. Laurent grabbed him by the shirt front and jerked him back to his feet before firing another punch into the man's surprised and now frightened face.

After the first punch, it was like a switch had gone on in Laurent's brain. All the frustration that had been building from the moment of the police's refusal to investigate Antoine's death to this moment when this man blithely had insulted Antoine hours after his death came to a furious head. Laurent threw the man up against his own bar and pulled back his arm to deliver another bone cracking punch. He saw Durand's terrified eyes, and how he brought his hands up to protect his face. Voices cried out around him, as people rushed forward. Out of the corner of his eye Laurent saw a man with a chair over his head, aiming at him. Laurent pushed Durand away and stepped out of the arc of the chair which missed him by inches.

There were shouts then and the sound of shuffling feet as servers and kitchen staff charged into the room. Some held rolling pins and heavy sauté pans, prepared to do battle to defend their boss. In a confused flash of thought, Laurent wondered how they could possibly want to protect this man. One look at their faces told him they weren't doing it out of fear. They were loyal to him.

Breathing heavily, his chest heaving with a mix of frustration and now a sense of confused futility, Laurent glared at Durand who had scrambled to safety behind the bar. The bartender was helping him mop up the stream of blood pouring from his nose. Amid the clamor and distress of the restaurant's diners, Laurent heard a single voice breathlessly explaining what was happening on the phone to the police.

*So now what?* he thought dispiritedly, as he watched panicked diners hurry out of the dining room while Durand's employees lined up in front of him to shield him.

Laurent felt a thickening in his throat. In the midst of his anger, he had allowed himself to be consumed by a blind fury. As he looked around at the chaos he'd caused, he saw the consequences of his impulsive actions staring back at him.

He'd come here for justice for Antoine but in a matter of moments he'd succeeded in escalating the tension he felt in his gut—the same one that now told him he was in the wrong—and worse than that, by coming here he'd actually managed to impede his search for the truth.

## 16

As soon as Maggie got to Toulouse—after a tedious and nerve-wracking five-hour drive mostly due to the fact that Laurent hadn't answered his phone for the last twelve hours—she went straight to Laurent's lodgings, winding her way through the remnants of the sausage festival. There at the bed and breakfast the concierge confirmed that Laurent had not spent the night there, but he assured her Monsieur was alive. After all, he had heard through the grapevine that Laurent had been arrested the evening before.

Anxious and blaming herself for not coming immediately to Toulouse when Laurent told her about Antoine's suspicious death, Maggie rushed from the bed and breakfast to the police station. She knew that, for all that Laurent chided her for being too blunt in social situations and not allowing enough time for small talk, Laurent himself didn't suffer fools gladly. She further knew that while he might say all the right things when produce shopping in the village markets in Arles or Aix, she had no doubt that when it came to asking questions and demanding answers, he tended to charge in like a bull in a bric-a-brac shop.

Yes, she definitely should have come yesterday.

As she entered the police station, she saw officers moving purposefully everywhere she looked, their voices blending into a concert of official jargon. She went immediately to the front desk.

"Excuse me," she said to the uniformed officer behind the desk. "Where do I go to bail someone out who has been arrested?"

The officer regarded Maggie with a stern gaze. After a brief exchange of information, Maggie provided the necessary details proving her relationship to Laurent and then completed the required paperwork. After that, she waited, her thoughts consumed with questions and concerns for Laurent's well-being. What had he done to get himself arrested? The charge paperwork said, *unprovoked assault*, which frankly sounded like Laurent—at least under certain situations. But who did he assault? And why? Did he already know who killed Antoine?

Finally, the sound of approaching footsteps drew Maggie's attention, and her heart skipped a beat as she saw Laurent being escorted towards her. His face carried traces of exhaustion and frustration, but a glimmer of relief sparked in his eyes when he saw Maggie.

In spite of that, his words to her were terse.

"I thought I told you to stay home," he said.

"You probably did," Maggie said. "I chose not to listen to you."

She leaned up on tiptoe to give him a quick kiss. After that, they navigated the necessary procedures to leave and then left, mostly without speaking. It seemed the charges against him had been dropped. As soon as they stepped out of the station, Maggie turned to Laurent, and he caught her up in his arms and gave her a hard hug.

"Forgive me," he said. "It's been a long night."

"You look terrible," she said.

He winced and ran a hand through his unruly hair.

"Let's get back to the bed and breakfast," Maggie said. "You can tell me what happened."

"Amelie?"

"She's with Grace and Danielle."

He gave her a strained smile.

"I am sorry, *chérie*. I am glad you are here."

An hour later, after Laurent had showered and changed clothes, he and Maggie left the bed and breakfast and walked to the square where they found an available table on the rue des Jacobins and ordered lunch.

"So what happened?" Maggie asked, proud that she hadn't bombarded him with an onslaught of questions before now.

"I paid a visit to Remy Durand," Laurent said as he closed the menu. "The night before he died Antoine told me that Durand was a problem for him."

"Do you think Durand killed Antoine?" Maggie asked.

"I don't know," Laurent said. "The police are determined to treat Antoine's death as an accident. I am the only one asking any questions."

Maggie could see the depth of Laurent's grief and frustration in his face. And the helplessness, too which she knew for Laurent was probably the worst feeling of all. A man of action, Laurent hated not being able to *do* something to fix a problem.

"Tell me about Antoine," she said in a soft voice. "I never heard you mention him before."

Laurent's face relaxed and his gaze was directed out past the terrace to the city street.

"Bentley and I were much closer," he said. "Even though Antoine was French and Roger wasn't."

Maggie had long ago come to grips with her feelings toward Roger Bentley. Now that he was dead, she was more inclined to forgive him and to listen to Laurent's memories of him.

Their first course arrived, and Laurent's eyes went to the plate of *foie gras* with toast points and local fig jam and then to the bottle of Sancerre as the waiter poured it. He took a sip of the wine and eased back in his chair.

"Antoine was always a good friend to me," he said after the waiter left. "I remember one time we had a game scheduled in a dingy bar café in Saint-Honorat Island. Not even any electricity or running water."

Maggie smiled. Laurent had taken her to Saint-Honorat for a picnic on one of their very first dates. The memory of that afternoon had been indelible for her. But of course, the reason Laurent was so familiar with the small charming little island was that it was often part of the venue where he committed his string of international crimes.

"Antoine had lured in the mark who'd flown in by helicopter," Laurent said. "The game was poker—not my strength—but it went all night. In the end, Antoine and I won, not honestly of course." Laurent shrugged. "And by then the mark had become suspicious. He went after Antoine because he was smaller but also because he was the one who had done most of the talking."

Maggie smiled. She remembered well the Laurent of those days—even though she'd known him only at the end of that period of his life. Then like now, he'd been taciturn.

A con artist who rarely spoke? In some ways, it made Laurent even more believable to his victims.

"The mark pulled a gun," Laurent remembered. "Before I could intervene, he shot Antoine."

Maggie sucked in a surprised breath.

"Oh, my goodness! He really shot him?"

"He did," Laurent said. "I disarmed the mark and forced him to fly us to the nearest trauma center in Nice. While they operated on Antoine, I had the mark transfer our winnings for the night to Antoine's wife's account. When I knew that Antoine would live, I gave the police the mark's information—along with the gun he used to shoot Antoine—and left him screaming and in handcuffs on his way to jail."

"You had some wild times before we met," Maggie noted.

Laurent grinned at her.

"His wife divorced him two years later," Laurent said, "but Antoine never blamed her."

"I wouldn't either," Maggie said with an arched eyebrow. "But is it strange that the two of you fell out of touch after sharing so much?"

Laurent shrugged.

"Our lives took different paths. I met you and that was the end of that."

"Wow, you are such a romantic," Maggie said.

"You know what I mean," Laurent said. He leaned over and took Maggie's hand. "I saw Antoine just two nights ago. I did not envy where he ended up, even with his fame and fortune."

"I'm just teasing you," Maggie said. "I'm glad if seeing him again made you grateful for all you've got."

"I did not need to see Antoine to feel that," Laurent said

admonishingly. "But I cannot accept that the police are willing to do nothing about his death. I feel I owe it to Antoine and to his son to find the truth."

Maggie didn't understand how a dead man or even his son—a boy Laurent had never met—could be owed anything. But she did understand the kind of man Laurent was and the mysterious code he lived by. It was important to him. And that was all that mattered. Reasons were irrelevant.

"Tomorrow we'll ask around town and see if we can find some answers," Maggie said, as she spread duck pâté on a piece of toast and added a small spoonful of fig marmalade. She raised an eyebrow at him before popping the morsel in her mouth. "Preferably without you having to spend a night in jail in the process."

## 17

That night after dinner as dusk settled in, Maggie caught a glimpse of the cityscape of Toulouse from where she and Laurent stood outside *L'Étoile Gourmande*. The ancient brick buildings of the town were tinged with hues of red and orange. The soft glow of streetlights illuminated the cobbled streets and the air held a subtle hint of the still cooking sausages, mingling with the faint scent of cigarettes and woodsmoke.

The evening temperature was mild yet and they had been enjoying an after-dinner stroll when they'd discovered that Antoine's restaurant appeared open for business—something neither of them could have expected. Laurent was angry at the fact, seeing it as further evidence of how the police were not taking his death seriously. Instead of brooding over it, Maggie encouraged Laurent to use it to their advantage.

"Let's go inside and see if any of the kitchen staff is available to talk about why Antoine might have been in the walk-in freezer that night," she said.

Assuaged, Laurent had just agreed when his phone rang.

He looked at the screen and showed it to Maggie. It was Antoine's son Marco calling. Maggie stood close to Laurent to hear the conversation.

"Hello, *mon vieux*," Laurent said, answering the phone. "How are you today?"

"Not great, honestly," Marco said. "Did the cops tell you they now think Papa was murdered?"

Maggie saw Laurent wince. This was a terrible conversation to have with a child—over the phone or in person.

"So it is now a homicide?" Laurent asked.

"I guess so. That's what the detective called it."

Maggie was glad the police seemed to have finally come to their senses about reclassifying Antoine's death. Perhaps this meant they would investigate properly, and she and Laurent could go home.

"It is good," Laurent said. "It means the police will be investigating now. Did they find something in the autopsy to make them change their minds?"

"They must have," Marco said.

Maggie thought he sounded very young, although Laurent said that he was in his mid-thirties. She was sorry he was going through this alone and found herself wondering if he was married.

"They sent me a copy of the autopsy," Marco said. "But I couldn't make heads or tails of it. If you give me your email, I'll send it to you."

Laurent gave him his email address.

"I'm just glad they're finally looking for who did this to him," Marco said. "I have to say that the last time I talked to Papa he sounded paranoid."

"How so?" Laurent asked.

"He kept telling me to *look over my shoulder*. Is that

weird? Do you think he was having a premonition about his death?"

Maggie arched an eyebrow at Laurent. Telling your son to *look over his shoulder* sounded more like Antoine was worried about *Marco* than himself. She watched Laurent's face and saw the pain and the helplessness written on it. Up until this moment, she wasn't sure what she was doing to help by being here in Toulouse except for giving Laurent moral support. She knew how long it took to process traumatic news. In her mind, looking into Antoine's death was precisely what Laurent needed to do not only to wrap his mind around what had happened to his friend, but also to help himself navigate through it.

When he hung up, she looped an arm through his.

"Is he coming to Toulouse?" she asked.

"The police told him it was unnecessary for purposes of identifying the body."

"He sent you the autopsy?"

"We'll look it over later back at the room," Laurent said.

"So the police have changed their tune," Maggie said. "I can't imagine what that poor boy must be feeling."

"*Je sais.*"

As Maggie and Laurent stepped inside Antoine's elegant *brasserie*, they were greeted by a beautiful woman standing at the hostess stand. She welcomed them with a warm smile, her demeanor radiating grace and professionalism. Around her, the air hummed with a gentle buzz of conversation, mingling with the soft melodies of a live piano.

You'd never know a murder had been committed here, Maggie thought as she took in the elegant surroundings. She couldn't help but be aware that for someone like Laurent's friend Antoine, the experience of dining was about more than food. Here, within these walls, every guest would be treated to an unforgettable dining experience—where flavors would dance upon the palate and forge cherished memories never to be forgotten. As Laurent had told her on innumerable occasions *that* was really what fine dining in France was all about. It was only partially ever about the food.

"I have to admit to being surprised that you are open for business," Laurent said to the hostess.

"Do you have reservations?" she asked coolly.

"How are you managing without Antoine?" Laurent pressed. "I thought only he set the menus."

"That is true," the hostess said, now looking visibly uncomfortable. "But our acting sous-chef has taken that over. I can assure you he has the experience equal to what you have come to expect from *L'Étoile Gourmande*."

"Without Antoine?" Laurent asked pointedly.

The hostess blushed and looked around as if looking for help.

"I am sorry, Monsieur," she said helplessly. "We are full tonight. Do you want to reserve a seating for lunch tomorrow? I believe I can squeeze you in."

"Who has taken over in Antoine's absence?" Laurent asked.

"Our sous chef is renowned on two continents for his culinary imagination and creations," the girl said, looking a little more confident to be able to recite the chef's credentials. "And he is very familiar with *L'Étoile Gourmande* since he used to work here."

Laurent had been about to turn away when he suddenly looked back at her, his eyes alert.

"What is his name?" he asked.

"Lucas Moreau," she said promptly.

Now Laurent did turn away, his hand on Maggie's arm as he steered her away from the surprised hostess and toward the door. As soon as they were outside, Maggie turned to him.

"What's the matter?" she asked.

"Lucas Moreau was an ex-employee of Antoine's," Laurent said. "Antoine told me that the man stabbed him in the back. So how is it he is now working at Antoine's restaurant a day after Antoine's murder?"

"Good question."

"Isn't it?" Laurent said, a flicker of suspicion hardening his gaze. "It's almost as if he knew there would be a position opening up."

## 18

Since it was clear that the police had no issue with the *brasserie* opening up so soon after Antoine's death, Laurent decided to take another shot at speaking with the detective about the investigation. Walking through the sausage festival that was starting to show signs of winding down, they bought sausage rolls that they chased down with beer and ate on a bench in the square. Maggie wasn't hungry so soon after dinner, but she knew that Laurent would eat for many different reasons. She watched the activity of the people around them while he brought up on his phone the autopsy report Marco had emailed to him and read it several times in silence. The temperatures had dropped in the last hour making it much less desirable for most people to want to sit outside eating shaved ice and gelato.

Finally, Laurent put his phone away.

"We need to talk to the detective in charge," he said.

Maggie glanced at her watch to see that it was nearly midnight, but she knew not to argue with Laurent. Plus, she had to admit there was a possibility that the detective would be more available to see them at this hour—if she hadn't gone off shift.

They walked to the Toulouse police station which at that hour was much less busy than their last visit. After just a few minutes waiting in the lobby of the station they were escorted down the hall to the same office where Laurent had gone that first morning after finding out about Antoine's death. Here they sat side by side in the somber atmosphere of the detective's office, their gazes fixed on the chief detective—a plain, middle-aged woman with broad shoulders and a posture that was ramrod straight. Her attire was functional and professional, and her expression was a mix of weariness and resolve.

"I am glad you came in," she said. "I'm sorry I wasn't here to talk with you before."

Maggie wasn't sure if the detective was referring to the time when Laurent came after Antoine was found dead and spoke with this woman's second in command—or when Maggie had bailed Laurent out for assaulting whom they believed should have been the detective's prime suspect.

"It has been a particularly complicated case," the detective said. "With a few surprises we did not anticipate."

Maggie forced herself not to look at Laurent. They both knew that the police considered Antoine's death a homicide now, but Laurent wasn't revealing the fact that he already knew. That was typical of him. He would never volunteer information just for the sake of doing so.

Detective Rousseau leaned forward, her voice thick with apology and concern as if she was about to deliver unsettling news.

"I did want to share with you the news that we now believe Monsieur Dubois's death was not an accident,"

Rousseau said, her words careful and measured. "The results of the autopsy revealed that he died as a result of a blunt force trauma to the back of his head."

A tense silence hung in the air as the weight of her words settled on them. It was all Maggie could do not to snort in derision. Such a head wound would've been obvious even to the most rookie police officer.

*You don't need an autopsy to tell you the victim was hit on the back of the head.*

"So it's murder," Maggie said.

Inspector Rousseau turned to look at Maggie and made a face.

"We're treating it as a homicide, yes," she said.

Maggie could tell that Laurent was bristling with fury.

"How?" he asked abruptly.

"I'm sorry?" Rousseau asked with a frown.

"What was he hit with?" he asked.

The detective hesitated and Maggie could see her struggling to make up her mind. Laurent was formidable even when he wasn't trying to be.

"The murder weapon was a meat mallet," the detective said finally. "It was left at the scene."

This was worse than Maggie had imagined. The crime scene contained a bloodied mallet in addition to a body with a head wound? And they were only *now* classifying it as a homicide? Either the police were in the pocket of whoever killed Antoine, or they were outrageously inept.

"We were just at *L'Étoile Gourmande*," Laurent said. "It is open for business as if nothing has happened."

"Yes, that's unfortunate," Inspector Rousseau said. "I fear that because we didn't initially consider the death suspicious, the crime scene has been compromised."

"By *compromised*, you mean scrubbed clean and restocked with lamb chops," Laurent said with disgust.

"Yes, well, I admit it is not ideal," Rousseau said, blushing, no longer able to dismiss or ignore Laurent's combative tone. "But there is no one to blame for that."

Maggie was astounded that the woman was refusing to take responsibility for the error. Could this be ineptitude? Surely nobody was this incompetent?

"Lucas Moreau has been hired at *L'Étoile Gourmande*," Laurent said.

Rousseau frowned.

"I don't know who that is," she said.

Laurent got to his feet and Maggie felt his fury pinging off him in waves.

"He is an angry ex-employee," he said bristling in frustration, "with an axe to grind against Antoine Dubois. He was fired for cause six months ago but the day after Antoine is killed, somehow, he's back at his old job."

"I am sorry I can't give you more positive news," Rousseau said, standing too, and to her credit looking guilty and flustered at Laurent's show of anger. "But I must ask you to stay away from the investigation and in particular from Remy Durand and his restaurant."

"Will *you* be staying away from Remy Durand?" Laurent asked pointedly.

"What are you implying?" Rousseau said, flushing darkly. "I assure you the Toulouse police will explore every possible lead to find the truth of who committed this murder."

Maggie put her hand on Laurent's arm, rock hard beneath her touch.

"Come on, Laurent," she said firmly. "The police are doing all they can."

She didn't want Laurent to say anything that might alienate the detective and she knew if they stayed even a few seconds longer, that was exactly what was going to happen.

## 19

The café terrace that Maggie and Laurent chose for breakfast the next morning was situated on the rue Dominique Baudis across from the Square Charles de Gaulle. It offered a protected spot from the brisk fall breeze as well as from the onslaught of tourists and locals who continued to swarm the streets thanks to the sausage festival. Maggie found herself enjoying the nippy weather as she sipped her espresso.

She glanced at Laurent who had been restless most of the night. Even though the police were finally admitting that Antoine's death was suspicious, Laurent clearly had no confidence in their being able to get to the bottom of what had happened. She couldn't blame him. Not if the level of incompetence she witnessed last night with Detective Rousseau was any indication of how the homicide department was run. It was partly the reason that she'd agreed to stake out a nearby restaurant this morning to observe the food critic Philippe Martin whose website revealed he would be dining there. Laurent insisted that Martin was a suspect in Antoine's murder. Maggie had considered discouraging Laurent from doing this since all he really had to go on was Antoine's recently shared list of people he didn't like. That constituted nothing more than rancor from the victim in the way of a lead—basically meaning there was no lead. But Maggie knew that doing something, even if it was next to nothing, was often helpful in the grieving process and so she bit her tongue. Still, it was a little disconcerting to see Laurent more interested in watching every person who came out of the restaurant across the street—the place where Martin's website claimed he would be this morning—than enjoying his own breakfast—something Maggie had rarely witnessed in all the years she'd known her husband.

"What is it exactly you're hoping to find out from the food critic?" Maggie asked as she scooped raspberry jam onto her croissant.

"I am not sure," Laurent said, his eyes on the restaurant across the street. "I just know that Antoine said the critic hated him. That's all I have to go on."

"Okay," Maggie said dubiously. "Except, is it really surprising for a restauranteur to accuse a food critic of being biased?"

"Antoine said Martin *hated* him," Laurent said.

"Yes, okay, but you know how passionate chefs can be. Isn't it possible that Antoine got a couple of bad reviews and turned that into an imagined vendetta against him?"

Laurent didn't answer. His eyes remained riveted to the door of the restaurant. Maggie decided not to suggest again that Laurent's ambushing a local food critic was probably not going to produce his hoped-for results. The fact was, she knew that Laurent needed to do *something* and, for lack of any other leads, this was probably as good as anything. On the other hand, now that the police were treating Antoine's death as a homicide, they would begin to give the investigation its proper due. Because of that, Maggie knew her main goal now was less about finding Antoine's killer than it was giving Laurent the support he needed to accept his friend's death. And of course getting both of them back to Domaine St-Buvard as soon as possible.

"There he is," Laurent murmured.

Looking up, Maggie saw the door to the bistro across the street open. Out of it came a tall well-dressed man with graying hair, and a discerning, superior look on his face. By the time Maggie turned back to Laurent, he was on his feet and heading across the street.

"*Excusez-moi*, Monsieur Martin," Laurent called as he crossed the street.

Philippe Martin glanced over at him in surprise but immediately accepted the handshake that Laurent was offering—as any normal Frenchman would—while his expression was guarded.

"My name is Laurent Dernier," Laurent said. "I understand you knew Antoine Dubois personally?"

Even from where she sat, Maggie could see Martin's expression tighten. She quickly tossed a handful of euros onto the table and gathered up her purse to hurry across the street to join Laurent.

"Who are you?" Martin asked Laurent as he watched Maggie cross the street toward him.

"I am a friend of Antoine Dubois," Laurent said. "You have heard the news, I assume?"

"Yes, yes, of course," Martin replied. His hand fidgeted with the edge of his jacket, twisting and untwisting it nervously. "It is terrible. But if you will excuse me—"

"Monsieur Martin," Laurent said firmly stepping in front of him and blocking his exit, "I understand you had a contentious relationship with Antoine. I am here to determine if that had anything to do with his death."

Martin's eyes widened. He licked his lips and looked from Laurent to Maggie.

"It...it is true that Antoine and I had our disagreements when it came to his restaurant," he said, haltingly. "But I assure you, my critiques are purely professional."

This was just as Maggie had expected. Everybody thinks the critics are out to get them but sometimes it's just because the truth hurts. Laurent wasn't convinced.

"Did your *professional* disagreements ever escalate beyond the realm of criticism?" Laurent asked. "Were there perhaps personal conflicts that might have fueled animosity between you?"

A bead of perspiration formed on Martin's brow.

"What are you suggesting?" he said, wiping the sweat from his face. "It's true I may have been negative in my reviews, but they were never personal. Antoine simply failed to live up to the standards I expect from a chef of his reputation."

Laurent leaned forward, his gaze piercing.

"Where were you two nights ago, Monsieur Martin?" he asked.

A flicker of unease crossed the food critic's face.

"I...I don't believe I owe you the answer to that," he said haltingly.

"Would you rather I encourage the police to ask it?" Laurent said.

Martin threw his hands up in frustration.

"I had no involvement in Antoine's death!" he said. "Our interactions were limited to professional settings. I...I never wished him harm."

"Monsieur Martin," Maggie said, keeping her voice calm

and placating. "We understand that tensions can run high in your line of work, especially when working with passionate people. But if there's anything you know, any detail that might help us find justice for Antoine, we are hoping you'll share that with us."

Philippe Martin's eyes darted again between Maggie and Laurent, his composure seemingly teetering on the edge of an eruption of some kind. To Maggie, it looked as if the weight of the man's secrets were bearing down upon him.

"Fine," Martin said his voice tinged with reluctance. "Look, there might have been an incident...an unfortunate exchange between Antoine and me at a recent culinary event. But it was just words, nothing more."

Maggie was surprised. Up until this moment, she thought any interview with the food critic was a waste of time. Now she wasn't so sure. There was something about him. He was definitely holding back something.

"Now if you will excuse me," Martin said. "I have another engagement on the other side of town."

"One last question," Laurent said.

"Yes, what?" the man said impatiently, the perspiration reappearing on his forehead.

"Your website indicated that you would be reviewing *L'Étoile Gourmande* under its new management later this month. Is that true?"

Martin cleared his throat noisily and looked away.

"I haven't updated my website," he said.

"So it's *not* the truth?" Maggie pressed.

"Okay, yes, it is. I do intend to review *L'Étoile Gourmande* sometime later this month."

"Is that because it's under new management?" Laurent asked.

Maggie could see the trap he was laying. How could

Martin have scheduled a time to review *L'Étoile Gourmande* under new management when before yesterday there was no new management?

"New ownership," Martin corrected him and then clamped his mouth shut as if he was sorry he'd said that much.

Laurent's eyes widened in surprise.

"New ownership?" Laurent said. "Since when is the restaurant under new ownership? And when did you learn about this?"

"Look, I don't know any more of the details than you do, Monsieur—"

"Clearly you do," Laurent said between gritted teeth. "What new ownership are you referring to?"

Martin made a strangled sort of half laugh.

"I was told two weeks ago that *L'Étoile Gourmande* was being purchased," he said. "That's all I know."

"That is not true," Laurent said, stepping threateningly closer to the man. "You know a lot more."

"Yes, okay, fine," Martin said, pushing past Laurent. "But the person you want to talk to is the new owner of *L'Étoile Gourmande.*"

"And who would that be?" Maggie asked, afraid that if Laurent asked it, it would be accompanied by a punch to the food critic's nose.

"Remy Durand," Martin said tartly as he turned and hurried down the sidewalk.

## 20

After their confrontation with Philippe Martin, Laurent felt that he had seen with his own eyes the animosity that Antoine had insisted the food critic had for him. But he still didn't know why. Immediately after he and Maggie left their street interview with Martin, they found a small bistro where Laurent put a call in to Antoine's son Marco. The bombshell news that Durand was about to become the new owner of *L'Étoile Gourmande*—and that it had been in the works for at least two weeks—was nearly impossible to believe.

After ordering lunch, Laurent left Maggie at their table and stepped out onto the street to call Marco so as not to disturb the other diners. In the short time that Maggie had been in Toulouse with Laurent she found herself deeply concerned with his general affect. Normally so cool and low-key, she caught him drumming his fingers on the table and even touching his shirt pocket as if looking for the packet of cigarettes he'd given up years ago.

She knew it wasn't just because of the abrupt and violent murder of his friend. He'd come into the weekend already a little shaky. She'd been naive to think a single weekend away was going to fix what was bothering Laurent. Topping it off with the murder of his old friend had just made everything a thousand times worse.

After a few minutes, Laurent came back to their table just as the waiter finished pouring a carafe of house red in their glasses. As Laurent took his seat, he ran a hand through his hair, a familiar gesture Maggie recognized as a sign of agitation and frustration.

"What did Marco say?" Maggie asked.

"He said as far as he knew his father never owned *L'Étoile Gourmande.*"

Maggie's mouth fell open in surprise.

"Then who owns it?" she asked.

"He said it's owned by a syndicate of owners."

"But surely he owned at least a part of the restaurant?" she said.

"Yes, but the syndicate contract prohibited it being automatically passed on to a beneficiary," he said sighing deeply, his eyes momentarily glazing over as if replaying the conversation in his mind.

"So Marco isn't Antoine's heir?" Maggie asked.

"He is, but not for the restaurant."

"Well, how did Remy Durand get a piece of it?"

"The only way for Remy Durand to become even a part owner of *L'Étoile Gourmande* was for Antoine or one of the other owners to sell his share to him," Laurent said. "Or to die."

"Who are the other owners?" Maggie asked.

Laurent shrugged.

"Marco didn't know. He thought the other portions were owned by corporations. He said, there was a wait list."

"And Durand was next in line?"

"Presumably."

Maggie paused and then took a sip of her wine. Laurent looked so distracted and unhappy, and she had no idea of how to ease his misery.

"How did Marco sound?" she asked.

"Sad, confused." Laurent reached over and picked up his wine glass. "He begged me to find out what happened to his father."

"So he doesn't have confidence in the Toulouse police?" she asked.

Laurent snorted. "Do you?"

Maggie had to admit he had a point. She reached across the table and touched his hand. She knew that Laurent's ability to appear unemotional and stoic was both his armor and his burden. And make no mistake it was an appearance only. It had taken her decades to realize that. It was a persona that had protected him in the past but had also isolated him. She desperately wished he would share his feelings with her. But she could at least imagine what they were. She sat back in her chair and glanced across the terrace. From here she could just see the tips of the Pyrenees on the Spanish side. She imagined this would be a lovely place to come for a vacation or even to live. She looked back at Laurent and saw he was staring into space, his eyes focused on nothing in front of him.

The lunch was good and normally Maggie would have expected Laurent to comment on it but today he didn't. In fact, if Maggie wasn't sure she'd imagined it, he almost appeared to hurry though his meal. Well, not *hurry* in the sense that an American might, she amended. But for someone like Laurent who sees food as one of life's great pleasures, it was the first time she'd ever seen him eat with no apparent interest in what he was putting in his mouth.

After that, they walked the square and then headed back to the bed and breakfast. Maggie knew better than to pepper Laurent with questions about how he was feeling or what he wanted to do now. She didn't know whether he intended to stay on in Toulouse to investigate Antoine's murder or if he was planning on going home. Admittedly, a part of her couldn't see how going home would help with whatever he was going through.

Once back at the bed and breakfast, they stopped to talk with their hosts who recommended a popular *brasserie* on the square for dinner that night. Back in their room, Maggie showered and lay down for a nap while Laurent sat at the desk in the room looking at his phone. It was odd seeing him do that since half the time he left his phone in restaurants or lost it between car seats. She'd never actually seen him access the Internet on his phone—or even, come to that, on his desk top computer in his office at home. She was curious what he was looking at but since it seemed to give him peace, she held off asking him about it.

A few hours later, when Maggie woke from her nap, she was able to lure Laurent into the bed next to her—not something she'd ever had much trouble doing in the past—ostensibly to encourage him to catch a few winks. He looked exhausted and she knew he hadn't been sleeping well. Plus, she of all people knew how exhausting stress was—especially when your mind was buzzing twenty-four seven. It was worse for Laurent who was naturally given to want to control any given situation. Maggie had once likened him to an overprotective sheep dog who would chew off his own paw to protect his flock. And of course she and the children were his flock. She wasn't entirely sure that trait of Laurent's wasn't partly the reason why Jemmy had left home with no suggestion of ever coming back to France for longer than a visit. In any case, for Laurent not to be able to control what was happening was easily a thousand times worse than it would be for anyone else. That much she knew as well as she knew her own name.

In any case, he did fall asleep and when he woke up, Maggie was happy to see that he looked refreshed and brighter. She was hesitant to ask him if he'd come up with any new approaches on Antoine's murder because she didn't want to spoil this pleasant respite from the stress of thinking about the investigation. While she knew she'd initially come to Toulouse to help support Laurent in finding justice for his friend, not so deep down she knew her first responsibility was to make sure her husband—the strongest person she knew—didn't end up spiraling someplace he'd never been before.

## 21

Le *Piment Rouge* was as charming as their bed and breakfast hosts had promised. As soon as Laurent and Maggie had stepped inside the little brasserie that night, the aroma of freshly baked bread and simmering sauces filled the air, mingling with the sound of soft jazz music playing in the background. The menu, written in an elegant script on an old-fashioned chalkboard, offered a delightful array of classic French dishes, from *coq au vin* to *crème brûlée*.

The restaurant staff was dressed in traditional Pyrenees and Spanish attire which added a festive note to the ambience. The servers moved attentively but unobtrusively between the tables, ensuring every guest felt at home.

Once shown to their table, Laurent ordered *poulet à la Toulousaine* for them both along with a demi bottle of champagne.

"I still can't get over that Durand is going to be able to buy into *L'Étoile Gourmande*," Laurent said, shaking his head. "Or that Lucas Moreau is already working there. It feels so pre-arranged, *tu sais?*"

"I agree," Maggie said. "We can probably talk to Moreau tomorrow. I think you might want to give it a beat before approaching Durand again."

Laurent snorted but he didn't argue with her.

"What did you think about our visit with Philippe Martin?" she asked as the waiter brought them a basket of bread and a small dish of olives.

"I think he's keeping something back," he said.

"I thought so too."

"Antoine believed Martin had a personal vendetta against him," Laurent said.

"If you want, I can do a deep dive on the Internet tonight to see if I can find that culinary event that Martin mentioned he attended with Antoine," Maggie said. "Maybe the heated exchange was really more than Martin is saying."

"*Merci, chérie*," Laurent said, reaching out to take her hand.

The soft glow of candlelight at their table danced on both their faces. That and the clinking of silverware and hushed conversations around them seemed to create a backdrop of romantic allure. Yet, there was still an unspoken heaviness that hung between them. Their eyes occasionally met, but words remained elusive. As usual, the quieter Laurent was, the more Maggie worried about what was going on in his head. They ate in silence for several minutes.

"Any more thoughts about how you're going to handle Mathieu Beaumont when you get back home?" Maggie asked, eager to talk about something a little less grim.

She knew that the thorny issue with the Aix politician was weighing on Laurent. His mini-houses were his pet project and he wouldn't easily give them up. Or at least he wouldn't have just a few short years ago. She wasn't sure what he was thinking these days.

"I talked to Windsor last week," Laurent said.

Windsor VanSant was Grace's ex-husband. He'd moved to Atlanta years ago, but he and Laurent had remained friends over the years.

"What did he say?" Maggie asked.

"Just that I should hire a good lawyer. He said that if Beaumont was trying to go through legal channels to shut me down, I needed to answer him in kind."

"At least you know it's not personal. He's only trying to get ahead in Aixoise politics."

"It doesn't matter whether it is personal or not," Laurent said with a frown. "The end result is the same."

Maggie couldn't argue with that. She'd hoped that his weekend away would prove a pressure release for Laurent from all the challenges back home. Naturally, Antoine's murder had put an abrupt end to that hope.

"The harvest felt different this time," she said casually.

He stared at his hands and Maggie knew him well enough to know that this was his form of tacit agreement.

"Do you know why?" she asked.

"Perhaps I am just getting old."

"That's not it."

He shrugged.

"You didn't look as if you were enjoying it this time," she said. "Are we having problems with distribution or production?"

"No, not at all. If anything, we are more in demand than ever."

"Well, was it because of all the problems with the pickers?"

Because of Beaumont's campaign to shut down Laurent's housing for the migrant workers, there had been rampant discord this year among the ranks. There was more petty theft and violence too, with Laurent having been called out to his mini-houses at least once a week to intervene in domestic disputes or drunken altercations. Laurent didn't answer.

"Are you thinking of making a change?" Maggie asked.

Laurent looked at her and frowned. She wasn't surprised to see that this appeared to be the first time that he had considered moving the pieces around in his life. For her, if something wasn't working, she was always ready to jettison the ill-fitting piece or add something new. Life was about moving components. Sometimes what was working great ten years ago was something that was holding you back today.

"In what way?" Laurent asked.

"I don't know. Have you ever thought of selling Domaine St-Buvard?"

He snorted.

"And do what, *chérie*? Move to Florida?"

"We don't have to leave Provence," Maggie said. "But farming is hard and every year we have more and more trouble finding and keeping good workers. I just think there comes a point when you need to ask yourself: Am I still happy?"

"So American."

"Well, we do get some things right," Maggie said with an arched eyebrow. "I wouldn't stay in a situation that was no longer working for me."

"So you would throw away twenty-six years of working the land?"

"No, because if we sold it, we wouldn't be throwing it away. We'd be reaping the benefits of our twenty-six years of stewardship. And if we rent it out, we wouldn't be throwing it away at all. There are many different ways to look at a problem."

"I am not convinced we have a problem."

Maggie sighed. As usual, it was going to take Laurent much longer to get to the same point where she was right now. She knew he was, if not unhappy, then at least no longer loving his life. What she also knew was that life was short. If there was a problem, her motto was to start working as soon as possible finding the solution to the problem instead of spending another five years being unhappy.

A few minutes later, on the way back from the ladies' room Maggie noticed two men at the bar who appeared to be openly watching her. Both were relatively young and one had a neck covered with tattoos. When she glanced back at them, they averted their gaze. She assumed they weren't drunk enough to be obnoxious. As she came back to the table, she couldn't help but mention the fact to Laurent. It wasn't every day a fifty-three-year-old woman got the attention of two young bucks out for a night on the town, she thought with a smile.

"Two guys at the bar were checking me out to see if I was wearing a wedding ring," she said as she settled back into her seat.

Laurent smiled wanly.

"Must I now kill total strangers to prove my devotion to you?" he asked.

"Haha, funny guy," she said. "Do you want dessert?"

"Of course."

After that Maggie made a point to only talk about things Amelie was up to, or their upcoming trip to Atlanta to visit with their niece Nicole and Jemmy. Luc had been hinting that he and Charlotte were trying to get pregnant, and Maggie had hopes that their visit home for Thanksgiving would coincide with a special announcement. She watched as Laurent scrutinized his Fenetra *tarte*—a delicacy of the region made with apricots and almond meringue that was not available in the area where they lived.

As she watched her husband, she couldn't help but think that a new baby was exactly the distraction that Laurent needed. Even if it was one on the other side of the world.

Later, as they left the restaurant, the night air around them felt heavy with a sense of unease. Maggie wasn't typically sensitive to atmospheric pressures or even gut feelings, but there was a chill in the air not totally attributable to the temperature that had her pulling her pashmina around her shoulders. The events of the last couple of days had left both her and Laurent on edge, their minds almost constantly racing with questions and uncertainties. She wasn't sure her being here was a good thing in that regard. All the obsessive questioning that Laurent would naturally be doing in his own head was now done out loud ad nauseum with her. The streetlamp on the side street of the restaurant cast a long shadow that seemed to amplify Maggie's growing apprehension.

"Are you warm enough, *chérie*?" Laurent asked.

Before she could respond, a sudden rustle of footsteps echoed from behind, causing both of them to turn. At first all Maggie was aware of was the shock of realizing that they had been followed. Right on the heels of that realization, she saw a pair of masked figures emerging from the darkness. Maggie heard the gasp come out of her mouth as Laurent stepped in front of her, facing the two men. She turned her head to look around, but they were facing a dead-end alley with the men standing in the only exit route.

She felt a flinch of terror as she saw that they both carried baseball bats.

"We have no money," Laurent growled.

As if a trigger, total chaos erupted on his words. Both assailants lunged forward. The man with the bat swung hard at Laurent who blocked the blow with his forearm, grunting in pain on impact before returning a hard punch to the man's face which sent him staggering. But before Laurent could draw his arm back for another punch, the second man's swing of the bat caught him on the side of the head with brutal force. The sickening thud of the bat as it connected with Laurent's skull echoed through Maggie's mind as she watched in horror as Laurent dropped to the pavement. Blood oozed from a gash on his forehead.

Maggie turned to the two men who were now walking toward her. She felt her adrenaline spike as she tried to muster the breath to scream as fear raged through her.

"Watch out for her nails," one of the men said.

"What are you worried about? You have the bat!"

"We're not supposed to kill her."

Maggie flung her purse in their faces and darted to the left, knowing her chances of getting around them were small. She felt harsh hands grab her and she bucked and twisted to shake them off. She was flung to the ground, the pavement rushing up to slam her in the face. Stars buzzed in her brain as she pawed impotently on the cobblestones, trying to ground herself, trying to get her knees under her.

She opened her mouth to scream and felt a sharp pinch in her side which robbed her of breath. Then she felt herself being lifted until darkness swallowed her vision. The sound of the car trunk lid slamming was the last thing she heard.

## 22

It was the nauseating scent of antiseptics that finally dragged Laurent into consciousness. That, and the effort of trying to register the faint beeping of medical equipment in the background. His eyes fluttered open, adjusting to the bright lights glaring down on him. Blinking away the remnants of his disorientation, Laurent found himself lying under a crisp white sheet on a hospital bed surrounded by bustling medical professionals. The room hummed with a sense of urgency and efficiency. Inspector Maxine Rousseau dressed in her police uniform stood by his bedside. She exuded an air of authority, and her presence seemed to provide an anchor in the sea of uncertainty that surrounded Laurent.

Her gaze met his. She leaned forward.

"Monsieur Dernier, can you hear me?"

Laurent nodded weakly.

"Yes," he managed to rasp. His throat was dry. "I can hear you.

Suddenly he remembered.

"My wife?" He looked around the room and then as

panic seized him, at the detective. "My wife was with me when we were attacked."

Inspector Rousseau took a seat in a nearby chair.

"Can you tell me what happened?" she asked.

"Is Maggie not here?" Laurent asked, trying to shove the panic down that was welling up inside of him.

He whipped back the sheet on the bed and lurched to an upright position. Instantly his mind swirled with fragments of memories along with a dull throbbing pain. He felt firm hands on his shoulders gently pushing him back into bed. He must have closed his eyes against the burgeoning nausea. When he opened them, he saw that two male nurses stood beside the bed. Or maybe just one.

"Not yet, Monsieur," one of them said. "Nice and easy."

"Where is my wife?" Laurent said, his voice hoarse and insistent.

Inspector Rousseau was standing again. She put a hand on Laurent's arm as if to keep him in place.

"We are looking for your wife, Monsieur Dernier," she said. "But I need you to tell me what happened."

Laurent groaned and ran a hand through his head.

*What happened?*

His mind raced as he tried to piece together the sequence of events. He remembered the dark street. The two men. The baseball bats.

"We left the *brasserie*," he said, his brain straining to remember. "We were headed for the bed and breakfast on rue du Poids de l'Huile. It was dark. The streetlamp was flickering."

Laurent noticed another detective standing by the window taking notes.

"Two men approached us," Laurent said. "They were

masked but Maggie said that two men had been watching her inside the restaurant."

"So you don't know if it was the same two men," Rousseau said.

Laurent narrowed his eyes at her.

"One of them had a full neck tattoo that the mask didn't cover," he said.

"Yes, okay. Go on."

"They came from the shadows. They went for me first. I...I..."

Laurent sought desperately to remember more but that was when everything had gone dark. He took a shallow breath and felt his throat close up.

"Why would they take her?" he asked in bewilderment, his voice choking with emotion as he looked at Rousseau. "Do we look wealthy?"

Inspector Rousseau's gaze softened.

"We don't know why they would take Madame Dernier," she said. "Her purse was taken so robbery is definitely a possibility, but we will find her. I promise you, Monsieur."

The whole time they talked, the hospital staff continued their work with the sounds of medical machinery in the background. Laurent turned away from Rousseau, his head pounding, and the movement prompted a terrible nausea deep in his gut. He felt a terrible urgency to get out of bed, to go back to the place of the attack. Inspector Rousseau leaned in closer.

"For now, Monsieur Dernier," she said, her voice carrying a tone of firmness, "you must focus on your recovery. We'll need your cooperation as we work to bring your wife home."

"Are there any clues at the site?" Laurent asked. "Did you find anything?"

"Not yet," Rousseau said.

"There was a car," Laurent said suddenly. "It was in the street. I'm sure it was theirs."

"Did you see a license plate?"

Laurent wracked his brain, but he couldn't remember seeing the car tag. Everything had happened too quickly.

With a final glance of understanding, Inspector Rousseau closed her notebook and promised that she or her staff would be in touch to keep him apprised of their progress. Laurent watched numbly, as Rousseau and the other detective left the room. He waited for a moment and took in a breath. He more than anyone knew the benefits of waiting, of testing the waters, of holding a finger up to the air to determine which way the wind was blowing. But if there were any more memories of that night, they weren't immediately forthcoming.

Slowly, he pulled back the bed sheet again and swung his legs over the side. He saw his clothing folded on the chair by the window and he stood carefully, waiting for the wave of dizziness to pass before making his way to the chair.

"*Pardon*, Monsieur!" a woman's voice came to him from close by. "You cannot leave. You have a serious head injury!"

Laurent ignored her and dressed, slowly and deliberately. He looked around the room leaning on the chair with one hand for balance. The room was spinning.

"Where is my wallet and phone?" he asked.

She gave a snort of frustration and then opened the drawer in the nightstand by his bed. She drew out a plastic bag and handed it to him.

"At least let the doctor look at you again before you leave," she said.

Laurent tucked his wallet into his pocket and turned on his phone. After a few moments of fumbling, he found the location finders app and quickly activated it. Instantly he saw the red pulsating dot that represented Maggie on the map. With a grunt of satisfaction, he slipped the phone in his pocket and turned to leave. If he had had even a shred of confidence in Rousseau and her idiot clown train of police detectives, he would've told her that he could track Maggie's whereabouts.

But then, if he *had* told her, he wouldn't be able to murder the two men who'd taken his wife.

## 23

Less than thirty minutes later, Laurent tightened his grip on the steering wheel of his car as he sped down the main road leaving Toulouse. He glanced at the map on his phone that showed him the digital path where Maggie had been taken and where her phone was now. He'd plugged in the address to his car's GPS system and its screen illuminated the car's interior, displaying a route that wound through twisting roads that climbed ever higher up the treacherous landscapes of the Pyrenees. The calm voice of the navigation system guided him with precise instructions through every turn.

With each passing mile, Laurent's anxiety grew. The road ahead narrowed as he followed switchbacks and hidden turnoffs, the scenery constantly transforming as he followed the GPS's guidance to more and more remote and rugged terrain. The majestic mountain range rose in the distance, its peaks obscured by wisps of clouds, while dense forests bordered both sides of the road.

Time seemed to blur as he drove, his focus unwavering from the image of the two men—masked and violent—who now had Maggie. He forced himself not to think of what they might be doing to her. There was no point in thinking like that.

As the GPS counted down the remaining distance, leading him deeper into the wilderness, closer to the spot where the red dot that represented Maggie had stayed static for the last two hours, Laurent's heart quickened. The car's tires crunched on gravel as he turned onto a narrow, winding path, leading him off the beaten track. His surroundings grew even more secluded. With each passing mile marker, Laurent's anxiety crested. Suddenly, the GPS chimed, signaling his arrival at the destination—the spot where Maggie was. He pulled the car to a halt, his hands gripping the steering wheel tightly as he surveyed his surroundings.

The location was hauntingly serene, a secluded clearing nestled amidst the embrace of nature. With the absence of the sound of the car's engine, he heard the wind whispering through the trees. He narrowed his eyes and squinted. A cabin was just barely visible in the thicket.

He stepped out of the car. There were no cars parked out front of the cabin. He moved closer on foot. The place looked abandoned. Even without smoke coming from the chimney or any cars parked out front, it was obvious there was nobody home. Its worn wooden exterior spoke of years of exposure to the elements.

He pulled up his phone and saw that the red dot that represented Maggie's cellphone was still there. Her phone at least was inside the cabin.

Approaching cautiously, Laurent noticed the footprints in the dirt leading to the cabin's entrance. The front door, slightly ajar, beckoned him forward, its creak echoing through the stillness of the surrounding forest when he pushed on it. The cabin's interior was heavy with an eerie silence, broken only by the sound of his footsteps on the wooden floorboards as he stepped inside.

His eyes scanned the space. He knew by now he wouldn't find Maggie here. How long had he known that? Since before he'd driven up and seen no cars? Now he was just hoping to find a clue that would lead him onward. The remnants of a fire lay in the hearth, but it was cold. Whoever had been here had been gone for hours. Disheveled bedding on the floor in one corner suggested a hasty departure. Laurent pulled out his phone and touched the button on the locator app to ring Maggie's phone—something he hadn't dared to do before now—and heard it buzz from a wooden counter in what passed as a kitchen. He went to it and picked up the phone. His stomach soured when he saw the photo of Amelie that Maggie kept on her screen. He held the phone and stared at it, thinking hard. Her captors could've destroyed the phone but instead they'd allowed him to follow it here to its inevitable dead end.

He felt tears sting his eyes as he held Maggie's phone. He'd actually held out hope that he'd find her. He could admit that now. He thought the red dot was leading him to her. He turned, his gut sick with disappointment and helplessness, and looked around the space as he tried to imagine Maggie here, tried to visualize the men who'd grabbed her. He rubbed a hand across his face, wiping the tears of frustration away. When he turned back to the kitchen, he saw the note.

It was written in a scrawling hand with a black marker. Laurent picked it up and read.

*Stop now if you want to see your wife alive*

## 24

Laurent's heart raced as he stared at the note. If there had been any question at all—even after finding Maggie's phone—about the intention of her kidnapping, this note put an end to those doubts once and for all. These men had his wife, and they were stipulating to Laurent the conditions on which he would see her again. He cracked his knuckles in mounting anger and felt adrenaline course through his veins, fueling his determination not to feel the despair that threatened to engulf him. He looked around. Every corner of the cabin held the potential for answers. It wasn't likely but it was something. He set about to meticulously search every inch of the space for any evidence that might shed light on Maggie's captors or their intentions.

An hour later, long after he'd already proven the disappointing truth to himself, he knew it was hopeless. They'd left her phone and the note. That was it. His gut churned with nausea at the thought of her here, sitting on the floor in this filthy place, maybe gagged and bound. He wanted to slam his fist into something.

The mere thought of Maggie suffering like this ignited a fierce anger within him, making his hands curl into tight fists. But alongside the rage, Laurent also felt a sense of helplessness creeping in. He struggled with the conflicting emotions, unsure of how to channel them into action. His rage quickly dissipated to a sickening spasm of self-hatred as he realized that it was his fault that this was happening to Maggie. He had failed to protect her.

He stepped out of the cabin and took several long breaths. As soon as he'd noticed there were no cars parked outside the cabin, he'd tried to recalibrate his expectations for what he would find. But he'd failed in that too and the disappointment now threatened to overwhelm him. He inhaled the cold mountain air in quick restorative gulps and stood on the threshold of the cabin, his eyes drawn to the majestic expanse of the mountains and the wilderness that stretched out before him.

*Is she out there somewhere?*

The silence around him was interrupted only by the whisper of the wind rustling through the trees. In that moment, Laurent knew he had no hope of wandering the mountains and finding Maggie. Out there was only chaos and darkness and death. Any answers that might help him must lie back in Toulouse.

Only in Toulouse could he find the people who knew who did this and why. Who were the two men? Were they working for someone else? Would they ask for a ransom? He instantly dismissed that thought. No, they'd clearly said what they want—for him to back off.

Now he was tasked with continuing his search—but do it such a way that the people holding Maggie didn't find out. He felt exhaustion creep over him as he stepped off the porch and headed in the direction of his car.

He thought again of the note that had been left for him.

*Stop now if you want to see your wife alive*

He didn't know if the men were professionals or just local thugs. He didn't know if this meant an organization was behind Maggie's kidnapping or if it was somehow personal. And if it was personal, was it against him or Maggie or Antoine? He ran a hand through his hair in frustration and felt his stomach cramp in fear.

In fact, the only thing he really knew for sure was that in order to find the people who had kidnapped Maggie, he needed to find the people who had killed Antoine.

## 25

It was late afternoon by the time Laurent drove back to Toulouse to the restaurant where he and Maggie had eaten the night they were attacked. Because Toulouse was a robust tourist town, the restaurant was already open for dinner. He parked his car on the street and stepped into the dimly lit bar area of the restaurant. A sense of unease throbbed in his gut as he approached the bartender. Memories of the night of the attack mixed with dread and guilt.

The bartender, a middle-aged man with a weathered face and a friendly demeanor, glanced up from polishing a glass as Laurent approached the counter.

"Can I help you, Monsieur?" he asked.

"My wife and I were here for dinner last night," Laurent said, his voice steady but tinged with an undercurrent of urgency. "My wife mentioned seeing two men at the bar. Sitting right here, as a matter of fact."

The bartender's brow furrowed slightly, his gaze sharpening with consternation.

"Ah, yes. I remember of course. You are the couple who was attacked in the street."

Laurent leaned in closer, his voice lowering to a hushed tone.

"My wife described them as wearing leather jackets. One of them had a full neck of tattoos. Had you ever seen these men before?"

"My memory is not very good," the bartender said evasively.

Laurent knew that bartenders tend to have very good memories that got better the wider one opened one's wallet. He peeled two twenty-euro notes out of his wallet, and both fluttered to the counter.

"Think harder," Laurent said.

The bartender's eyes narrowed as he eyed the bills on the counter.

"I am sorry, Monsieur. I do not remember seeing anyone like that."

Laurent knew he was lying. More than that, he knew that he was afraid. The bartender began to nervously mop the countertop with a bar towel.

"I'm sorry, Monsieur. I'm afraid the bar is always quite busy," he said.

Laurent felt a churning of frustration and anger welling within him. He left the money where it was and added his business card to the counter.

"You are aware that my wife was abducted that night?" he asked.

The bartender nodded, his eyes downcast and focused on the counter.

"I am, Monsieur. I am very sorry that happened to your wife."

Laurent was sure the man knew the two men and before the week was over, he would be back to question him again. Only this time, instead of bringing euros, he would bring a fist wrapped around a tube of euro coins. Some people needed encouragement to do the right thing. He turned and walked out of the restaurant, heading for the spot in the street where the attack had taken place.

He walked into the street but saw nothing that told him more than he already knew. There were no tire marks, no dropped items. It didn't matter which way the car had been pointed since Laurent already knew where it had gone after leaving here. Frustrated and fighting the feeling of encroaching helplessness, Laurent went back to his car and drove to the bed and breakfast. In his mind, the two men's attack on Maggie felt planned. Taking her to an isolated spot seemed to point to a local knowledge. Plus, the fact that no ransom note had been delivered told Laurent that her abduction was not random or driven by money. All of it seemed to point to the idea that the men were a part of a local crime syndicate.

If Laurent assumed that Maggie was still alive—and at this point, he had to or he would lose his mind—then he had to believe he had some control of keeping her that way. The threatening note left in the cabin for him tied his hands. But one way or the other it was clear that finding out who killed Antoine was key to finding out who held Maggie.

Since the police were either in the pocket of the mob or simply unable to organize a competent investigation, what Laurent did now mattered more than ever. As he pulled into a parking spot in front of his bed and breakfast, he took out his phone and called Detective Rousseau to see if she had any information about Maggie's abduction. As he waited for the receptionist to pass his call through, he found himself holding his breath until Rousseau came on the line.

"I am sorry, Monsieur Dernier," Rousseau said. "But the

good news is that there have been no reported bodies in the area."

Laurent felt a flash of fury. They were surrounded by a mountainous wilderness. Professional killers would have no trouble disposing of a body such that it would never be found. The fact that Rousseau felt her news of *no found body* was encouraging to Laurent filled him with even more disgust at her incompetence.

"I promise to keep you informed of any news," she assured him.

"*Merci*," he said before disconnecting. He didn't bother asking if there were any leads on Antoine's murder. She wouldn't tell him if there were. He sat in the car staring straight ahead with his head pounding before digging out two paracetamols from the glove box and swallowing them with a few swallows of water from a liter bottle in his car door before getting out. As he walked toward the bed and breakfast, he called Grace—something he'd been putting off. He'd already received two calls from her that he'd let go to voice mail. She'd texted him too saying that she was having trouble reaching Maggie.

He leaned against the front porch of the bed and breakfast and waited for her to answer. The cobblestone street in front of him was lined with neatly trimmed trees, and what leaves that were left rustled softly in the cool breeze. Down the street, he could see evidence of the bustling activity of the main square, with its ongoing sausage festival, kiosks, cafés, and artisan shops. Beyond that were the spires of the city's historic churches rising above the rooftops, their bells chiming, adding a melodic backdrop to the scene but also adding a wrench to Laurent's heart.

"Laurent! Thank goodness!" Grace said when she picked up. "What is going on? Maggie isn't answering her phone."

"We've had a problem here, Grace," Laurent said.

He'd already decided that he would need to tell her the truth. He heard her sharp intake of breath and he steeled himself as he told her what happened. When he was finished, he appreciated the calmness in her voice. He knew she was upset. He knew she was afraid. But she wouldn't show it in front of the children.

"Now what?" she asked.

"Now I find her," he said. "Put Amelie on the phone so I can wish her sweet dreams."

"Laurent?"

"Yes?"

"You'll find her," Grace said. "I don't doubt that for a minute."

Laurent sighed. He wished he felt half as sure.

## 26

The next day, after a sleepless night where all Laurent could think about was wondering what kind of a night Maggie had spent until he thought he might go mad, he set out for the center of town to find a coffee and a croissant before then going on to *L'Étoile Gourmande*.

The early morning sun cast a warm, golden light over the cobblestone streets which even at this early hour buzzed with the cheerful chatter of locals manning their various sausage kiosks. After drinking his coffee and eating his croissant standing on the street, Laurent walked the two blocks to the now familiar façade of Antoine's restaurant, his heart heavy with trepidation.

As he stood across the street from the restaurant, he found himself replaying in his brain the memory of the man he'd known so many years ago. Even then, Antoine's passion for cooking had been evident. Laurent was impressed with the idea of all that Antoine had overcome in order to create this restaurant, this new life for himself. The fact that

Antoine hadn't owned it solely himself—and hadn't shared that fact with Laurent—seemed to suggest that Antoine was ashamed about the fact. Did Antoine have money problems? All Laurent had seen when he met back up with him was a successful, happy man living the dream and fulfilling his life's work. He made a mental note to ask Marco about it the next time he spoke with him.

Taking a deep breath, he pushed open the front doors. The restaurant wouldn't open for diners for another four hours and the hostess stand was vacant as Laurent maneuvered through the tables toward the kitchen, the aroma of various savory dishes filling the air. Laurent expected the kitchen to be focused on preparing for the upcoming lunch hour. He intended to be quick and unseen. He slipped into the kitchen, his footsteps noiseless against the tiled floors.

The atmosphere shifted from the deathly quiet of the dining area to the typical controlled chaos of a restaurant kitchen. Line cooks and prep cooks moved with precision, chopping, sautéing, talking, walking in and out of the freezer and the walk-in pantry, all in preparation for the upcoming dinner hour. Laurent made his way discreetly to Antoine's office unobserved by the focused workers. The door to the office was closed, but when Laurent turned the doorknob, he found it unlocked.

The lock wouldn't have prevented him from entering but it was convenient not to risk being observed. Inside, the office revealed itself once more as it had three nights before when he and Antoine had sat here and told their stories, laughing and enjoying their memories. Photographs adorned the walls, capturing Antoine's many moments of triumph, serving as a reminder of the passion and unique talent that had fueled Antoine's culinary journey.

The lingering presence of Antoine's spirit was almost visceral for Laurent and for a moment it was all he could do to stand there and look at the two chairs where he and his friend had sat. He shook the melancholy feeling away. He didn't have time to indulge in it. Instead, he focused on the desk against the wall under the observation window that opened up into the kitchen. No one looked in his direction. They were all too busy.

Laurent began his search methodically, scanning the room for anything that might provide insight into Antoine's murder. He combed through the file folders on Antoine's desk, searching for any peculiarities. He rifled through the desk drawers which revealed a collection of personal items —a handwritten work calendar, a stack of letters, and a file labeled "Confidential." Laurent opened the file, his eyes quickly scanning the contents—invoices, contracts, and a series of correspondences. Names, dates, and cryptic references danced across the pages. Why were these categorized as confidential?

Was Antoine doing something illegal?

Laurent pulled out his cellphone and photographed each document. His mind raced as he sifted through the folder's contents. He didn't know what any of it meant, but he would comb through more thoroughly at his leisure later.

As he closed the file, his gaze settled on a framed photograph on Antoine's desk. It was a picture of Antoine with Marco when the boy was around twelve. Laurent remembered Jemmy at that age. He tried to imagine how he'd feel if a total stranger had to call his son up to tell him his father had been murdered. He swallowed hard and found himself once more promising Marco—and Antoine—that he would find out who had done this.

Laurent had been so focused on the documents he'd discovered that he literally jumped when a strident voice pierced the air.

"What are you doing here?"

Looking up, Laurent saw Lucas Moreau standing in the doorway of the office with a scowl etched across his face.

## 27

Laurent was momentarily taken aback by Lucas's sudden appearance, but quickly composed himself and met the sous chef's hostile gaze.

"What are you doing in my office?" Lucas demanded, his arms crossed defiantly.

"Your office?" Laurent said with a snort. "That was awfully quick, wasn't it?"

Lucas flushed but Laurent could tell he'd hit a nerve.

"I'm conducting a personal investigation into Antoine's death," Laurent replied.

Lucas crossed his arms, his eyes narrowing.

"What makes you think you can find anything here? Antoine's gone, and good riddance. He was a terrible chef. He held us back with his outdated ideas."

"He said he fired you," Laurent said. "For lack of ability."

He'd made that last part up but in his experience, egging people on generally got them to say things they might not normally. Unfortunately, in this case, a smug smile played at the corners of Lucas's lips, his arrogance clearly unaffected.

"Antoine was a relic," Lucas said. "His death may be

tragic, but it was necessary to clear the path for true innovation."

While that sounded very much like someone who might have cleared the path himself to get what he wanted, Laurent forced himself not to jump to conclusions. His instinct told him there was more to Lucas's animosity than met the eye. He pressed further.

"Did you have any specific issues with Antoine?" Laurent asked. "Anything that might shed light on his murder?"

Lucas's expression hardened, a flicker of anger crossing his face.

"Antoine was holding us back," he repeated, almost as if he was reading from a script. "He couldn't accept new ideas, always clinging to his outdated methods, refusing to adapt."

Laurent found himself weighing the sous chef's words and his manner. Was he merely a disgruntled employee, seizing an opportunity to vent his frustrations? Or had he done something to help him realize his own ambitions? Examining the young man's face Laurent tried to see if there was something in his expression that hinted that he might know something about Maggie's abduction. If he did, he was pretty cool. Or cold-blooded.

At that point, Lucas abruptly turned away, his voice dripping with contempt.

"If you'll excuse me, I have work to do. Unlike Antoine, I have a restaurant to run."

Laurent watched as Lucas disappeared back into the bustling kitchen. The sous chef's words had offered a glimpse into the possible motivation for Antoine's murder that Laurent had already suspected, but whether they held any true relevance to Antoine's murder remained to be seen.

With a final glance around the office, Laurent shut all

the desk drawers and stepped out of Antoine's office. Winding his way through the dining room before exiting the restaurant, his mind was awhirl with what little he felt he'd discovered. He'd nearly reached the front door when he spotted a man leaning against the hostess stand watching him. Laurent went up to him.

"Do you know me?" Laurent asked.

The man, whom Laurent estimated to be in his sixties, exuded a rugged charm that spoke of years spent working out of doors. But while his sun-weathered skin and calloused hands told him that, the man's piercing blue eyes suggested he also held a secret or two.

"I know of you, Monsieur Dernier," the man said. "Antoine spoke of you."

"You are a friend of Antoine's?" Laurent asked.

"Jean-Luc Bouchard," he said, extending his hand. "We should talk. But not here. Come."

Bouchard guided Laurent out of the restaurant, down the sidewalk and then into a narrow side alley tucked behind the restaurant. A faint scent of tobacco smoke mingled with the aroma of spices and food where the kitchen staff obviously had their cigarette breaks. As Laurent and Bouchard turned into the alley, they entered a secluded enclave shielded from the noise and chaos of the main street. At the moment, the area was empty of kitchen workers.

Bouchard stopped and pulled a cigarette pack out of his jacket, offering one first to Laurent who shook his head.

"I have known Antoine for many years," Bouchard said as he lit his cigarette. "I was his main local supplier. I have a farm on the outskirts of Toulouse."

That surprised Laurent since the man was dressed in a wool suit complete with vest.

"I am trying to find out what happened to Antoine," Laurent said. "The people who killed him also abducted my wife."

Bouchard's eyes widened but Laurent could tell the man knew about Maggie's kidnapping.

"I am sorry to hear that," Bouchard said.

"Do you have any idea who might have taken her?" Laurent asked.

Bouchard sucked in hard on his cigarette and then flung it to the cobblestones and ground it out with the toe of his work boot.

"I would only be guessing," he said.

"That's more than I have," Laurent said.

Bouchard looked around and even though they were alone, Laurent got the feeling that Bouchard didn't trust that fact.

"Look," Bouchard said. "I don't know who killed Antoine or who took your wife. But there is an organization in Toulouse called *La Main Noire*. You have heard of it?"

Laurent shook his head.

"It is a crime syndicate headed by a man named Emile Chevalier," Bouchard said.

"What does that have to do with Antoine? He was a chef."

"Chevalier is responsible for overseeing certain operations in Toulouse related to the culinary world."

"What kind of operations?" Laurent asked.

"Drug trafficking, money laundering and human trafficking. *La Main Noire* is sponsoring the Merguez Festival."

Laurent ran a hand through his hair in frustration, a confused look on his face.

"Why?" he asked.

"Chevalier's job is to infiltrate various levels of society in

Toulouse in order to hold influence over certain figures in law enforcement and local government," Bouchard said.

"You understand?"

Laurent nodded grimly.

"This kind of influence allows *La Main Noire* to operate with impunity, covering their tracks and hindering investigations," Bouchard said.

"Investigations like into the murder of Antoine Dubois?"

"That I do not know," Bouchard said. "Was Dubois killed by *La Main Noir*? Perhaps. But to find out for sure you would have to discover why."

"How would I discover that?"

"By talking to people. But you must be careful of who you talk to. Abducting your wife was a warning."

"I'd heard of an organized crime syndicate in the area," Laurent said. "But it seemed to me that because the kidnappers used local spot where they initially took my wife, it sounds more likely it's two individuals desperate to cover their own involvement in Antoine's murder, rather than the work of a coordinated criminal syndicate at work."

"*La Main Noire is* local," Bouchard said. "Its members would know any and all local spots around Toulouse and the Spanish border and yes, even into the mountains—no matter how remote or otherwise inaccessible."

"Why are you helping me? Aren't you at risk doing so?" Laurent asked.

It had crossed Laurent's mind that this man might be working for whoever it was who killed Antoine. Pushing Laurent toward the idea that the local mafia was the culprit would fit perfectly with the plans of someone trying to cover his own tracks. For that matter, Laurent didn't know if *Bouchard* didn't have a private motive himself for wanting Antoine dead.

"I am, of course, Monsieur Dernier," Bouchard said. "But I felt it was important to impress upon you the seriousness of the situation."

"You don't think my wife's abduction didn't make that point fairly clear?" Laurent asked.

"Of course, Monsieur. I was just trying to be helpful."

"Where can I find this Emile Chevalier?" Laurent said. "I think I need to talk to him."

"*Non, mon vieux*," Bouchard said, his face gone suddenly ashen. "That is literally the last thing you need to do."

## 28

Discouraged with his morning's efforts but reminding himself that any information at all might be the piece that helped him find Maggie, Laurent went back to his lodgings to regroup.

His bed and breakfast was a charming, two-story house located just a block off the main square of Toulouse painted in a soft, buttery yellow, with white trim and flower boxes overflowing with geraniums beneath each window. A small wrought-iron gate opened to a cobblestone path leading to the front door which was framed by climbing ivy.

Once back in his room, Laurent looked around and his eye landed on Maggie's silk camisole. He felt a sudden and painful stab in his heart at the sight as if she had suddenly materialized in the room. In all the years of their marriage there had been so many celebratory moments—most having to do with the children or the vineyard—and of course many challenges as well. But in every case no matter what they were grappling with, he and Maggie had always ended up on the same side, with the same viewpoint. That hadn't always been the case in the beginning.

But even then, those times of misunderstanding—and often outright lying—had been exciting in their own way, like discovering an exotic dominion and being forced to learn its ways for survival. He smiled sadly as he looked at Maggie's camisole, so carelessly tossed onto the bed. The two of them had always found moments to acknowledge and appreciate the touchpoints of their lives, no matter how incremental. Those moments provided a respite from the mundaneness of their lives and reinforced their commitment to each other.

Laurent sat down on the side of the bed and thought of the jeopardy he might be putting Maggie in by continuing to search for her. He ran a hand through his hair and tried to imagine what she was feeling right now, what she was going through. She was smart, the smartest woman he ever knew. He knew she would be careful—if she had any choice in the matter. His stomach seized with fear as he thought of the men who'd taken her and what they might do to her.

*What they might be doing to her.*

He stood up and paced to the other side of the room, his feelings a painful jumble inside him threatening to burst out of his skin. He could only distract himself from his fear by imagining all the ways he would disembowel the men who'd taken her when he finally caught them.

And catch them he had no doubt he would. Or die trying.

He went to the bathroom and splashed cold water on his face, then shook the droplets away like a dog after a bath, not bothering with the hand towel. He thought back to his conversation with Rousseau this morning. The warning note didn't say anything about not involving the police. He didn't know if Rousseau was in the pocket of the people who took Maggie, but it was probably best not to take chances.

He would refrain from calling the police from this point on. Besides, what were the chances they could help him even if they weren't corrupt or complicit? No, talking to them could only succeed in getting Maggie killed.

He ran his hands through his hair again before picking up his phone to call Antoine's ex-girlfriend Claudine. He'd gotten her number off one of the pages he'd taken from Antoine's office. Claudine was a common name and normally Laurent would assume that the number was listed in Antoine's phone to which Laurent had no access. Why had Antoine jotted it down? Laurent had no answer for that. What he did know was that he needed to be very careful that the people he talked to were untraceable. He wouldn't go to the police or confront Remy Durand again, but he had to assume that the people holding Maggie didn't know about every causal hookup that Antoine had.

"*Allo?*" a woman's voice said, answering.

"Claudine?" Laurent said.

He didn't know the girl's last name, or he would've addressed her as Mademoiselle.

"Who is this?" she asked guardedly.

"I am a friend of Antoine's," Laurent said. "Is it possible we can meet?"

There was a hesitation on the line.

"Okay," she said finally. "Can you come now?"

Laurent scooped up his car keys.

"I'm on my way," he said.

## 29

Claudine's apartment was just a few blocks from Antoine's restaurant which made Laurent think that the restaurant was likely the key to how the two had met. Her apartment building was set squarely in the heart of the old section of town. It was a charming structure with a weathered façade of ochre and terracotta that exuded a sense of history and character.

Laurent passed through a delicate wrought-iron gate at the building entrance, its design a nod to the artistic craftsmanship of the region. He took the outdoor stairwell to the third floor where he faced a worn hall with three apartment doors on each side. He could smell the scent of decades of garlic-infused meals trapped in the thin plaster walls. He found Claudine's apartment easily and rapped on the door before taking a step back into the hall. Because of his size, he was well aware that he could be unintentionally intimidating. He knew that asking Claudine what she knew would be more constructive in the long run if she wasn't threatened by him. At least at first.

She was clearly waiting for him because the door

opened immediately after he knocked and when it did, Claudine stood on the threshold facing him. Laurent's eyes widened when he saw her. He hadn't expected to recognize her. His face gave away his surprise.

"You're the hostess at *L'Étoile Gourmande*," he said.

"I was," Claudine said, moving into the interior of her small apartment to allow him in. "I am taking some time off."

As Laurent stepped inside, he was immediately enveloped by a pervasive scent of sandalwood and jasmine. In a glance he saw that her apartment featured a minimalist aesthetic with a monochromatic color palette. The living room was furnished with a simple gray sofa adorned with colorful, embroidered cushions. The walls were a soft shade of dove gray.

"Antoine didn't mention that the two of you worked together," Laurent said.

"I am surprised he mentioned me at all," Claudine said, gesturing to the couch.

Natural elements played a prominent role in the apartment's décor, but Laurent couldn't help noticing an abundance of crystals of various sizes and colors on the shelves and windowsills, their shimmering facets catching the light and casting delicate prismatic reflections across the room. Laurent was vaguely familiar with the idea that New Age believers felt these stones were valuable for their supposed metaphysical properties, believing them to enhance positive energy or some such thing.

Dreamcatchers swayed gently in one of the open windows. A small meditation corner was set up near a window, furnished with cushions and a tapestry featuring sacred symbols and mandalas. The wafting smoke mingled with the faint scent of old books and polished wood.

As he moved into the living room, Laurent noticed a bookcase with shelves holding an array of books that referenced topics such as astrology, chakra healing, and energy work. Throughout her apartment were subtle affirmations and inspirational quotes framed and hanging on the walls. It occurred to Laurent as he looked around that for all the crystals and incense and soft flowing fabrics, the atmosphere in the apartment was a somber one. A soft melodic lullaby was playing from the kitchen, lending another layer of sadness to the place it seemed to him.

As he sat on the couch, Laurent noticed there were no photographs of Antoine. His gaze settled briefly on a small, delicate figurine standing on a shelf amid other ceramic and crystal figurines, this one a miniature sculpture of a mother cradling a baby in her arms. Laurent had seen the figurine somewhere before. A memory tugged at him from long ago, but he couldn't place it. Turning his attention back to Claudine he marked that she looked nervous. Or was it fear?

"I was wondering if you knew what Antoine might have been involved with in the days before his murder," Laurent asked, keeping his voice as gentle as possible.

Tears seeped from her eyes, and she reached for a ready box of tissue on the coffee table.

"We often fought over the kinds of people he allowed into his kitchen," she said.

"What kinds of people?" Laurent asked.

She shook her head.

"Bad people," she said. "Yet Antoine listened to them."

"Did he act wary of them?" Laurent asked. "Or maybe even afraid?"

"You're asking if they owned him in some way," Claudine said. "I didn't see that. I saw Antoine work with them willingly."

"Do you think he was doing something illegal?"

Claudine blew out a breath and looked around the room. For a moment Laurent got the idea that she wasn't comfortable speaking in her own home.

*As if she thinks she might be bugged?*

"I don't know," she said. "He asked me to trust him." Her tears started up again. "And then he told me it was none of my business."

That must have been around the time that the relationship was breaking up, Laurent thought. Claudine stood up and massaged the small of her back.

"I try to trust the universe," she said. "You know? It helps to know that all of this is mandated. But it still hurts."

"Was there anyone who came into the restaurant who might have meant Antoine harm?" he asked.

"Well, you know about the food critic, yes? Philippe Martin?"

"Antoine mentioned him. Was it more than just Antoine being annoyed because he got poor reviews?"

"I used to see Martin come into the restaurant all the time," she said.

Laurent was aware that she hadn't answered his question.

"Again, that is hardly incriminating for a food critic," he said.

"In disguise?" she asked.

Laurent's eyebrows shot up.

"Martin came to *L'Étoile Gourmande* in disguise?" he asked.

"On more than one occasion. I'm sure he didn't know that I recognized him. But I stand at the front and I see everyone who comes in."

Laurent frowned. Was it typical for food critics to come

to restaurants in disguise? Perhaps they needed to hide who they were in order to get typical service and dishes. He found that he could almost believe it. Almost.

"Can I get you something to drink?" Claudine asked.

"I am fine. *Merci*," Laurent said. "Can you can think of anything mysterious or odd about Antoine and the restaurant? Anything at all?"

Claudine sat back down. "Odd, how?"

"Strange comings and goings? Altercations?"

She frowned as if in thought.

"I know he had trouble keeping staff," she said.

That surprised Laurent. The reputation of *L'Étoile Gourmande* would've attracted endless numbers of kitchen workers eager to be a part of its glory. He made a mental note of the supposed kitchen turnover rate to see if there was anything in the documents that he'd photographed in Antoine's office that might shine a light on why that was. For a moment he remembered the fierce loyalty he'd witnessed in Remy Durand's staff when they defended their boss.

"Oh!" Claudine said as if suddenly remembering something. "And of course there was the feud between him and Jean-Luc Bouchard."

## 30

Laurent could hear the sound of some sort of fountain or running water somewhere in the apartment as he digested what Claudine had just told him. The scent of incense seemed more pronounced than before.

"What kind of feud?" he asked, beginning to feel a nagging dread that he'd let Bouchard off the hook way too easy.

"Well, you could ask around the kitchen because I'm sure they know the details better than I do," Claudine said. "But it has something to do with a cassoulet recipe that Bouchard accused Antoine of stealing. Do you know the menu?"

Laurent nodded. He'd seen that the dish *Cassoulet de Perdrix*—partridge cassoulet—was a unique twist on the region's most famous fare. Now that he thought about it, he realized that this variation of the popular dish was practically the showpiece meal of the restaurant. If Antoine had truly stolen it, it was an insult to the real owner that would be hard to bear.

"I suppose Bouchard didn't have proof that it was his recipe originally?" Laurent asked.

"I really don't know," Claudine said. "I suppose if he had proof, he would've presented it, though, yes?"

"Presumably," Laurent said. "But the two continued to work together?"

"Toulouse is not Paris," she said. "Here, you must work with whomever you have. Antoine and Bouchard needed each other. They couldn't afford not to work together."

"But there was bad blood between them."

Claudine got up to arrange a series of scented candles on the coffee table between them before delicately and with great ritual lighting each one.

"*Absolument*," she said sadly. "In fact, if you ask around, I'm afraid you will be hard pressed to find anyone who will sing Antoine's praises. Did you know him well?"

"A long time ago."

"Ah, well. People change. Perhaps Antoine was not the man you once knew."

~

After leaving Claudine's place, Laurent went directly to *L'Étoile Gourmande* to confront Bouchard, but he couldn't find him in the alley or the kitchen. Frustrated at not being able to ask Bouchard directly about the stolen recipe and the feud between him and Antoine and why he hadn't mentioned it, Laurent found a seat at a nearby bistro and used his cellphone to call up Philippe Martin's website where he saw that the food critic was scheduled to eat lunch today at a place called Café du Capitole off the main square of Toulouse. Laurent paid his tab and headed over there.

Moments later, he stepped into the Café du Capitole.

The aroma of garlic and fennel wafted through the air, mingling with the soft murmur of conversations and the clinking of glasses. Even at lunch time the interior lighting cast a warm glow in the dining room and created an intimate atmosphere as Laurent scanned the restaurant in search of the food critic.

He spotted Martin at a corner table and approached with a determined stride. The food critic's table was adorned with a pristine white tablecloth, featuring an array of small plates artfully arranged with colorful culinary creations. It looked like a tasting menu. Each dish was meant to reflect the creativity and craftsmanship of the chefs who sought Martin's discerning palate—and the rave review that would make the difference in their bottom line.

As Laurent drew closer, he noticed Martin meticulously examining each dish with a critical eye. The food critic's intensity was palpable, his focus unwavering as he carefully tasted and evaluated the dish before him. Laurent felt an unanticipated wave of revulsion at the man—someone who considered his taste buds attuned to the subtleties and nuances of gastronomy. Someone who could make or break a restaurant regardless of the skill, hard work and money invested in it.

"Bonjour, Monsieur Martin," he said.

The food critic looked up, momentarily startled, before his features softened into an expression of unhappy recognition.

"I have nothing to say to you," Martin said, waving Laurent away as if he were an annoying fly.

Laurent pulled out a chair and sat down, prompting a huff of indignation from the food critic. Beside the man was his cellphone, screen side down. It dinged as Laurent joined the man.

"I have a few more questions for you," Laurent said.

"Look, I'm sorry about what happened to your wife," Martin said petulantly as his phone dinged again. "But how can I help? I certainly don't hang out with hoodlums or underworld kingpins."

"Is that who you believe abducted my wife?" Laurent asked.

"I have no idea who did it!" Martin said, snatching his glasses off his face in petulance. "But I am working here and you have no right to interfere."

Laurent turned to the waiter over Martin's shoulder and lifted his hand to get his attention. Martin turned in his seat to see who Laurent was waving to. When he did Laurent reached across the table and knocked the man's glasses to the floor. Martin snapped his head around and then with a grunt of annoyance scooted his chair back to bend down to retrieve them. That was when Laurent turned the man's cellphone screen over and saw the string of text messages having to do with online betting.

When Martin saw that Laurent had touched his phone, he blushed scarlet and snatched it up and tucked it into his top jacket pocket while the phone continued to ding indicating more bets were being made.

"I cannot help you, Monsieur," he said sharply. "And now I must ask you to leave."

"I'm told you make it a habit of coming into *L'Étoile Gourmande* in disguise," Laurent said.

Sweat popped out on Martin's brow and his chin began to tremble.

"I...you...that is an outrageous lie!" he said.

"The hostess at *L'Étoile Gourmande* says she's seen you on numerous occasions wearing a fake mustache."

Laurent had exaggerated what Claudine told him, but it worked. The man was apoplectic.

"I'd have to say that wearing a disguise is very suspicious behavior," Laurent said as he stood up. "Especially when the object of your stalking ends up dead."

As Laurent left, it occurred to him that Martin being a gambler might not mean much in itself. But in Laurent's experience it meant he could be vulnerable to people who might want to control him. Laurent took the long way back to his bed and breakfast, from there, passing the few kiosks of the Merguez sausage festival still open for business. It appeared that even the tourists were tiring of sausages. As for Laurent, his appetite had not recovered since the moment Maggie had been taken. He trudged back to his lodging, feeling as if every path he'd taken had led to a dead-end. Maggie had now been gone twenty-four hours. He was fresh out of ideas.

As he neared the exterior door to his room at his lodging, a sense of unease came over him. Climbing the stone steps to his front door, he felt a buzzing premonition that told him something was wrong. His heart sped up. Suddenly, his eyes made out a dark shape on the doorstep. He approached cautiously and took in a quick intake of breath.

It was the body of a mangled rabbit. A note was stuck to the rabbit's fur beneath the bloody slit in its throat.

The words etched onto the paper were as cold as the poor creature's carcass.

*Your last warning*

## 31

Laurent stared at the note left on the dead rabbit. It was written using French-style handwriting. The script was characterized by a meticulous crafting of each letter with graceful, looping strokes that connected smoothly. Unlike the last note which had been largely printed, this one was in cursive. He studied the note intently. There were two kidnappers. Clearly, they were taking turns writing the notes. He held the note up to the light. Was there something feminine about the hand? Or was he trying to read that in?

He let out a sigh of frustration. He didn't have the resources to check the note for DNA or fingerprints and now more than ever he didn't want to be seen going to the police. The only thing he knew after all his efforts that he hadn't known yesterday was that the kidnappers were willing to give him one more chance to stop investigating. Next time the delivery to his doorstep would likely be a body part.

He paced his room, both hands raking through his hair in frustration. Even what little effort he'd made in investigating Antoine's murder was clearly too much as far as Maggie's captors were concerned. What now? What could he possibly do that they wouldn't see? Desperate and with no other idea of what to do, Laurent jammed the note in his wallet and left the room to walk to town where he remembered seeing a stationary store.

An hour later, Laurent pushed open the heavy glass door of a local stationary store, a small bell chiming softly to announce his arrival. The shop, tucked away on a quiet side street, was a treasure trove of paper goods, pens, and elegant writing instruments. Shelves lined the walls, filled with an array of stationery in every conceivable color and texture, while display cases showcased luxurious fountain pens and finely crafted notebooks.

As he stepped inside, the subtle scent of fresh paper and ink filled the air, mingling with the faint aroma of polished wood. Laurent approached the counter where an elderly gentleman with silver-rimmed glasses and a kind smile stood ready to assist him.

"Bonjour, Monsieur," the man greeted him. "How can I help you?"

Laurent reached into his coat pocket and pulled out the note, carefully unfolding it.

"Bonjour," he replied. "Would you have sold a card like this?"

The shopkeeper took the note and examined it closely. He ran his fingers over the textured surface, inspecting the quality and weight of the paper.

"Ah, *très intéressant*," he murmured. "This is a very fine paper, indeed. The texture and weight suggest it might be handmade, possibly from one of the local artisan workshops."

Laurent watched as the shopkeeper moved to a nearby shelf and pulled out several samples of high-quality stationery.

"Let's see," the man said, laying out the options. "These are some of the finest papers we carry. Perhaps one of them will be a match."

Laurent compared the note to the samples, scrutinizing each one. After a few moments, he found a close match: a creamy, slightly textured sheet that felt identical to the note's paper. The shopkeeper nodded in agreement.

"Yes, this is from a small workshop just outside Toulouse. They specialize in handcrafted paper. It's quite possible that your note was written on one of their products."

Laurent's mind raced with confusion. Did it make sense that the same people who scrawled their threat to him at the cabin on the back of a piece of cardboard now took the time to write to him on an artisan-created stationary?

"*Merci beaucoup*," he said dejectedly.

"Of course," the shopkeeper replied. "I hope you find what you're looking for."

As Laurent left the store, the bell chimed once more, and he felt a vague sense of premonition. Perhaps it was a dead end. Or perhaps it was a clue that he was too stupid to understand. But whatever it was, it was just possibly a step closer to uncovering the identity of the writer of the anonymous note.

When he returned to his lodging, he disposed of the dead rabbit. He couldn't help but wonder if it had been his visit with Claudine or with Philippe Martin that had raised the alarm to

Maggie's captors? He sat at the desk in his room and stared at the note and tried to think. What did he now know? The discovery that the stationery had probably originated in or around Toulouse was hardly world-shattering. But combined with the fact that *whoever* was his mystery writer, he was obviously watching Laurent closely seemed to confirm to Laurent that the kidnappers or their employers must be in Toulouse.

*Does that mean Maggie is here too?*

Was it possible they'd taken Maggie to the mountains to throw him off the scent? Had they turned around and driven her back to town? Wouldn't that make sense? He thought about some of the things that Bouchard had said and while he still wasn't sure he could trust the man, it did seem less likely that local run-of-the-mill thugs could manage this level of surveillance. That pointed in the direction that the murder and abduction were the work of the local syndicate crime organization after all.

Frustrated and finding it impossible to simply sit in his room and do nothing in spite of the warning, Laurent left again and found himself wandering the square until he found himself back at *L'Étoile Gourmande*. The restaurant was in the middle of dinner service. He looked around and studied the diners. He spotted the girl who'd shown him the text thread about Antoine's death at the hostess stand. Laurent wondered if that was a promotion for her. She looked terrified. He walked back toward the kitchen, close enough to eye the few line cooks working in the kitchen but refrained from approaching them. He had no doubt his next warning would be a piece of Maggie herself delivered to him.

Discouraged, he left the restaurant and stood outside for a moment when he suddenly recognized Bouchard walking down the street, his arms swinging good-naturedly as if he hadn't a care in the world. His easy-going gait enraged Laurent. With a surge of adrenaline, Laurent quickened his pace, closing the distance between them. He ran across the street, knocking into Bouchard with a force that carried both of them into a nearby alley where Laurent threw Bouchard up against the wall.

Bouchard gasped and put his hands up in a defensive gesture.

"Why are you doing this?" he stuttered as Laurent grabbed him by the front of his jacket.

"Where is she, you bastard?" Laurent snarled, his breath coming in ragged gasps.

"I...I have no idea, Monsieur!"

The fear seemed to roll off Bouchard like a noxious odor.

"You're lying," Laurent said. "You knew Antoine was involved with *La Main Noir*! You sold him to their enforcer because he stole your recipe!"

Bouchard's face looked wild with fear.

"No, you've got it wrong," he said as Laurent drew his fist back threateningly. "Antoine was trying to get out of his contracts with the syndicate!"

"I don't believe you," Laurent said. "Antoine wasn't involved with the syndicate. He would never allow *L'Étoile Gourmande* to be used for money laundering."

"Maybe not," Bouchard said. "But even if he wasn't allowing them to money launder he still had a problem with them."

"What problem?" Laurent asked, his eyes narrowed suspiciously.

"*L'Étoile Gourmande* had become too popular," Bouchard said. "It was cutting into the syndicate's illicit businesses being run through the *other* restaurants they controlled."

Laurent hesitated. What Bouchard said had the ring of truth to it.

"Like *Café du Midi*?" Laurent asked.

"Yes. But there are others. All Antoine had to do was keep a low profile and they would've let him alone. As it is, *L'Étoile Gourmande* has taken over half of all the food and wine profits in Toulouse."

Dropping his hands to his sides, Laurent glared at Bouchard in disgust.

"As for the recipe," Bouchard said, "Antoine and I sorted that years ago. He didn't give me credit for it, but he at least paid me."

Laurent knew he couldn't trust Bouchard but found himself believing at least that the man didn't know more about Maggie's whereabouts. He ran a hand through his hair and saw two of the restaurant's kitchen helpers step out from the back door of the restaurant. They saw him and looked startled before darting back inside. Did they think Laurent was undercover immigration police?

"What do you know about Lucas Moreau?" Laurent asked.

Bouchard shrugged.

"He hated Antoine and the feeling was mutual."

"Why?"

"You know how these things go in a kitchen," Bouchard said evasively. "Tempers run as hot as the grill. Hotter."

Laurent hoped he wouldn't have to punch Bouchard in the face after all. His thoughts must have been conspicuous on his face because Bouchard quickly amended his statement.

"Look, yes, there was some verbal abuse in the kitchen. There always is. It's a stressful environment and Antoine was hard on his staff."

"Go on," Laurent growled.

Bouchard looked around before speaking.

"Antoine slept with Lucas's fiancé," he said.

As soon as he heard it, Laurent did not for a single second believe that Bouchard was lying. For some reason, even though he hadn't seen Antoine in decades, Laurent knew the ugly truth when he heard it.

"But that's all I know," Bouchard said. "No love lost. That's it."

"Could Lucas have killed him?"

Bouchard wrinkled his nose.

"How? He wasn't allowed within a hundred meters of *L'Étoile Gourmande.*"

Laurent grunted. He didn't know what else to ask the man but was loathe to let him go.

"You know these people who are holding my wife," Laurent said, his voice laced with anger and dread.

Bouchard nodded, defeated.

"Will they hurt her?" Laurent asked.

*Will they kill her?*

"Monsieur, no. She will be returned to you. I am sure of it. They have no reason to kill her. Just bide your time. Stop raking up the dirt around Antoine's death. Yes, he was murdered. Yes, the syndicate likely called for the hit. Finding out *who* pulled the trigger? That will not help you get your wife back. In fact, it will prevent it from happening."

Laurent's fists clenched, his voice trembling with fear and determination.

"Why would they do this?" Laurent said it more to the air around him than directed at Bouchard.

"It's just business," Bouchard said. "Like the pharmacy chain they own, PharmaZen. They launder the money and can operate freely after that. These people do business in the shadows to control those who threaten their interests."

And now *those who threatened them* would be himself, Laurent thought bitterly. But what else could he do? He couldn't stop. He couldn't leave. He stepped back to let Bouchard scurry away. Then Laurent turned and walked away with Bouchard's warnings ringing in his ears. He made his way down the street until he reached a park bench where he sat for a moment, staring straight ahead. Then he took in a long breath and got to his feet. It was time. Time to collar the bear in his lair.

It was time to talk to Emile Chevalier.

## 32

In the end, attempting to contact Chevalier had taken most of the rest of the evening and night. Once he'd made the decision to talk face to face with the person he believed had sanctioned Maggie's abduction, Laurent went to a cell phone store in town and bought a burner phone. From there he went back to his lodgings and set up the preparations he believed necessary to facilitate the meeting.

He sat by the window in his room at the bed and breakfast, the chill of the night air seeping through the old glass panes despite the thick curtains drawn halfway. He gazed at the misty cobblestone street outside, the dim streetlights casting a depressing glow that flickered in the night, reflecting his dark, contemplative mood.

It wasn't easy doing any of this on his cellphone, but Laurent had managed it a few times in the past from his home computer, so he at least knew the general procedure. He accessed a section of the dark web that he'd been to before and entered Chevalier's name. An hour later, he'd drilled down to the level of a labyrinth of various criminal enterprises and businesses until he had a single phone number.

He immediately called the number which connected him to a recording that referenced swimming lessons in Arles. He ignored the artifice, knowing that it all came down to what message he would leave on the call. When the tone sounded, he spoke clearly into the receiver.

"My name is Laurent Dernier. If you don't know who I am I would ask you to contact a man by the name of Guy Dupont in Montpelier. He has a lengthy dossier on me and if you know Monsieur Dupont, you know he can be trusted to tell you the truth."

Laurent knew that if Dupont were still alive, he would understand that Laurent needed him to pass on Laurent's credentials. They had worked together in the old days on the coast. If Dupont was no longer alive, his reputation alone would likely be enough to do the trick. Laurent paused. He wanted to hint that the call had to do with Antoine, but he didn't want to tip his hand before time.

"I am calling for a meeting with the Enforcer in Toulouse and can promise a mutually beneficial and highly profitable result for all parties," he said.

That had been the hardest part of the script to say with feeling. More than anything, Laurent wanted to kill everyone connected with Maggie's kidnapping, starting with the man at the top who'd ordered it. He forced himself to sound ingratiating until he could be close enough to wrap his hands around the bastard's neck.

"Reach me at this number to set up a time and place to meet," he said.

When he disconnected, he took in a long breath. He had done all he could for now. He looked around the room. As usual, the prospect of doing nothing was a feeling of something just short of torture. He stood up and showered and dressed again. It was already late in the evening, but he knew he wouldn't be able to sleep until the bait he'd tossed out had caught something.

An hour later, he received a text message on the burner phone that he'd given as his contact number.

> Warehouse behind Piscine Léo Lagrange. One o'clock. Come alone

∽

Waiting the four hours until he could make his way to the rendezvous point was the most grueling expanse of time that Laurent had endured so far. The swimming center cited in the text would be closed as would the warehouse behind it. Since he'd found the address on his phone and saw it was well outside the center of Toulouse, Laurent decided to walk to the meeting place. He could benefit from the time to temper his inclinations. Perhaps this way he wouldn't immediately grab Chevalier by the throat and demand answers.

Or kill him before he had the chance to answer.

At precisely one o'clock, Laurent stepped into the dimly lit, cavernous space of the abandoned warehouse, the air heavy with dust and an indistinct musty odor. Shafts of pale moonlight penetrated the slits in the worn-out roof, casting long shadows over the cracked concrete floor. The interior of the warehouse was filled with dilapidated wooden crates stacked haphazardly and lining the walls. The sound of dripping water echoed from the deeper recesses of the interior. Puddles had formed on the uneven floor, reflecting the dim light from Laurent's cellphone flashlight beam and creating shimmering patches of illumination amidst the darkness.

As he ventured further into the warehouse, Laurent noticed steel support beams that soared towards the high ceiling, their surfaces rusted and worn. The occasional sound of scurrying rodents and other denizens of the warehouse reverberated through the space. Even for Laurent who very rarely felt off-balance, the warehouse's atmosphere was eerie and suitable for a place where secrets were whispered, and clandestine deals made. The absence of any natural light and the constant creaking of the structure added to his sense of foreboding, as if the very building was holding its breath.

In this desolate setting, Laurent waited, his heart pounding in anticipation, his brain reminding him that this meeting with Chevalier was a high stakes encounter that could determine Maggie's fate.

A door opened somewhere deep inside the warehouse and Laurent heard several men walking toward him. He hadn't expected anything less. A man like Chevalier wouldn't come without protection. Laurent turned to face them, holding up his illuminating cellphone as they approached.

"Good evening, Monsieur Dernier," Chevalier said as he stopped in front of Laurent.

His two men quickly patted Laurent down.

"I wasn't quite sure what to think when you reached out to me," Chevalier said. "But your references were impressive. Are you still in the game?"

Laurent hated the fact that this scoundrel might believe they were anything alike, or worse, that Laurent might be interested in working with him. He took in a breath and set his jaw.

"I have come about my wife," Laurent said. "I am here to negotiate for her release. We will leave the area immediately never to return. Or you can just kill me now and let her go home to our children."

"No time for small talk, eh, Monsieur Dernier?" Chevalier said wryly. "That is not how we do business in the west. Have things changed so much where you come from?"

Laurent held the man's gaze. He noticed that the two bodyguards were alert and ready, their hands resting near their belts where Laurent could see they were armed. When he didn't answer, Chevalier sighed as if disappointed.

"And if I don't have your wife?" Chevalier asked as he fished a cigarette out of his vest.

One of his men leaned over to light it for him.

"In that case," Laurent said, "then I would ask you to help me."

"Why would I?"

"First because I imagine the kidnapping is reflecting badly on you. If I think the syndicate is responsible, then so do the police."

Chevalier laughed without mirth.

"I don't care what the police think," he said. "Anything else?"

"I am told that you have a vested interest in preserving a semblance of order and stability in Toulouse," Laurent said, feeling his control beginning to slip away. "A kidnapping disrupts the city's peace and could have negative repercussions on your operations."

"I can't imagine how," Chevalier said.

"The Toulouse police are not the only law enforcement in France," Laurent said.

"Is that a threat? Because I imagine you would have to live long enough to alert anyone."

"You would risk another unexplained death? On top of Antoine's? And my wife's?"

"As I understand it, your wife is not dead. But you would be surprised at how many bodies can pile up without causing unwanted distress from law enforcement—even outside Toulouse."

Laurent's disgust was tempered by the statement that Maggie wasn't dead. Even so, he could feel that the man was playing with him. Why not just tell him the truth? Why not come out from behind the cryptic handwritten notes and animal carcasses left on doorsteps and just tell him to his face!?

"I am happy to stop investigating Antoine's death," Laurent said. "And to leave Toulouse. *With my wife.*"

"Why would I care if you investigate Antoine's death?" Chevalier said, his voice, low and gravelly. His words were measured and laced with more than a hint of menace.

"I am asking you again," Laurent said, biting off every word, his patience all but gone. "Let me leave Toulouse with my wife."

"I am sorry I can't help you, Monsieur," Chevalier said, his sharp eyes cold and intractable. "But I did not take your wife."

Laurent realized that in his desperation he'd been so focused on having a direct confrontation with Chevalier, man to man, that it hadn't occurred to him that the crime boss might deny his involvement. There was very little argument against that particular tactic other than calling the man a liar. And Laurent wasn't ready to do that unarmed.

"If that is true," Laurent said, knowing the meeting was ending and that he had only a very few seconds to make his point, "then I would expect that your interest in maintaining control in Toulouse might prompt you to assist me in finding my wife."

"This again?" Chevalier said. "I am sorry, Monsieur, but I am comfortable with the level of control, as you put it, that I have in Toulouse—your wife's unfortunate kidnapping notwithstanding."

Laurent was now nearly quivering with rage and disappointment knowing he had failed and that any further attempt to wring the truth from this man, would only get him killed. Chevalier smiled coldly at Laurent and signaled to his men that it was time to go.

"Good luck, Monsieur," he said. "A little advice before you go? And please forgive the culinary metaphor but Toulouse is after all a gastronomic haven." He grinned openly, showing white straight teeth. "But I can only imagine that any more pot-stirring on your side cannot possibly be beneficial to your goals—or to the survival of your wife."

As Laurent clenched his fists by his side in impotent rage, Chevalier turned away.

"By the way," Chevalier said over his shoulder as he walked away with his two men flanking him. "I was impressed you were able to find me. But you'll want to lose that number."

# 33

Hours later, Laurent sat alone in his room looking at the papers and documents from Antoine's office that he'd photographed with his phone two days ago, his mind consumed with thoughts of Maggie and his bone-wracking disappointment in his meeting with Chevalier. Regardless of what the crime boss had told him, Laurent was not at all sure that Chevalier wasn't responsible for Antoine's murder and Maggie's kidnapping, just as Bouchard had suggested. If he was, Laurent had directly spoken to him and given him the message that he wouldn't give up. Either Laurent had just signed his own death warrant—and Maggie's—or Chevalier was uninvolved in Maggie's kidnapping. If that was so, it meant that someone else had killed Antoine. And for that, it meant starting all over again with finding some kind of clue or lead.

Laurent couldn't find anything in the documents that seemed relevant to anything. They all just looked like the sort of documents one would have when running a restaurant. So why were they labeled as confidential? He felt a splinter of frustration and stood up to stand by the window.

He thought about Philippe Martin's behavior when he'd ambushed him at the restaurant yesterday and then immediately remembered that Maggie had intended to go on the Internet to find the culinary event that Martin had referenced when he and Maggie had first talked to him. All Laurent had was his cellphone and he was barely able to write and send text messages on it, let alone do any kind of in-depth research, but he sat down on the bed and manfully tackled the job, spending an hour using both Martin's name and Antoine's in conjunction with any recent culinary conferences in France and then in Europe. Nothing.

He typed in their names over and over into various browser windows that popped up, but the result was always a collection of irrelevant information. He knew he wasn't putting in proper keywords or prompts but, since he didn't know how that worked, he just kept typing in *culinary conference* and *Antoine Dubois*. The results came back slightly different every time and always useless. Mostly he ended up uncovering an overwhelming number of unrelated search results—articles, recipes and random cooking web pages along with video tutorials that had nothing to do with Antoine. Once he started finding increasingly outdated articles and forum threads amidst a sea of completely unrelated culinary content that took him even further afield, he tossed his phone on the bed in frustration.

*Is it because I'm using my phone? Do I need to find an Internet Café?*

But he knew that wasn't the problem. *He* was the problem. It would take hours if not weeks for him to become familiar enough with researching on the Internet to find anything of use to him. Before today, he'd always stepped away from the new technology, leaving it to others—to *les enfants*—and now he was paying the price.

Or rather Maggie was.

Just then, his phone rang, and he snatched it up with hope bearing down on him that by some miracle it might be Maggie.

"How are things going?" Grace asked softly.

Laurent sat on the side of the bed, his disappointment strangling him yet knowing he couldn't let it show.

"Getting there," he said, hating to lie to her but knowing she likely didn't believe him anyway. "Because of the note they left me, I'm not sure any line of investigation I do is safe."

"Oh! Of course. I hadn't thought about that."

"Tell me how the little one is," Laurent said.

He was changing the subject—as much for his own sake as for Grace's. Thoughts of Amelie could at least briefly help distract him from his current torture—a mindfulness that was literally turning him in agonizing circles.

"She asks about you both daily," Grace said. "Sometimes hourly. You know how she is. Insistent. Won't take no for an answer. Philippe caught her walking down the road this afternoon. She said she was going to Toulouse. I've tasked him with watching her more closely. But all in all, she's fine."

"That's good," Laurent said, hating to think of how upset Amelie was about his and Maggie's absence.

"She is doing a project at school that is helping to distract her," Grace said. "She was asked to write a letter to a famous person from the past—someone she admires. She chose Anne Frank."

Laurent was moved at his granddaughter's choice of heroine. Amelie was strong-willed if a little reckless. The fact that she would choose a person to admire who was noted for her quiet resilience and calm in unimaginably horrible circumstances pleased him.

"Tell her I'm proud of her," he said. "Give her a kiss from me and tell her we'll both be home soon, and I expect a good report on her."

"I will, darling," Grace said. "Is there anything I can do from this end?"

"Yes, actually, there might be," Laurent said.

Quickly he outlined for her the trouble he was having finding the information about Philippe Martin and any possible fracas that might have happened at a culinary conference.

"I can't even find his LinkedIn account," Laurent said in frustration. "Whatever *that* is."

"Leave it to me, darling," Grace said.

∽

Laurent sat at the small wooden desk in his room as frustration and exhaustion weighed equally upon him. Hunger gnawed too. He couldn't remember the last time he'd thought to grab something to eat. His eyes burned with weariness as he stared again at the documents that he'd photographed from Antoine's desk and files. The more he read, the less he knew, the less anything made sense to him, the less any of it felt like it was connected to Maggie's kidnapping.

Over and over again he came to the same painful conclusion: the only lead remotely within his grasp lay squarely within the parameters of where he'd been warned not to go. His heart sank as he contemplated the agonizing choice before him—go in pursuit of this single lead which would surely risk Maggie's safety or stay put and hope that the kidnappers would play fair and return her if he did as they demanded.

He stood up and walked to the window. He wasn't the kind of man to do nothing. He'd always been a man of action even if that action was tactical and looked more like lying in wait. This time there was nothing of merit or worth behind his inaction. Nothing at all. The torment of indecision gnawed at his very soul. Go or stay? Reach out or sit tight?

What did Maggie's abductors want from him? Just inaction? They hadn't asked him to leave town. Why not? What was he missing? Had Chevalier's final comment to him been a doubling down on the message in the note telling him not to get involved? Laurent's determination hardened, suddenly overshadowing his doubts. With a heavy sigh, he decided to follow his sole lead.

*If not, I might as well just give up and go home.*

He picked up his phone to look at the document he'd found and had looked at twenty times without really understanding what he was seeing. But this time his eye landed on something he hadn't seen before. He took in a breath and felt his heart rate quickening.

Right from the beginning he'd looked at Remy Durand. Was he just the most obvious candidate? Or the most likely? From the very start, Laurent's instincts had told him that the rival restauranteur knew more than he was telling. Laurent scrutinized the document on his phone and nodded to himself. When he zoomed in on the document, he saw that it was succinctly written in a wobbly, possibly even drunken hand. There was also evidence of wine stains on the edges.

"In the event of my death" Antoine had written in his shaky but unmistakable script, "I hereby sign over my share of *L'Étoile Gourmande* to Remy Durand."

The document was dated two years ago.

## 34

The night before, Laurent had watched the *Café du Midi* until the last diner left and the last kitchen and cook staff had emptied out. When he saw Durand leave, he followed him home.

Now he stood in the shadows outside Remy Durand's apartment. The wind had gusted up, driving a flurry of snow against the front door. It seemed to Laurent that there was an eerie gloom over the front of Durand's building making the sleek, modern structure appear forbidding against the black backdrop of night.

As far as Laurent was concerned, he'd found the smoking gun he'd been looking for in addition to the biggest motive so far for anyone wanting Antoine dead. He'd spent a few precious seconds considering the worth of showing what he'd found to Rousseau before deciding to skip her and go straight to the source. If Rousseau *was* in the crime syndicate's pocket, he'd be throwing away his only ace by presenting it to her. This document—actual physical evidence!—was the single best thing that he could have ever imagined. It gave Durand the ultimate motive. In Laurent's mind, he saw the moment when it was laid before a jury—irrefutable and damning.

Unfortunately, after the incident where Laurent had assaulted Durand at his restaurant, orchestrating another meeting with the chef would have prompted an uncomfortable situation. Normally, he might approach Durand in a way that showed that he was sorry for their earlier altercation. Or he could send him a message asking to meet to talk about what had happened or even suggest that Laurent felt Durand could be helpful in finding who killed Antoine. But Laurent didn't have that kind of time and anyway he didn't have the stomach to negotiate with someone who might well be Antoine's killer. He'd done it plenty of times when he worked as a con man on the Côte d'Azur but even then, it hadn't been his strong suit.

Because of the pressing time frame and the fact that Durand probably had people watching for Laurent, the only opportunity he would have to question the man would have to be an invasive one. There was no help for that.

The night was cool, casting a soft shadow over the narrow street lined with closely packed buildings. He watched Durand walking down the sidewalk in front of his building and Laurent stepped out from the muted glow of a nearby streetlamp, blocking his path.

"Monsieur Durand," Laurent said, his voice calm and controlled.

Durand turned to face him, his face an immediate mixture of surprise and then fear.

"I mean you no harm," Laurent said, as he stood between Durand and the entrance to his building.

Because of the late hour, the street was quiet, the only sounds the quiet hum of the city.

"I have nothing to say to you," Durand said. "If I tell the

police that you accosted me a second time, this time I won't agree to drop the charges."

"I have a single question," Laurent said. "After that I will leave you in peace."

Durand paused, clearly weighing his options. After a moment, his shoulders slumped slightly.

"Fine," he said.

Laurent pulled out his phone with the photographed document on it and saw Durand flinch when he did. It was clear the man had expected Laurent to pull out a weapon. To Laurent, that in itself was an admission of guilt.

"I found this in Antoine's things," Laurent said, handing the phone to him. "Do you recognize it?"

Durand frowned and took the phone and studied it before handing it back.

"That was years ago when we were still speaking," he said. "Antoine had lost at cards to me, but later paid me what he owed me. I told him to destroy that. Trust me, I would've gone to my lawyer by now if it was still valid."

"But you're still getting a share of *L'Étoile Gourmande*."

"Because I'm *purchasing* it!" Durand said heatedly. "It's all legal and above board! You're trying to imply with that..." He waved to the phone in Laurent's hand, "...that I had a motive to kill Antoine! I didn't need a drunken IOU to get his restaurant!"

"You just needed Antoine dead."

"I think we're done here," Durand said. "Thank you for not assaulting me this time. The doctor said I was lucky you didn't break my nose."

It was all Laurent could do not to correct the error.

"Why did you hate him so much?" he asked instead.

"Because he was despicable," Durand said as he turned

to face the door to his apartment building. "Did you know him at all?"

Laurent was beginning to wonder.

"So, it was personal," Laurent pressed.

"Yes. But also private," Durand said as he punched in his security code. "Note the difference?" Then he slipped through the wrought-iron gate and disappeared.

Laurent watched him go. He had to admit that since Durand had been able to buy his share of *L'Étoile Gourmande* anyway, the IOU chit wasn't much to go on as far as motives went.

But whatever secret—and private grudge—Durand held against Antoine, now *that* might be a whole different matter.

## 35

The next morning, Laurent sat in a bare-bones café off the main square, his gaze sweeping over the scene before him. The striking pink hues of the city's grand town hall dominated one side of the square, its imposing presence a testament to the town's centuries of history. The weather was sunny but cool. An icy breeze carried the scent of freshly brewed coffee and the ever-present aromas of the sausages still being sold from a few remaining kiosks. Locals and tourists alike still crowded the cobblestone streets, stopping now and then to peer at the posted café menu before deciding against its rudimentary fare and dingy interior.

Across from where Laurent sat, a fountain gushed water, its sound intermingling with the lively chatter all around him. As Laurent gazed across the street, he found himself thinking more and more about the idea of Amelie writing a letter to Anne Frank. He wondered what Amelie would say to her. Would she ask how Anne stayed brave and never gave up hope? Would she ask how she'd kept her courage hiding from people who hated her and wanted to harm her for so many years? As Laurent thought an idea began to form in his brain.

The people holding Maggie somehow knew what he was up to. That meant they must be watching him. Either the two kidnappers themselves were in town along with Maggie—and the mountain cabin was just a ruse—or the syndicate had enough personnel to have people surveil Laurent. He dropped a few coins on the table and got up to head back to his lodging.

If he was being watched, he would give them nothing to see, he thought as excitement began to build in his chest. The bed and breakfast was a comfortable walking distance of six blocks from the center of town. If Maggie's captors were watching, they would merely see Laurent return to his lodging—the picture of dejection and capitulation—and assume that in order to keep Maggie safe he was obeying their edicts.

But to Laurent, doing nothing was not a good alternative to doing anything that would reap results. Every problem needed an action to solve it. Doing nothing was not an option. He walked purposely down the six blocks through town to his bed and breakfast passing street after street of picturesque townhouses with wrought-iron gates and balconies and the omnipresent window boxes filled with geraniums and petunias.

Once back at the bed and breakfast, after noticing with a grimace that there was no gruesome message left on his doorstep, he went inside and closed the blinds.

He went to the bed and lay down for a few minutes expecting just to rest, but woke hours later, his mind and body refreshed. He hated wasting the time to sleep. He knew he'd needed it. He'd been so exhausted that he was having trouble trusting his own thoughts.

Laurent prayed that she hadn't been killed yet. But he knew that must be the abductors' end game. *They will kill her.* He hadn't allowed himself to think that before this moment but now he knew it was so. And refusing to think the words wouldn't stop it from happening. If they'd had any thought of releasing her, they would have told Laurent to leave town. Leaving would have told them that Laurent was compliant to their demands. Asking him to do nothing, was just buying time for something. But what?

He forced himself not to think any more about it because that would only weaken him and right now he needed to be strong and resolute if he ever did. He sat down with the pens and markers he'd found in the drawer of the room desk and a thick blank post card. The plan he'd come up with on the walk back from the café was a simple one. He'd been unsure if it was a solid plan or if he'd been too tired and desperate to truly judge it. Now as he picked up the heaviest marker, he found a conviction rippling through him that it was a good plan.

He stood up and realized his back and legs were cramping from being in one spot for too many hours at a time. That was when he realized that light was coming through the blinds of his room. He wasn't sure how long he'd nodded off for, but it was morning already. He looked at the card he'd created. If they hadn't already decided to kill her, nothing he did would matter, he thought grimly. But in that case, Laurent needed to know sooner rather than later.

A rescue plan was very different from a killing mission. He needed to know which one he was preparing for.

He looked at the notebook of notes and then sat down and carefully copied the single sentence he'd settled on onto a large card. Then he propped up his cellphone on the desk in his room and set the photo function on it to video. He picked up the card and held it in front of the phone camera, his eyes looking directly into the lens. He watched the countdown function on the camera go to ten seconds and then he shut off the camera. He didn't need to say anything. The message said it all. If Maggie was already dead, then the video also sent the message that Laurent was coming for them.

He sent the video to Grace with a text message asking her to post it to Maggie's Facebook, Tik-Tok and Instagram accounts. Within seconds, he got a text back from Grace.

> are you sure?

> yes

Then he left the bed and breakfast, walking into town until he found an open café where he ate a breakfast of bread and two cups of strong coffee. After that, he found a quick print shop where he made fifty copies of the card. Even more than the act of driving out to the cabin in the mountains, last night's work had made him feel for the first time as if he was actually doing something to get Maggie back. Instead of reacting to these bastards, he was playing a tune that he was forcing *them* to dance to.

However it played out, at least Laurent was the one directing things now.

He glanced at the stack of cards in his hand and felt a grim satisfaction as he read the sixteen stark words printed on them.

*Proof of life by tonight or I go to the National Police with what I know.*

## 36

The rest of that day was long and filled with anxiety. Laurent spent it delivering his stack of cards—in case the social media avenue wasn't productive—roaming from restaurant to café and bistros to the public restrooms and the message pillars of all the nearby parks. He put them on the bulletin board in the town center, in the library and in the floral kiosks that ran through the popular and well-visited Jardin Pierre Goudouli.

The whole time, he kept his eye on his cellphone. He hadn't needed to put his phone number on the message. They knew how to contact him.

He felt sure that if Maggie's captors were watching him as closely as he knew they were, then getting them to see his message should be no problem. It had been Amelie's school project that had given him the idea: how to talk to someone with whom it was impossible to communicate? And since Maggie's captors weren't dead yet, it was actually a little easier to find ways of contacting them.

Laurent blanketed the town with his cards, leaving one

in Antoine's kitchen and also Remy Durant's, as well as one in Martin's letterbox. After leaving one at every pharmacy, *tabac* and café. on the square, he stood in front of a CCTV camera and held up the message so it could be read.

After that, he went to Maggie's Facebook page—not her personal page that she filled with family photos but the one she used for posting her expat stories with photos of the shops and markets around St-Buvard and Aix. There he saw the video that Grace had uploaded this morning. He was momentarily startled to see himself in the video. His face was haggard and haunted. But it was his eyes that shocked him the most. He looked like a man ready to kill someone.

As Laurent made his way to yet another café along the square to drink yet another cup of coffee, although he was sure he'd had way too many already. He thought of how most of what he'd done to try to find who had taken Maggie involved waiting, drinking coffee, staring into space and watching people to see if they were watching him.

Would the bastards reach out? He glanced at his phone. Or was he about to embark on the next part of this mission? He forced himself not to get ahead of schedule. He knew what he must do in any case. This was the last time he waited for them. It was the last time he responded to their provocation. He was done letting them call the tune.

He was momentarily distracted by a little girl running across the terrace to her father. The moment Laurent saw her, his chest felt as if it were clenching in pain. The way the child raced after her papa—her hand outstretched to find him—reminded him of how Mila always knew she was safe with him. He remembered those years so well. He'd never expected to feel what he'd felt as a father. He had Maggie to thank for that.

Until this week, he'd never bothered imagining what his

life would have been like if he'd never met Maggie. He only had to look at how Roger Bentley had ended up: a man he'd loved and respected but who had never managed to truly leave his criminal past behind. And of course, Antoine.

He'd never taken for granted a single Christmas at Domaine St-Buvard with his children gathered around him or the fact of his standing in the community where people stopped him on the street to ask his advice. He thought of how his wine was judged nationally as some the best in the country and how the very seasons had given him a template for patience and expectations that had helped settle him and, in the end, created the man he was always intended to be. And none of that—not the love or the family or the traditions or the pride of accomplishment or even the security of his day-to-day life—none of it would have been possible if not for this one impetuous American girl whom he'd met and fallen in love with so many years ago.

He remembered that moment this morning when he'd held Maggie's camisole to his face to inhale the scent of her. Tears burned his eyes with the ferocity of his emotion.

*I'll get her back because there isn't a future for any of us without her.*

Just then his phone rang, and he felt his nerves jump. His heart began to pound as he reached for the phone.

"Any news?" Grace asked.

"*Non*," Laurent said, fighting the disappointment cascading over him at his words. "I saw the Facebook post."

"You'll let me know if they reach out?" Grace asked.

His hesitation was her answer.

"Never mind," she said. "Don't worry about me. I'm just calling to tell you what I discovered about Philippe Martin. I'm sending you a video clip now."

Laurent pulled his phone from his face to see that a video file had shown up in his text messages.

"What is it?" he asked, not sure if he could click on the video without disconnecting from Grace.

"Let's just say," Grace said, "that if you're looking for a reason for why this Martin guy might have hated your friend Antoine, this would do it."

"Thanks, Grace," Laurent said, eager to hang up so he could watch the video.

Grace must have realized that because she quickly explained what was on the clip.

"It's a cellphone video that someone captured a year ago at a culinary conference in Lyons," she said. "In it, you can see Antoine and Martin together. Antoine sounds drunk but he's still very articulate. He accuses Martin of unprofessional bias and the ten people surrounding them found it very funny. If I were Martin, I'd want to kill Antoine too."

"*Merci*, Grace," Laurent said.

"Do you think it'll be enough to prove motive?"

"Not on its own," Laurent said. "But, add to it the possibility that Martin might have been attempting to buy goodwill from a dangerous group of people, then possibly, yes."

"Why would he need to buy goodwill?"

"I think he has a gambling habit," Laurent said. "If he owes the syndicate money, they might have allowed him to do a distasteful job for them in order to wipe the slate clean."

"Goodness," Grace said. "That would definitely do it."

But even as he spoke, Laurent was already dismissing his own theory. The fact was, Martin might well have motive for wanting Antoine dead but if the syndicate wanted the chef dead, it wouldn't have allowed a nonprofessional like

Philippe Martin to handle the job and possibly botch it since that would only lead back to them. On the other hand, Laurent had to admit that Antoine's murder did not look like a pro had done it.

"How are you holding up, darling?" Grace asked.

"I'm fine," he said gruffly. "If I don't hear something in another hour, I'll probably just go to Philippe Martin's apartment and kill him."

"Now, now, dearest," Grace said. "Try to have faith. Like you said, just because he was publicly humiliated, doesn't mean he murdered Antoine."

"Only that he is half a man," Laurent said.

"Always a possibility, dearest. Call me when you hear something."

As soon as Laurent hung up, he watched the video clip several times. For him personally, the act of derision that Antoine had heaped upon Martin in the clip would have been sufficient cause for murder. But Laurent wasn't sure if Martin was that kind of man. He seemed mild-mannered in an oily sort of way. On the other hand, Claudine had insisted that he often came to the restaurant in disguise in order to watch Antoine. That at least took guts.

Laurent looked at his watch. It was ten o'clock. The deadline was nearly here. If he didn't hear from Maggie's captors, he would go to Martin's place. Whether he killed him or not, he would at least question Martin to the point where he would be forced to tell Laurent the truth. Feeling antsy, he got up and began the walk back to his lodgings to do anything to keep busy and to stop the constant buzzing of his panicked, anxious brain. He had no sooner reached his bed and breakfast as his phone dinged, alerting him to the arrival of a text message. Laurent stiffened in anticipation of the call he'd been waiting for all day. If it was proof of life, there was a next step after that he would take. He didn't know what that was, but he would find it. If it wasn't proof of life...He let that thought hang and saw that the message was from a new contact. He opened the door to his room and went in and stood by the window. He opened the message.

It was a photo of Maggie. Alive.

Laurent shoulders sagged with relief. In the photo, Maggie was sitting on a straight back chair with her hands tied behind her back. Her usually vibrant eyes looked at the photographer with a dull stare. Her hair was unkempt and disheveled. Despite the weariness etched in her face, there was a glimmer of steel in Maggie's expression—one that Laurent knew well. It was a fierce determination that shined through her weariness.

Laurent studied every detail of the photograph. The background of the photo was nondescript—just a wall and nothing to indicate where that wall was. There was a table beside Maggie with a newspaper on it. By pinching the photo to zoom in, Laurent could see the front of the paper. It was a colorful photo of a big fried pickle kiosk. Laurent remembered that photo from the front page when he'd walked past the newspaper paper racks in Toulouse this week. With anxiety thrumming in his gut, he got up and went out the door and down the hall to the lobby of the bed and breakfast. It was late and there were no guests in the lobby and no one at the front desk. Laurent moved behind the registration counter to the bookcase that held newspapers and magazines. He quickly found what he was looking for. He pulled the newspaper out and stared at it. The photo of the big green pickle kiosk took up nearly the whole of the page above the fold. Just like the paper in Maggie's photograph.

For a moment it was all Laurent could do to keep from

hurling his lunch. He leaned against the counter and felt perspiration form on his cheeks as a tsunami of despair crashed over him.

The photograph was taken two days ago.

# 37

Maggie twisted in the chair with her eyes still closed although she had awakened moments before. She could feel her hands and feet were still bound, although more loosely this time and with her hands in front of her. She felt headachy and sick to her stomach. She opened her eyes and looked around. It was a one room cabin. She was sitting in an armchair that smelled of mildew and urine. She appeared to be alone.

She felt a throb of discomfort in her left bicep. She knew instantly it was the site of the injection she had been given. Fear blossomed in her gut as she realized how much effort and thought had gone into her abduction. It was the second time in two days that her captors had drugged her before they moved her. She turned her head and vomited onto the wooden floor of the hut. As if the act of vomiting had exhausted her, she rested and listened for the sound of men's voices and creaking floorboards. But there was nothing. She was alone.

The memory of what had happened to her was vague and terrifying. She hated awakening because every time she did, she remembered hearing Laurent's angry, helpless shout. He was seeing what he couldn't prevent from happening. For Laurent, that was the worst thing in the world. Maggie leaned forward and felt another wave of nausea wrack her. She'd been sedated for hours so that now every movement brought on another wave of dizziness. She was thirsty but saw a bottle of water had been placed next to her chair. As she drank, the water quenching the relentless thirst the drugs had caused, her mind was reeling with the same unanswerable questions with which she'd tortured herself from the beginning.

For hours she tried to imagine why she'd been taken and could only hope that her abduction was either a case of mistaken identity or the result of someone grown desperate to end Laurent's poking into Antoine's murder. Was the kidnapping a warning? She swallowed hard. Or would her lifeless body be found in the next mountain cabin as the real warning?

Suddenly the front door opened, and both her captors entered from the porch. Even from where she was sitting, Maggie could smell the smoke on them. She couldn't imagine why they would bother smoking outside. It was hardly as if they worried about offending her. Neither captor spoke to her but the taller one, the one she'd mentally nicknamed "Benson," whom she called "Hedges," seemed to be having trouble breathing. Maggie knew that some people with respiratory issues had problems in high altitudes.

Her captors were similarly dressed and she'd already guessed that they were related. They were definitely the two men she'd seen in the bar that night. They had been careful to hide their faces under hoods which Maggie took as a good sign. However, she recognized tattoos covering

Benson's neck. While they kept their faces covered, she could tell them apart by their movements. One was jerky and anxious, the other possibly stoned. Both had been smoking almost continually.

At first she had tried talking with them. She was aware that she needed to force them to see her as a real person. It was the only way she was going to be able to talk her way out of this—if that was even possible. But they never responded to her, so she gave up trying. They maintained a professional distance as if afraid to form any personal connection that could interfere with their objectives. Which was a worry.

They hadn't hurt her, but they had not engaged with her beyond handing her water or food and letting her use the toilet but only with the door cracked with one of them standing right outside. Since she remembered them from the bar, she knew they were really just boys. The way they interacted with her—even minimally—told her they had never done this before.

She watched them now as they took up their posts in the cabin. Both looked at their phones, ignoring her. She could tell by the window that the light was leaching from the sky and it would soon be dark. That meant another day gone. Had they asked for ransom? Had they reached out to Laurent? Do the police know what has happened? Maggie tried to remember what had happened to Laurent and although she'd been fully conscious when the men stuffed her in the trunk, she'd also been quickly drugged and kept that way since. Her memory of what they'd done to Laurent was hazy. But Laurent was the strongest most capable person she'd ever known. In their life together, she couldn't even remember two times when he'd been stumped or flummoxed about anything.

Laurent would find her. Somehow. That much she knew. Meanwhile, she prayed—not just for herself—but that Laurent would find the strength to stay tough for the duration of however this nightmare played out.

*Because if I don't make it, Amelie is going to need him more than ever.*

## 38

Laurent went back to his room, fighting the bone-grinding discouragement that after all his efforts he still didn't know if Maggie was alive. What did it mean that they didn't send a photograph taken today? He forced away the full implications of that thought and tried to tell himself that at least Maggie's captors appeared to be capable of being threatened into action.

What did *that* mean? Especially since they'd answered him without really answering him?

He looked around his room and forced down the familiar feeling of creeping helplessness as he realized he wasn't sure what to do next. He sat down on the bed and looked at his phone. He went to Maggie's Facebook page for lack of anything more concrete to do and saw that the Facebook video post that Grace had put up was gone. He'd already called Grace as soon as he got the proof of life photo and told her to take down all posts of the video, mostly because he was afraid of one of the children seeing them, although Maggie had commented more than once that none of the children followed her on any of her accounts. Today he was very glad for that.

He thought for a moment and then opened up a browser window on his phone and typed in *Facebook Antoine Dubois*. Instantly a list of articles referencing Dubois or *L'Étoile Gourmande* came up. He briefly scanned Antoine's very truncated Wikipedia page and then texted Grace in frustration.

> trying to find background on Antoine. Can you search his social media?

> anything in particular you're looking for?

Laurent thought for a minute and then texted her back.

> friends, hobbies, interests, potential enemies

> on it

Laurent tossed his phone on the bed and thought for a moment. Worse than spending two hours uselessly scouring the Internet in hopes of finding a lead was sitting here doing nothing. He thought about contacting Roger Bedard in Nice. Bedard was a police detective he and Maggie had known for decades. Roger had access to the kinds of police tools that might prove helpful. Possibly he would even be able to capture Antoine's email or some other kind of valuable digital evidence.

But their long acquaintance aside, Bedard and Laurent had a murky history, and Laurent wasn't eager to trigger him if it could be avoided. He went back to the files and documents he'd photographed from Antoine's office and ran through them once more. But the act of doing this felt too passive and useless to Laurent so he entertained himself for a few minutes imagining tracking Philippe Martin down. As far as Laurent was concerned, Martin wasn't off the hook, but neither did he seem as culpable as a few hours ago. Finally in frustration, Laurent picked up his phone and called Bedard.

"Laurent?" Bedard answered, his voice guarded.

"I need your help," Laurent said.

Twenty minutes later, after briefly outlining what he was doing in Toulouse—without mentioning that Maggie had been abducted—Laurent ended the call after Bedard agreed to check online databases, public records and any other background information on Antoine. Laurent couldn't delve into Antoine's bank statements, or other financial transactions. But knowledge of any unusual or suspicious financial activity such as large deposits, unexplained withdrawals, or payments to unknown entities could provide clues about Antoine's connections or motives. Bedard on the other hand had access to any manner of financial expert or forensic accounting that might help shine a light on any financial irregularities.

But of course, all that was irrelevant if it really was the syndicate who'd killed Antoine.

Laurent had been careful not to tell Bedard that Maggie had been abducted because, he knew Bedard would react by rolling into town with a full battalion of police with sirens and lights flashing. That would not be good for Maggie.

Bedard had been in love with Maggie since the day they'd met—during Maggie and Laurent's first year of marriage and concomitantly during a rough patch for them. Laurent knew nothing had happened beyond a stolen kiss which he'd already dealt with long ago.. And over the years, Bedard had made up for it more than he'd ever harmed Laurent. In fact eight years ago Bedard had lost his prestigious position as Chief Inspector of Aix when he compromised himself to save Laurent from prison—for Maggie's sake of course. Since then, he'd been in charge of all crimes having to do with the Department of Motor Vehicles on the Côte d'Azur. Not a terrible assignment as far as location went, but a significant comedown for someone as ambitious as Bedard.

As for Roger Bedard's feelings for Maggie, Laurent had never felt threatened or jealous of Bedard. He knew where he stood with Maggie. He knew her feelings and he was secure in her love. He'd long ago ignored any nonsense that he'd heard that said some people could love more than one person at a time. He didn't doubt that true. But he knew his wife. And he knew there was only room in her heart for him.

Twice, he'd stood up and walked to the door with the intention of going out to look for Philippe Martin and see if he couldn't beat a confession out of the man. Twice he'd talked himself out of it. Even if Martin had killed Antoine, it was hard to imagine him hiring two men to kidnap Maggie. That was on a whole different level and not one that Laurent could envision a man as benign as Martin doing.

And if Martin couldn't tell him where Maggie was, what was the point of rattling his chain?

Laurent continued to pace his room, wracked with indecision. Who else could he call who would be safe to talk to? He'd already gone straight to the source by confronting Emile Chevalier—and with no apparent consequences. Nobody else had the clout to orchestrate the kidnapping. It had to be him. Laurent ran a frustrated hand through his hair.

For all that he was working to find out who killed Antoine, Laurent could not escape the niggling notion that, if by solving Antoine's murder he got Maggie killed, what would have been the point?

His phone rang and he saw from the screen that it was Grace.

"Yes?" he said, trying to keep the strident anxiety and dread out of his voice.

"Don't despair, darling Laurent," Grace said. "This is early days yet. We aren't at the finish line."

Laurent felt tears spring to his eyes. In so many ways Grace was like Maggie. He knew that was likely the shared American characteristics in them. They had the do-or-die, take-the-hill, don't take no for answer and definitely never accept defeat attitude of most Americans he'd ever known. He found himself wishing for just a moment that he had that impermeable shield of hardy Americana to protect him against what he knew only too well could happen.

"I know, *chérie*," he murmured.

"I have some news," she said. "But I don't know how it helps."

"Tell me."

Grace quickly filled him in on a social media picture that told a story of sous chefs, line cooks, kitchen helpers and wait staff down through the years complaining that Antoine had consistently, constantly stepped out of line with them.

"Rape?" Laurent asked.

"No. Sexual harassment," Grace said.

"Ah," he said.

"It's still bad, Laurent."

"Yes, of course," he said. "*Je sais*. Of course."

"Have you looked at the kitchen staff for suspects?" Grace asked. "I mean, honestly, he sounds like a pig. Sorry."

"Do not apologize, Grace," Laurent said. "I am glad to have the information."

"There's this one girl who accused him of getting physically violent with her. She posted a photo of her back eye and everything."

"Did she go to the police?"

"I don't know. But I thought you'd be interested in her name. Eloise Durand. Must be Remy Durand's daughter, don't you think?"

Laurent felt a sudden cold invade his core.

*So this is the personal matter that Durand has against Antoine.*

Was it motive enough to kill? Laurent thought of how *he* would feel if someone had hit Mila or Amelie. He had to admit that for him it would have been more than enough motive.

"Are you still there, Laurent?" Grace asked.

"Yes," he said. "This is good information. Thank you, Grace."

"Please don't get discouraged, Laurent," Grace said. "You'll find her. I have faith. Now you just need to have some, too."

"I know," he said as he cradled his head in his hands. *"Je sais."*

After hanging up Laurent thought about calling Rousseau to see if she knew about this connection between Durand and Antoine but decided it would be a waste of his time. She probably knew all about it. He'd already decided that emailing a copy of the IOU where Antoine had supposedly signed over his share of *L'Étoile Gourmande* to Durand was also not likely to interest the detective—especially if she was in the pocket of the crime syndicate. Of course, this didn't move the prospect of guilt away from the crime syndicate in any way. If anything, it strengthened the likelihood.

Had *La Main Noir* rewarded Durand for his loyalty and

money laundering services by assassinating the man who'd hurt and humiliated his daughter?

Laurent clenched his fists, the frustration and helplessness boiling inside him. He had come to his limit of just sitting and doing nothing. With no other idea of what to do, he grabbed his car keys and drove to the street where Philippe Martin lived. He swore to himself that he wouldn't hit the man. He would just ask him a few questions. And then he would not take no for an answer to any of them.

After parking on Martin's street, Laurent climbed the stairs of the man's apartment building, his heart pounding in his chest. This wasn't yet a last-ditch effort. He had to believe that somehow Martin would tell him something which would lead to Laurent's next step, his next lead. At the top of the landing, he raised his fist to knock on Martin's door but stopped, perplexed. The door was ajar.

With the hair prickling the back of his neck, Laurent used two fingers to push the door open and stepped inside. Instantly the metallic smell of blood filled his nostrils. A feeling of dread needled into him as he walked into Martin's apartment, following the scent as it got stronger and stronger until he found the body in the kitchen, face down in a red pool of blood already congealing around him.

## 39

A gaping wound in Martin's neck glistened in the dim light. Laurent's eyes traveled to the butcher knife beside the body, its blade coated in gore. The nauseating smell of blood hung heavy in the air, mixed with the rancid scent of decay. The silence in the room was deafening, broken only by the sound of Laurent's own rapid breathing.

He stepped away from the crime scene into the hallway knowing that if any evidence of himself was found here, he'd be arrested for Martin's murder. He glanced into the living room, his eyes scanning the area for anything out of the ordinary—two wine glasses, a broken vase, anything that didn't fit. He didn't have enough time to examine the apartment and he didn't know what he was looking for. He saw a shard of broken glass on the living room carpet in front of the couch, but before he was tempted to investigate further, a noise from the hallway made him freeze. It sounded like the shuffling of feet.

Laurent went to the door and stood next to its open hinges, waiting until the two building residents receded down the hallway. He stepped out into the hall, looked both ways, and walked quickly to the stairwell. As soon as he was out onto the street, he slipped into the shadows. He found he was breathing a little quicker than normal.

What did Martin's death mean? Did it mean he *didn't* kill Antoine? Did it mean that Antoine's killer killed him? But why?

Laurent glanced back at the apartment building and saw how dangerous it had been for him to risk coming back to talk to Martin. Anyone could have seen him enter or leave the building. But now that Martin was permanently off his suspects list, who else was there? He briefly considered Bouchard but in a city the size of Toulouse, he'd never find him unless the man wanted to be found. So what now? Laurent furrowed his brow in thought, his mind racing to piece together the elusive connections that he was sure were right in front of him, but he just couldn't see. If he couldn't talk to anyone and he couldn't properly analyze any physical clues he stumbled onto, what was left for him to do that wouldn't endanger Maggie?

As he got to his parked car, he thought about calling the police to alert them to Martin's death and decided there was no harm in that. If, on the remote possibility that Rousseau was not in the pocket of the syndicate and she really did care about solving Antoine's murder and Maggie's abduction then having her people process Martin's crime scene was the only logical move in the direction of solving the other crimes.

It wasn't much but it was better than nothing. Laurent left his car and walked down the street until he found a pay phone tucked between two shuttered produce shops. He checked for the existence of CCTV cameras, found none, and made the call, disguising his voice. After that he went to a nearby bar and ordered a whiskey and soda, his brain working in double time.

He sat and drank, closing his eyes to concentrate better and to block out the world and his own churning stomach and think. The only possible lead he had—the only one that wouldn't alert the kidnappers that he hadn't stopped investigating—was the abandoned cabin where the men had first taken Maggie. With no other lead to go on, returning to the last place he knew Maggie had been felt desperate, but it was at least something. Perhaps he'd overlooked a clue? Or perhaps the kidnappers might return? That thought gave him a glimmer of hope as it melded with the image of his confronting them in person—and well away from any well-meaning bystander who might attempt to stop him from putting them both in permanent body casts.

Feeling a little cheered by this thought, he glanced up at the television set that the bartender had on over the bar to catch the weather report. The volume was muted but Laurent was able to read the caption crawl that predicted a heavy dumping of snow in the region surrounding Toulouse.

Instantly, Laurent felt this was a sign. He wasn't even going to chide himself for thinking such a mad thing. He was way past deriding the value of any idea—no matter where it came from or how farfetched. At the moment, even Claudine's New Age nonsense didn't seem quite so crazy.

*If you have nothing substantive to go on, go with whatever remotely presents itself, no matter how feeble until something concrete reveals itself.*

He was well aware that that thought was the very definition of desperation.

*But that's where I am right now.*

It was true that anything he did put Maggie's life in

danger. But doing nothing also did that. He tossed a few euros on the bar and pulled on his jacket. Whether Maggie was in town or still out in the mountains somewhere was suddenly irrelevant. It didn't matter. Nothing did. Nothing mattered except for the fact that he couldn't just sit here and do nothing another moment.

## 40

The air was thick with tiny ice crystals that glimmered as they fell and melted on the windshield as Laurent drove due west. Both sides of the road were banked with snow as he navigated the sharp turns, his tires fighting to grip the asphalt. As he gained elevation the surrounding landscape transformed before his eyes, going from vibrant autumn colors to a frosty, monochromatic tableau.

As he drove, Laurent had the inescapable, nearly visceral sensation that what he was doing was a hopeless waste of time. He didn't have the feeling he was moving toward Maggie at all. He might as well be driving in circles. He was just off the main highway and roughly twenty miles out of Toulouse, when he was forced to slow down. Up ahead was a herd of sheep congregating in the road. When he got closer, he stopped and saw they weren't sheep but goats.

Laurent knew that sheep farming had a long history in the area because much of the land surrounding the foothills was pastoral. But this herd was clearly intent on crossing the pasture to head up the narrow mountain pass that was just visible from the road. He watched the goat herder, an elderly man dressed in an outfit that could have belonged to Laurent's great grandfather—tweeds, leather boots, and an anorak with the hood pulled up against the chill.

The wind was cold and biting. High above, dark clouds loomed, threatening to release their snowy payload. As he watched the herder, it occurred to Laurent that this fellow was probably an inhabitant of the mountains. As the goats gathered on the verge of the narrow mountain road, Laurent put his car in park and got out. The shepherd looked up in mild concern as Laurent walked over to him.

"Can I help you, Monsieur?" the old man called out when Laurent was still ten meters away.

"I have lost something," Laurent said, slowing his advance so as not to frighten the man.

"Unless it is a goat or kid," the man responded, "I am not sure I can help you."

"It is my wife," Laurent said.

Several goats bleated lazily while others nibbled at the grass poking out of the snowbank along the roadside, oblivious to the gentle prodding of their shepherd trying to move them forward.

"Now I *know* I cannot help you," the shepherd said with a laugh.

Laurent pointed in the distance.

"I tracked her to a cabin on the other side of that knoll," he said. "Another ten kilometers that way."

The old man turned to look in the direction that Laurent pointed and then turned to look back at him with a frown.

"That place is a ruin," he said. "If your wife is meeting her lover there, it will not be a pleasant experience."

Laurent almost smiled.

"I was hoping you might know of other cabins in this area," he said.

The old man cocked his head as if trying to understand him better.

"I might," he said.

Laurent could see that the man was wary of him. He had to admit, the story of looking for a wayward wife in this rough terrain was outlandish. But it had the ring of truth to it. He didn't want to mention that it was a kidnapping lest he spook the old fellow. He realized then that in his urgency and desperation, he had broken his own rule of social engagement, a rule he'd scolded Maggie for ignoring from the moment she moved to France.

*You should always take the time to make small talk before getting around to saying what it is you want.*

Perhaps he had lived with his American wife too long. He was becoming more and more like her.

"You must have the *chèvre* market locked up in Toulouse," Laurent said, glancing at the man's herd.

The man's face opened up as he turned to admire his herd.

"I have been supplying the best restaurants in Toulouse for the last twenty years," he said. "And my father before me."

"Even a place as prestigious as *L'Étoile Gourmande*?" Laurent asked.

"Yes, of course," the goat herder said proudly and then paused. "Well, before it was famous."

Laurent wasn't sure if the man had heard of Antoine's passing but he decided he didn't want to sidetrack him by telling him about it.

"Antoine Dubois is a hard man," the shepherd said, his eyes still on his goats. "My wife dislikes him."

"Any reason why?" Laurent asked.

The shepherd waded through his herd of goats, gently prodding the more obstinate ones and calling out to them in a mixture of coaxing and commands. A sheepdog that Laurent hadn't noticed up until this moment darted around them, barking and nipping at their legs to keep the animals moving along the narrow road.

"She said I shouldn't expect friendship with Antoine," the shepherd said. "Which of course I never did. Even though we have known each other for many years. But neither should I expect thievery."

"Antoine stole from you?" Laurent asked.

The man looked at Laurent suspiciously. "Do you know him?"

"A long time ago," Laurent said, hedging.

"Was he a thief when you knew him?"

Laurent hesitated and then reminded himself that nothing could hurt Antoine now.

"He was," he said. "But then so was I."

The shepherd nodded as if unsurprised.

"My wife says Antoine only took what I allowed him to take," the old man said.

"To be clear," Laurent said, "you are referring to the price for your *chèvre*?"

The man laughed.

"Yes. He didn't come into my home and rob me! Although to hear my wife talk, you would think he had. No, after years of working together, in the end we could not agree on a fair price."

"Is there another goat cheese source in Toulouse?" Laurent asked.

"There is not."

"If you refused to supply to him, where does he get his *chèvre*?"

"Oh, he pays a middleman to get my cheese."

"That makes no sense. He'd have paid more, surely using a middleman?"

"I'm sure he does," the old man said with a shrug as if Antoine's reasonings were beyond him.

Laurent felt a pinch of anger at Antoine. Would he be so petty as to pay *more* than he needed to—all to show a lowly goat herder who was boss? He found he hated the picture of Antoine that that thought formed in his mind.

"A very sly creature named Bouchard who will always manage to be there to fill in the gaps," the shepherd said.

When Laurent made a face, the goat herder asked in surprise: "Do you know him?"

"I do."

"Ah well, perhaps I shouldn't be surprised. Bouchard is known far and wide for his ability to procure any delicacy for any of the chefs of Toulouse—whether legally sourced or not—and that includes *chèvre*."

"I am sure I saw *chèvre* advertised on the menu at *L'Étoile Gourmande* as locally sourced," Laurent said with an eyebrow raise.

The old man shrugged.

"Antoine has no problem advertising any of his menu items as locally sourced even if he gets them from Lyons or Marseille," he said.

It was pretty clear from what Laurent was hearing that Antoine had not really changed that much from the days when the two of them were cheating innocent victims on the Côte d'Azur. He was sorry to hear it. It was exactly what Bouchard and Claudine had both said—that Antoine hadn't changed from the old days.

Laurent looked out over the cold pasture with the mountains black and forbidding in the background. What could have made Antoine revert to old ways when so much good had fallen into his lap? Why would he steal when he no longer needed to? Or had there been something else driving Antoine?

"The weather is turning," Laurent noted. "Will you be able to get to the mountain pass tonight?"

"Don't worry about me, Monsieur. I have trod this path since I was a boy," the man said before turning to look at Laurent. "I know where every shelter is, owned or abandoned. Some of the cabins are impossible to find unless you know where they are."

Laurent held his tongue and waited. The cold breeze riffled through his jacket, and he found himself shivering. He'd left his knit cap in the car.

"Do you have a piece of paper, Monsieur?" the old goat herder said. "I am happy to draw you a map."

## 41

The snow fell softly outside the cabin window, turning the sky a hazy gray as darkness crept into Maggie's view. The air in the cabin was musty and, eerily silent except for the occasional scurrying of rodents and the sound of the wind whistling through the cracks in the walls.

Maggie held the water bottle to her mouth, not drinking but not wanting her captors to know. Once they did, they'd take the bottle from her and tie her hands again. Every second free of the plastic ties was a relief for her scraped and reddened wrists.

She watched the two young men closely. They were still careful not to take their masks off or speak to her. She wondered if that meant that their voices were distinctive in some way. The tall tattooed one she called Benson was wheezing. She'd seen him use an inhaler frequently. But he continued to smoke so Maggie wasn't sure what good the inhaler was doing.

The men sat around a rickety wooden table and shuffled a well-worn deck of cards. The scent of stale smoke and sweat hung in the air and the occasional clink of coins punctuated their low, murmured conversations between them. Benson looked over at her often, before returning to his cards with a grunt. She'd been with them long enough to know that he was the one to watch. He was the one to worry about.

She sipped from the water bottle and found herself flashing back to when she'd first come to live in France and how strange everything had been. Laurent used to tease her for not attempting to learn the language. But in her defense, she hadn't expected to stay. When it became clear that she would be here a while, she had finally buckled down to learn it. There had been so many differences between her and Laurent in the beginning—mostly culturally—but also things that were just exotic and strange enough that instead of repelling each other, tended to fascinate each other and draw them in closer.

She could only imagine the true hell Laurent must be going through right now. In the midst of what she was experiencing—something she'd define as equal parts terror and dread—the very thought of Laurent was her unwavering pillar of strength and support. She imagined him strategizing and working tirelessly to find her. This mental exercise was a way to help her tap into his strength and to stay strong, knowing that he would expect nothing less from her. She knew her moment would come, and she needed to be ready. Laurent would do his part. She needed to do hers.

In their years together, raising a family, building the wine business and learning to live with each other, their bond had formed, built on mutual support and love, strengthened and reinforced over and over again. As different as they were from each other, through all the miscommunications, trials, and misunderstandings, they'd built an understanding of each other It was this knowledge of who they were *together* that was enabling Maggie to stay strong now and to remain hopeful. If she knew one thing, she knew that Laurent would leave no stone unturned in his pursuit to find her.

Benson threw his cards down and scraped his chair back noisily on the wooden floor. Maggie tensed because both men were on their feet now. Hedges went to his pack, leaning against the door and rooting around for something while Benson pulled out his cigarettes as he stormed out onto the porch. The cellphone of Hedges began to ring. He turned to look at her and then hurried outside to take the call.

So far, they'd always driven by night and then found a place to hole up in by day. For all Maggie knew they had just been driving in circles.

The light had already leached out of the sky and she felt a dart of panic slam into her at the thought of being drugged again so soon after last time. While the two men were outside, she set the water bottle down and looked around the cabin. With her hands untied, she had just seconds to make the most of the moment. She could hear them talking on the porch but could not make out what they were saying.

Finding a weapon was unlikely, but there might be some way to leave a bread crumb or otherwise help Laurent to know she'd been here. As soon as she thought of it, her eyes found the item on the floor. She didn't have time to think about it. She was out of her chair and her fingers closed around it before quickly returning to her seat. She looked around as desperation welled up inside her. She could hear them talking louder now as if wrapping up their phone conversation. She reached out for the wall behind her, unmindful of splinters and worked for long seconds, the perspiration dripping from her face in the cold cabin.

When the door flung open, she twisted in her seat and faced them. Hedges was hurriedly putting his balaclava back in place over his face.

"Why didn't you tell him we were out of the stuff?" Benson said to Hedges.

Because they assumed she was a tourist, they didn't assume she could understand them, for which Maggie was grateful.

"I didn't want to call attention to it," Hedges said. "She won't give us any trouble. She's sat quiet, hasn't she?"

Maggie stared at them, keeping her face impassive. They were both looking at her now, but it didn't matter. Her moment had arrived. And they never saw it coming.

All she could do was hope that Laurent would find what she was leaving for him.

And of course understand what it meant.

## 42

Three hours later, Laurent was sitting on a frozen tree stump in front of the second cabin he'd been able to find from the map the goat herder had made for him. The air around him fluttered with tiny snowflakes, swirling and dancing in the biting wind. The once colorful trees were now barren, their branches creaking under the weight of the snow.

The first cabin he went to had been long abandoned, its roof caved in and the interior coated with evidence of the weather. It obviously had not been used for shelter of any kind for years. From there Laurent drove slowly up the mountain road until he was forced to leave his car and trek the rest of the way to the second cabin on foot. He'd already searched the cabin and, while essentially unfurnished, he decided it could certainly serve as a shelter from the elements. Touching the fireplace grate had told him nothing. The ashes were banked and cold.

The walls of the cabin were cracked and gaping. Thick cobwebs clogged the corners. Even though the fireplace was cold, Laurent was convinced this had been where Maggie's abductors had stopped. It occurred to him that they were doing one night in each cabin and moving on. After searching every nook and cranny in the house, he went outside to survey the surrounding grounds. He found no tire tracks but only two sets of boot prints. Either Maggie was no longer with them, or they were carrying her. He prayed that didn't mean she was injured. Laurent forced himself to draw conclusions without getting emotional. That wouldn't help anything.

One set of footprints was deeper than the other. Either that man was considerably heavier, or he had carried Maggie. Laurent stared at the cabin as evening began to gather around him, slowly blotting out the view of the mountain landscape beyond the cabin.

As he stared at the cabin, relishing the pain of the cold as it penetrated his thin jacket, he tried to imagine Maggie truly being here. If she had been, any telltale scent of her perfume no longer lingered. As he pulled his eyes away from the cabin, the feeling of helplessness returned but was quickly supplanted by the urge to take action.

He pulled out his phone and saw he had an email from Bedard. He felt his mouth go dry as he opened it and scanned the contents. His heart sank. Bedard had not been able to access Antoine's emails without tipping off Rousseau which Laurent had asked him not to do. Laurent already knew everything Bedard had uncovered. Antoine had done five years at Fleury-Mérogis—Europe's largest prison—for grand theft. Since then, his police record had showed him to be a model citizen, with the exception of an arrest for domestic violence a few years ago against an eighteen-year-old girl.

*That would be Durand's daughter.*

The charges for the assault had been dropped. Laurent felt a wave of disgust. Naturally.

He knew that Antoine's association with *La Main Noire* would ensure that nothing of consequence showed up on his police record. Bedard ended his email by asking for more information on why Laurent needed this information—assuming rightly that Laurent would not be reaching out to him unless he was desperate.

Laurent regretted contacting Bedard. It had come to nothing and now Bedard knew something was in the wind. In all likelihood the man had already tried to contact Maggie and had of course failed. Laurent sent a cryptic email back to Bedard saying the information was very helpful and that he or Maggie would call him tomorrow to fill him in.

Slowly, he got up and moved back inside the cabin. The emerging moon cast an ethereal glow on the landscape, revealing glimpses of the rugged terrain that surrounded the cabin. Laurent had already decided that attempting to make his way back down the steep mountainous trail to his car would be folly in the dark. Breaking his neck to then lie undiscovered until spring wouldn't do Maggie any good. Or Amelie. Or Jem, Mila, or Luc...

His shoulders slumped in defeat and discouragement, Laurent turned around and made his way back to the cabin. Suddenly, a memory came to him of Maggie in the hospital after Jemmy was born. She'd handed the baby to Laurent, her eyes bright with pride and love. He'd never told her that it wasn't until that moment, when he first held his son, that he felt as if his life had truly begun. Up until that moment, he'd just been waiting.

Laurent thought momentarily of Jemmy who was living in Atlanta and rarely coming home or even calling. Laurent's eyes stung with tears and he immediately felt the cold chill. How had that happened? How had the boy whom he'd loved so intensely grown into a young man he didn't understand? How had the toddler he'd carried and who'd gazed at him with limitless adoration end up learning that there were other things in the world that mattered more to him?

Inside the cabin, the air was cool and musty with hints of pine. Moonlight filtered through cracks in the walls, and the creaking floorboards under Laurent's weight echoed in the silence. He found a solitary candle in one of the kitchen drawers which he lit and set on the single battered wooden table in the center of the cabin. The light flickered and cast dancing shadows across the room. In a way, the tiny flame seemed to provide a small beacon of hope in the darkness as though he was sitting a vigil. Because that's what this was, he realized. Waiting and watching for something to happen. He thought of Jemmy again and tried to let go of him in his mind and be at peace with the life Jemmy had made in America—a life that didn't include Laurent or Maggie.

*Maggie might be able to do it*, he thought sadly as he watched the flickering flame. *That's the American in her, being able to see the world and then adjusting to what she sees. But all I can do is want what I thought I'd been promised.*

He looked around the cabin's darkened interior. A rickety chair was set near a cracked window which when he moved to it allowed him to gaze out into the black wilderness, his eyes scanning the silhouette of the far tree line. The night sky reminded Laurent of the vast universe stretching out before him and reminding him of the infinite possibilities and mysterious forces at play. How in the world, for example, could he ever have imagined that he would one day have a granddaughter from a woman he'd never even known was his daughter? And what about Luc?

Luc was the illegitimate son of Laurent's brother Gerard who'd done everything in his mean, short life to destroy all that Laurent had ever loved or cared about. But Laurent had come to love Luc as dearly as his own son. When Gerard was murdered in a dark alley in Paris, Laurent hadn't rejoiced, but he hadn't mourned him either. How was it possible that from that debased miscreant would come a young man like Luc? Laurent hadn't thought it possible that anything good could come from Gerard. But then there was Luc, he thought with a smile. *Like one of the glittering stars that shone above this very cabin.*

He shook his head ruefully and settled into the solitude of the cabin. He felt his heart filled with a mixture of hope and fear. Hope that she could be found. Fear that he'd already lost her forever.

The next morning Laurent awoke stiff and cold. He'd slept sitting up in the single chair in the cabin and wondered if Maggie had also slept in that chair. It had been uncomfortable and hard. He'd not wanted to give away his presence by lighting a fire, so he was cold too, as well as filled with despair, just as Maggie probably had been. Laurent had taken some small comfort thinking she had been here. He was well aware that Maggie hadn't had even that nominal succor.

He stepped outside the cabin and scanned the trees around the house. When he did, he saw animal tracks on the ground. He wondered briefly what kind of animal was roaming the area. Finally, he sighed. There was nothing else to do but go back to Toulouse. He didn't have any hope that there would be a message of some kind waiting for him there. He had a phone, and the kidnappers knew how to reach him on it. If they wanted to communicate with him, they could.

He went back to the cabin to give it one last survey. Just as he was turning away to leave, he thought he saw something that he hadn't noticed before. He narrowed his eyes. At first it looked like a piece of caulking—nearly imperceptible in the dark crevices of messy spackling—in the wall. He walked over to it behind the chair and reminded himself again that it was likely the place where they'd put Maggie when they'd been here—if they had indeed been here.

He knelt by the irregularity in the wall and dug his fingers into the crevice. Immediately he touched something that didn't belong there. It wasn't spackling. He felt his pulse quicken as he pried the item out of the wall. It tumbled to the floor and fell apart into two pieces. Laurent picked up the pieces and stared at them in his hands, one part metal, one part plastic, which he proceeded to reconnect. He knew what it was. But that didn't help him. The question was, what in the world was it doing wedged in the wall?

The second he asked himself that question was when he felt a jolt to his brain that nearly staggered him.

Maggie had left it for him.

## 43

Laurent stared at the inhaler in his hands, his heart pounding.

He turned it over and over examining it and then looked again where he'd found it crammed into the crack of the wall. His first response was an overwhelming swamping of relief because this was another piece of evidence that Maggie was still alive. But after that brief emotional spike, a tingling sensation raced down his neck as he held the inhaler in his hand, and he felt his anxiety ratchet up again

*Why would she hide this? Why would she think this is helpful to me?*

He frowned and looked around the room. There was a small trash bag of take-out food, a couple of empty soft drink cans and a plastic plate that had been used as an ashtray. He looked again at the inhaler in his hand.

*She's trying to tell me that one of her abductors is having a problem breathing.*

Laurent felt a rush of purpose and clarity.

*And he is going to need to replace his inhaler.*

Laurent felt like laughing out loud. It was his first real surge of hope since Maggie had been taken. He thought about calling the police. He even went so far as to pick up his cellphone, but the image of Maxine Rousseau's arrogant clueless face immediately came to him. He saw her with her arms crossed, saw her refusing to listen to him. She'd been wrong in the beginning about Antoine's death—stubbornly, perniciously wrong. She had refused to even consider that Antoine's death could be viewed any other way that accidental and as a result had allowed the contamination of the crime scene.

Laurent felt a surge of disgust rise up in him.

No. He would handle this himself. He turned and let himself out of the cabin, slamming the door solidly behind him. The guy who owned this inhaler needed to replace it. He would be looking for a place to do that. That meant Toulouse. It was the closest point of civilization to this section of the mountains. Laurent guessed there were at least twenty pharmacies in Toulouse that sold inhalers.

But there was only one that Bouchard said the syndicate regularly funneled their money through.

Laurent hurried down the side of the mountain toward his car.

## 44

Maggie sat on a worn, threadbare rug, her back against the rough wooden wall of the cabin. The light from the flickering lantern cast long, shifting shadows that seemed to stretch and shrink with each movement by the two men in front of her. The air was thick with the odor of aged wood, mingled with the faint scent of smoke from the cold fireplace. Since she'd fallen asleep in the trunk for most of the drive, she wasn't sure if they'd driven all night. Mercifully, although she'd been gagged, she hadn't been drugged this time.

Her two abductors remained masked and respectful, never laying a hand on her more than necessary to ensure she stayed put, yet Maggie found their very silence unnerving. They communicated in low murmurs, their words usually too quiet for her to make out, adding to her sense of isolation and dread. The cabin itself, much like the other two, was a claustrophobic space with sparse furnishings which did little to ease her anxiety. The creaking floorboards were the only sound that punctuated the silence.

Maggie's heart pounded in her chest, each beat a reminder of her vulnerability but also a galvanizing drumbeat of resolve. Since she'd been taken, she'd spent nearly every waking minute wondering what these men wanted and what would happen next. Her senses were heightened to the point that every creak and crack of the old cabin made her jump, her body tense and ready to react.

Outside, the wind howled through the trees. The mountains themselves felt like an impenetrable barrier trapping her in this nightmare. Her thoughts were constantly focused on escape, but with the ever-present watchfulness of her captors and the hostile, unforgiving terrain outside there was no plan Maggie could imagine that seemed remotely plausible. A cold fear settled deep within her. Even so, she felt there was something different about this morning.

She'd been given her usual meal of potato chips and warm cola as soon as they'd moved into the new cabin. Benson had untied her hands so she could eat. She noted that he was perspiring heavily and talking more than usual. It was just a low mutter as were Hedge's irritated replies to him, but still, it was different. Maggie imagined they were comfortable speaking around her—even in low voices and whispers—because they assumed she couldn't understand French. Now that they were speaking more, she found herself straining to understand what had changed.

She watched as Benson paced the room, his movements erratic and jumpy. At one point, he rummaged through his backpack, his frustration mounting with each passing second. Maggie guessed he was searching for the inhaler she'd hidden, and a small, defiant part of her felt a flicker of hope. Without his inhaler Benson was in some distress, gasping and periodically running outside as if sucking in lungfuls of the mountain air might help. Every time he opened the door, Hedges shouted at him.

"They might be watching the cabin!" he said when Benson stumbled back in, his face gray and pallid.

"I need my inhaler," Benson wheezed.

"Why is that my fault? Suck it up!"

Maggie felt a needle of hope pierce her. She'd only intended for somebody to find the inhaler and realize that she'd been in the cabin. But now she realized there was another possibility. She might have forced her abductors to alter their routine.

"It's a medical disability, you idiot! I can't breathe!" Benson huffed.

"Then maybe you should've taken better care not to lose the thing!"

"I'm going into town to get another one. I can't do this!"

"What will the boss say if you just piss off? We're supposed to watch her!"

Hearing Benson talk about going into town made Maggie wonder if they were close enough to Toulouse for him to do it within an hour or so. She was careful to keep her face impassive, so they didn't realize she understood them.

Finally, with a burst of anger, Benson snatched up the car keys from the table and stormed out of the cabin, the door slamming behind him with a force that made the walls tremble. Hedges, who had been watching him, glanced over at Maggie. Then he jumped up to retie her restraints, his rough hands making her wince as he secured them.

"You better not even breathe while we're gone," he muttered in French, before he turned and hurried out of the cabin, yelling for his confederate to wait for him.

As the door closed behind him, the cabin fell into an uneasy silence. The only sound was Maggie's own breathing that matched her racing heartbeat as she realized her chance had come.

## 45

Maggie waited until she heard the car roaring to life outside the cabin and then the sound of it slowly fading in the distance. Then she looked about, searching for anything that might help her escape. All she saw were the same worn, dusty surfaces, the same oppressive shadows she'd memorized when they'd first brought her here. Suddenly, her eyes locked onto a rusty metal screw protruding from the side of the kitchen counter not far from where she sat. If it had been in the floor, she wouldn't have stood a chance, but it was hip level to where she was in her chair.

With her heart in her throat, Maggie began to scoot her chair to maneuver herself closer to the screw, inch by agonizing inch. It took many minutes and a sheen of sweat coated her forehead before she was near the nail. As soon as she was close, she stretched her body, reaching out with her fingertips, until she could just barely touch it. Praying she could pull it out, Maggie stretched her hands out even further and wrapped her fingers firmly around the nail, feeling the sweat make her hand slick. Using all her strength, Maggie pulled at the nail, but it was solidly lodged into counter. She paused, tamping down her frustration.

*Don't give up! Think!*

She took in a long breath and reconsidered the screw's position. Her hands were tied together but at least not to the chair or behind her back. The screw would be reachable with her wrists if she scooted even closer. Slowly she edged herself across the floor, knowing that one mistake and she would end up on the floor with no hope of recovery. She lifted her hands and positioned the knotted part of the rope on her wrists against the protruding screw and began to saw against it with a back-and-forth motion. She listened intently for any sounds outside the cabin that her abductors were returning. Sweat dribbled down her cheek even though it was cold in the cabin.

The rope slowly began to unravel but progress was slow as she continued for what felt like an eternity. Finally, one of the ropes broke apart, freeing Maggie's right hand. She quickly worked to release her left wrist, which was easier now that she had a hand free. Then, she reached down with trembling but determined hands and untied the ropes around her ankles. After two days in captivity, her captors had grown tired of tying thick knots every day and had made only the most rudimentary knot to hold her feet in place.

Maggie stood up, rubbing her sore wrists and looked around for a weapon. She spotted a heavy wrench on the table and grabbed it, feeling a surge of determination as she did. This was real. This was *happening*. The adrenaline coursed through her veins. She moved towards the cabin's window, cautiously peering outside just in case her abductors had reconsidered and returned.

Her breath was coming in short, fast pants now.

Had she thought this far ahead? Had she really thought she'd find a chance to make a run for it?

It didn't matter. She was doing it. She turned to look around and found Hedges's heavy jacket hanging on a peg. He'd left in such a hurry and left it behind. Maggie quickly pulled it on. It had a thick lining and an artificial fur hood. She ran into the kitchen and threw open the cupboards. She found a package of ramen noodles and a self-opening can of Vienna sausages which she stuffed into the pockets of the jacket.

How far was Toulouse? Could it be more than twenty miles? If not Toulouse, was there a village nearby with a pharmacy? It didn't matter. Maggie had no idea, no map and no compass. Whatever was outside the cabin door was just whatever she would have to deal with.

She stepped outside and the sun was shining, so Maggie didn't immediately feel the cold. It would be a different story in a few hours. She stepped off the porch and surveyed her surroundings.

The bare trees were silhouetted against the sky, their branches coated white from last night's snowfall. The sky was a deep blue. The only sound was the soft crunching of snow under her boots as she stepped off the porch onto a path of packed snow made by her captors' comings and goings for the last few hours.

As Maggie breathed through her mouth she could feel the cold air on her tongue.

Then, with a sudden spurt of urgency, she set out walking, determined to get as far away from the cabin as she could while it was still light. She wasn't cold yet. The heavy parka was doing its job. As she walked, she told herself the stories her grandfather had told her about the brave Allied pilots during World War II who had trekked the Pyrenees to get to safety. Shot down over enemy territory, many of these men had found themselves stranded and alone in a hostile land. They had trekked through the harsh, unforgiving terrain, driven by a fierce determination to reach safety and freedom.

Maggie could almost hear her grandfather's voice recounting their tales of courage and endurance. These men had faced insurmountable odds—cold, hunger, injury, and the constant threat of capture. Yet, they had pressed on, one step at a time, guided by the hope of survival and the will to persevere. She took a deep breath, drawing strength from the visions of these brave men. She pictured them trudging through snow-covered peaks, their faces set, their spirits unbroken despite the overwhelming odds.

The image filled her with determination.

She set her jaw and felt her muscles tightening in readiness. She was doing this. And nobody but God Himself would stop her now.

## 46

That evening, as soon as Laurent arrived back in Toulouse, he went straight to the nearest PharmaZen pharmacy not far from his lodgings and parked on the street in front of it. While he knew it was a shot in the dark, Bouchard had mentioned that the syndicate ran their money through this pharmacy, so it was at least a good possibility. He didn't know when the thugs had left the cabin or when Maggie had hidden the inhaler. If yesterday, they might already have come into town and replaced the lost inhaler. But if they were moving Maggie from one spot to the next to avoid being found which seemed to be the case, then just maybe they hadn't had time to come to Toulouse yet.

It wasn't much to go on, but it was all he had.

He sat in his car and watched as people came to and went from the pharmacy. He scrutinized every man who entered the store. One man stopped on the street in front of the pharmacy and looked around first. Laurent's skin prickled as the man looked over his shoulder. Most innocent people didn't do that. He was young, too, and appeared nervous. And he had a full neck tattoo.

Laurent's heart was pounding with anticipation as he watched the young man walk into the pharmacy. Then he got out of the car, crossed the street, and waited outside the pharmacy. He didn't have to wait long. Within minutes, the man exited the store and began to hurriedly walk down the street, already peeling the paper off his new inhaler. Laurent got in step behind him, waiting for his moment. That moment came when the man passed an alley. Not bothering or caring if anyone might see Laurent came up fast behind the man and shoved him hard into the alley.

The man stumbled and dropped his inhaler onto the pavement as Laurent threw him up against a wall of the alley.

"Where is she, you bastard!" Laurent snarled.

The man faced Laurent, his mouth open to explain or complain but he never got the chance. Laurent drove his fist into the man's stomach. The tortured emotions and fear that had been barely contained for the last two days exploded from Laurent.

"Help! Help!" the man called weakly, as he fought to bring his hands up to protect his face.

With a grunt, Laurent's fist slammed into the man's face, so absorbed that he didn't hear the second man materialize behind him. Instantly, Laurent's vision exploded into a blinding flash of light and pain. He felt the earth lurch beneath him as he sank to the ground. Darkness crept in around the edges of his consciousness. His brain wouldn't connect with his arms or legs. He felt the kick when it connected with the side of his face though. And then another, solid and methodical, at his face, his kidneys, his head. As the blows and kicks rained down upon him, each one pulled him further and further into the darkness, where he heard their voices as if they were coming from a long way away.

"Kill him, Jean-Claude! The bastard knocked my tooth out!"

"Nobody is supposed to know we're in town! Let's go!"

"Finish him! Do it now!"

# 47

That night was the coldest of Maggie's life. The cave where she finally found refuge after trudging through ankle-deep snowbanks all afternoon was made up of near-frozen rock walls that were rough and uneven. At first fearful of animals who might want to share the cave with her, she was eventually too cold and too tired to care. Stalactites hung from the ceiling, their jagged formations casting ominous shadows as the light from the waning moon filtered through the cave entrance.

Outside the cave, the world was cloaked in a blanket of white. Snowflakes fell from the dark sky, dancing in the air before gently settling on the ground. If Maggie had not been so miserable, she would have thought it beautiful. The cold air carried a crisp stillness broken only by the occasional rustle of branches or distant howl of the wind. She'd collected twigs and branches before realizing she had no way to start a fire. Instead, she settled away from the entrance, with the hard floor, uneven and rocky, against her hips. She was able to arrange her backpack to create a padding, but nothing helped the constant cold.

Her breath hung in the air, forming wisps of steam that dissipated into the darkness. She pulled her jacket tighter around her, hoping to ward off the bone-chilling cold. The only sound in the cave was that of her teeth chattering. As the night wore on, she found it impossible to sleep. The cold had become an active, relentless adversary—no less a threat to her than the two men hunting her.

*Where is Laurent? Is he looking for me?*

Maggie blew warm breath on her fingers and stared out into the night, her eyes trying to make shapes out of the blackness. Would the men still be searching for her in the night? Would she see their flashlights if they were? She tried to understand what might drive them to come after her. They'd seemed lazy and reactive to her, and not terribly smart. They were definitely following orders. They did not strike her as people who would venture out into the cold dark night to try to find her. Only someone as desperate as herself would do such a mad thing.

When morning finally came, Maggie was surprised to realize that she must have dozed off after all. It was still very cold, but she had survived. She stood up and tested her joints, massaging her hips and knees. She looked out the entrance of the cave and saw a dusting of snow in front of her that was unmarked by footprints, human or animal. She would have thought that any sensible woodland creature would have tried to join her in the cave last night. Past the cave entrance, she saw the morning had brought cold fog over the rocky trail.

While the men had obviously not ventured out at night to recover her, she had no doubt that they wouldn't hesitate once it was fully light. Although not in any way warm, the day was brightening by the minute. Maggie had no idea how far from the cabin she'd walked yesterday. But she was hungry and tired and fearful. And she was fifty-three years old. If the two men had provisions, warm clothing, and any kind of incentive to find her she would be no match for them.

What could that incentive be? Who hired them to do this? Had they asked Laurent for a ransom?

The thought of spending another night in the cave forced Maggie to get moving. She had to find help. The longer she hesitated. whatever head start she had would be erased She stepped outside and listened but all around her was quiet. Not even birdsong or the sound of rushing water. Not even the noise of the wind in the trees. She stepped out further and felt the cold breeze against her face. She had no compass and no way to know which way Toulouse was or even if the distance was walkable. If she chose the wrong direction, she would be walking into the mountains toward certain death.

Yet she couldn't not start moving.

One foot in front of the other. She forced her mind to focus on those WWII pilots. Their legacy of courage and tenacity was now her guiding light. She would honor their memory by fighting for her own freedom, by refusing to let fear dictate her fate.

As for which way to go? She would go with her gut, and her gut told her to walk toward the sunrise. That would be south. A few yards past the cave entrance the landscape opened up before her, displaying an unforgiving expanse of snow-laden peaks and treacherous slopes. She stopped and reconsidered. She turned away from the vista of mountain peaks and started walking in the other direction.

The snow-covered trees, their branches weighed down by the weight of winter, seemed to stand as silent sentinels beside her. Their skeletal forms created a haunting scene, casting elongated shadows across the pristine white canvas. Maggie made a conscious effort not to look at them.

Before long, each stride required more effort, as the powdery snow gathered around her ankles and threatened to swallow her boots. The terrain was uneven and unpredictable, demanding her utmost concentration. Twice she'd nearly twisted an ankle and once she came down to her knees, unharmed but shaken. The man whose jacket she was wearing had stuffed gloves into one of the jacket pockets for which Maggie had spent long minutes praying in gratitude. Without them, she had no doubt she'd already be suffering from frost-bitten fingers—or worse, she wouldn't be able to last out here at all.

Majestic peaks reached towards the heavens all around her, their snow-capped summits in stark contrast against the crisp blue sky. But Maggie felt the beauty of the surroundings almost mocking her. With each arduous step, she found herself drawing upon some inner resolve she didn't know she had, summoning courage from the very depths of her being.

The morning hours dragged by. She noticed when the sun reached its mid-day zenith and began to edge relentlessly toward the west as she trudged into the afternoon. The air was crisp and biting, nipping at her exposed skin and causing her breath to form into frosty clouds. She continued to tug her coat tightly around her, but the cold found its way through the smallest gaps. Her hunger gnawed constantly at her too. She'd eaten a few of the tinned sausages last night in the cave and was determined to save the rest. She'd been tempted to scatter the ramen noodles for the birds, realizing the noodles would likely be bad for her insides in their raw form. But she didn't know if she might need them. She stopped once to eat snow, letting it melt in her mouth before swallowing. And always she looked in every direction as if somehow, she might see some landmark to indicate where she was and where she was headed. To that end, she felt as if her senses were heightened. Every rustle of a branch or distant sound sent a surge of anticipation through her.

And always the fear was there. It lingered in the front of her mind, an ever-present companion as she moved painfully, awkwardly through the rugged terrain. Although it was true that the two men had been her jailers, they hadn't talked much. She wondered if that would change when they weren't worried about being overheard. Maggie had to believe she would hear them coming in the quiet that surrounded her. Surely, she'd get enough warning that they were near. She looked around. But what would she do if she did hear them? She couldn't run. There was no place to hide.

Plus, her trackers were well fed and warm and well rested. If they were at all savvy—savvy enough to track her in the snow—she would undoubtedly be recaptured. Maggie shook off the despairing thought and forced herself to replace it with anger. What good did it do to anticipate her capture before time?

She picked up her pace and set her shoulders in a determined hunch against the chill and trudged on into the winter wilderness.

## 48

It was late afternoon when Maggie found the cabin. She had spent the last several hours praying she was going in the direction of a road or a town. She clung to the hope that help was right around the next bend, that her pain and effort would be rewarded. That was the desperate prayer that was throbbing in her head as she crested the rise and found herself staring down the slope at the cabin.

It was nestled in the shadow of the dense, looming trees around it. Maggie crept closer, wary now as she stood behind a large oak tree and scanned the area around the cabin. She was cold and exhausted. The cabin's exterior was like the other two she'd been in—worn and splintered by the harsh elements. But this one seemed to exude an eerie sense of abandonment, even though a single lantern glowed in the window. The roof sagged under the weight of the recent snows.

Maggie watched the lantern with an unsettled feeling. Her first reaction had been one of jubilation. *Rescue!* But then doubt crept in. She took in a shaky breath, drawing the cold air into her lungs and forcing herself not to cough. The only sounds were the distant, mournful howl of the wind through the trees and the occasional creak of the cabin's ancient timbers, almost as if the structure were whispering secrets. The longer she stood there watching, the more the lantern's flickering light felt less like a beacon of welcome than a silent warning telling her to stay away.

She was cold and hungry and tired. Out of habit she glanced at her wrist where her watch used to be. She looked up into the sky but didn't trust herself to be able to determine what time it was by looking at the light. She glanced back at the cabin. All she knew for sure was that this place was shelter and right now she needed that.

*But who would leave the cabin with a light on?*

It occurred to her that she should wait and see if anyone came to the cabin. Could she tell just by looking at them if they were friend or foe? She edged closer to the cabin going from bush to bush, hearing the snow and gravel crunch under her boots. Even with the lantern in the window there was something about the cabin that told her nobody was inside. She prayed her instincts were good. She inched closer. Any moment now she half expected her two captors to jump out of the cabin door, having lured her with the lantern and its promise of comfort and warmth. She crouched in the bush and waited, her heart thumping in her chest.

What were her options? She was exhausted, hungry and freezing. She needed to go inside that cabin regardless of what was waiting for her. She straightened up behind the bush where she was hiding and walked to the front porch. She reached for the doorknob with a shaking hand and wasn't surprised to find it unlocked.

Taking in a long breath, she entered the cabin. Instantly,

her eyes scanned the interior, her heart pounding in her chest as she realized that it was in fact vacant. The relief seemed to turn her legs to jelly, and she stumbled across the floor to the nearest chair which she lowered herself into. She sat there, breathing hard, giving herself time to recover while looking about her as she did.

The inside of the cabin was sparse, with the flickering lantern casting erratic shadows that danced eerily across the rough wooden walls. The air was stale, carrying a faint odor of mildew and aged wood, mixed with the lingering scent of woodsmoke. A large, stone fireplace dominated one wall, although the hearth was only filled with ashes, suggesting a fire had been in it not long ago. A throb of doubt started in her chest. Someone had been here not too long ago.

The furniture in the cabin was minimal but more than the other cabins had. Maggie took in the rickety wooden table with two mismatched chairs, a threadbare rug across the floor, a single, sagging armchair near the fireplace and three single cots, each with blankets.

Unlike the other cabins, there was something particularly foreboding about this place. It was being used and not just for temporarily stashing kidnap victims. Maggie noticed a refrigerator in the corner of the room and got to her feet. She pulled open the door and found milk—spoiled—and some cheese. She quickly ate most of the cheese, without bothering to look for mold.

A chill lifted the hair on the back of her neck, and she looked around to see if there was an open window to account for it. She could see nothing. She rubbed the goosebumps from her arms and took in another steadying breath. Now that she was a little warmer and had something in her stomach, her brain began to function better. Whoever lived here would be back. This wasn't an abandoned cabin like the others. She couldn't stay—at least not until she made sure that whoever lived here wasn't in the same network as the two men who'd kidnapped her.

She walked over to the cots and touched the blankets. If she took one of these, she might last another night in a cave if she found another one. She looked around for a backpack or something to carry the bedding in since the one she carried was too small. That was when she saw the small wooden desk under the window. She went over to it and pulled open its front drawer.

What she saw made her pull out the desk chair and sit down.

The drawer was crammed with notes and sheets as well as identification papers, passports, and travel itineraries suggesting the movement of individuals across borders. There were photographs too. Photographs of individuals and families, most of them looking terrified, their expressions filled with despair and obviously photographed in moments of duress. Some photographs showed people being transported in unmarked vehicles. Maggie looked around the cabin interior and this time she saw it for what it was—a way station for human trafficking victims.

Turning back to the drawer, she pulled out sheets with handwritten notations—dates and numbers that seemed to indicate money spent or expected.

Whoever used this cabin was not afraid of these documents and photos falling into the wrong hands. She dug deeper into the drawer and found a collection of maps marked with specific locations and routes. Were these the trafficking routes used? Yellow markers highlighted so-called safe houses, border crossings, and other significant points integral to the trafficking network.

It was a complete description of the crimes committed and the crimes intended.

But who did it incriminate? Maggie shuffled through the documents and looked for a name or anything else to tie to these deeds. And that's when she saw a handwritten name on a document notating the size of the next group of people who would be delivered and to whom. The delivery was to be made to A.D.

*Antoine Dubois.*

Maggie leaned back in the chair, stunned. It had to be him. This changed everything. If Antoine was trafficking in people, his compatriots were the lowest of the low. It wasn't surprising that they would deal with disagreements by way of murder. Grimly, she scraped the files and photos together and then turned and spotted a nylon bag on the floor next to one of the cots. She crammed the files into the bag, added a thin wool blanket from the bed and went to the fridge to take the rest of the cheese.

The primal urge to flee—to get out *now*—clawed at her insides as she again rubbed her arms through her jacket and braced herself to step back out into the cold. It was still light out, but it wouldn't be for long.

One thing was for sure, any thoughts she'd had about hiding in the woods to see who came back to the cabin were immediately quashed. There was no way the people who used this cabin would have any intention of helping her.

She stepped out onto the porch and felt the first razor blade of the mountain air slice fully into her face.

## 49

Maggie stood for a brief moment on the cabin porch and then stepped off and walked around the house where she noticed car tracks. Her stomach hardened at the sight. The tracks had filled in a little with snow. She tried to remember when it had snowed last to determine out how long ago the owners of the tracks had left. In the end, she couldn't manage that but she could at least follow the tracks, hoping they would lead her to a proper road. She shifted the backpack on her shoulder and went forward, praying she was going in the right direction toward Toulouse.

As she walked, Maggie's mind whirled with what she'd discovered and what it meant. She wasn't completely sure why she had taken the papers. It was true they were evidence of a crime, but Antoine was past the point of being able to answer for his part in it. Is that why he was killed? She shook her head. It didn't matter that Antoine was safe from prosecution. What mattered was getting this information to the authorities as soon as possible. There were vulnerable people being hurt and just possibly these documents could track them down and help save them.

After that, Maggie just put her head down and trudged on through the unforgiving snow-packed trail, her exhaustion and despair growing with each step. The terrain seemed to stretch out endlessly in a maze of icy slopes with towering peaks all around her that seemed to taunt her. She'd long since lost whatever car tracks she'd been following. Instead, the once-promising path had become a treacherous labyrinth, leading her deeper into the heart of the wintry wilderness. Panic began to grip her, its icy tendrils tightening around her chest as the biting cold penetrated her clothing, seeping into her bones and numbing her extremities.

She told herself stories, she reminded herself of the brave Allied pilots, she brought her children's faces to mind over and over again. An hour later, the weather began to turn, and it started to snow again.

Maggie tightened the hood around her face. A cap and scarf would have been better since she knew she was losing most of her heat through the top of her head, but she was glad for what little she had. The snow was coming down harder now and whipping against her skin. The trees and rocks that she passed were being quickly swallowed up by the silent, graceful snowfall. Her steps slowed. She knew she must find shelter soon—even if it meant backtracking to the traffickers' cabin. It was either that or risk freezing to death.

As her fatigue weighed more and more heavily upon her, Maggie pushed forward, telling herself she would turn around but not just yet. Her vision had narrowed to just the small patch of snowy trail in front of her. She was careful not to trip over hidden rocks and downed tree trunks. She found herself thinking again and again of her grandfather and his tales of the brave lost men during the last world war. She imagined it was just this cold when the men had attempted their escape. Some of them were alone, most of them weren't dressed for a trek through the Pyrenees. And all of them were hungry and afraid.

*They did it and I can do it.*

She forced herself to plow through the thickening snow, her boots sinking deeper with each step, her legs feeling as if weights were tied to them. The pack pulled at her shoulders, and more than once she thought about just leaving it. She had been walking for hours. The thought of giving up crossed her mind every minute now. The memory of that cabin with its lantern flickering beckoned to her. Sometimes she imagined a gentle whisper in her ear that told her to just lay down and close her eyes. Just let the snow consume her.

Suddenly she stopped. She became confused about what to do next—turn around or drop to her knees. In that moment of befuddlement, a flicker of movement caught her eye in her disorientation. She turned her head and peered through the white haze of falling snow. What she saw at first made her blink in disbelief. It was a group of moving figures whose bright orange jackets standing out against a white backdrop. Maggie rubbed her eyes, unsure if she was seeing properly, and strained to refocus. Then she heard the voices.

Her heart leapt with a mixture of relief and trepidation. She couldn't be sure that they weren't a hallucination or the people hoping to recapture her. But she knew she wouldn't last another hour in the mountains alone. With an ardent prayer on her lips, she stepped off the path and raised her arms to wave to them.

# 50

The first thing Laurent saw when he opened his eyes was the dark, grimy walls of the alley around him. He blinked a few times before registering that he was laying on the ground, eye level with a pile of crumpled trash. A single flickering streetlight somewhere in his periphery offered dim illumination. He groaned and a sharp, metallic scent filled his nostrils, mixing with the stench of garbage that filled the alley. He could taste his own blood, warm and coppery in his mouth. Each breath he took brought up a bitter wave of bile as he fought the nausea swirling through him.

Slowly, he moved to a sitting position, his battered body radiating with pain, each movement a painful memento of what had happened with the two men in the alley. He lifted a hand to the back of his head and brought his fingers away —disjointed and sticking out at unnatural angles—covered with blood.

Confusion swirled within him, like a thick fog obscuring his thoughts as he struggled to remember what had happened. He turned to vomit on the ground and then leaned against the wall, limp and spent as his physical pain juddered though him. He glanced around and saw his cellphone on the ground. It was smashed to pieces. He brought his arm up and looked at his watch. It was late morning. He'd laid undiscovered in the alley all night long.

As he struggled to muster the willpower to stand, Laurent's mind became a battleground of emotions with anger and disgust at himself the clear winner. Anger for not checking to see if the man he cornered in the alley had been alone. Disgust because he'd allowed his desire to vent and punish overwhelm everything else. And because of that weakness, he'd lost his last chance to find Maggie.

He pulled himself to his feet and leaned against the alley wall, waiting for his dizziness to subside and the pain to stop vibrating through him. Then he dragged himself to the alley entrance. He blinked in the morning light before staggering from the alley onto the street, his body feeling every bit of the brutal beating he'd taken last night.

Every breath Laurent took was accompanied by a sharp twinge of pain which made it difficult for him to draw in air properly. That meant broken ribs. At least two. His lips were split and cracked, as he ran his tongue over them. The taste of his own blood lingered in his mouth. It was a constant reminder of the violence he'd endured.

And how completely he had failed her.

## 51

Maggie would always remember that moment when she waved to the group standing in the clearing, knowing her voice would be lost in the wind. Lifting her hand was the most she could do but in the end it was enough. She watched them run toward her like one blur of orange moving and morphing with the background, her eyes stinging with tears of relief. Three men and a woman, all dressed in orange parkas with the word *sauvetage* printed on the backs of their jackets. Rescue.

"Are you all right?" one of them said as the group descended upon her.

"Where did you come from?"

"Are you hurt?"

Just then Maggie's knees gave out from under her, and she sagged to the ground.

"You're all right now, Madame," one of the men said as he put a hand on her shoulder as if to hold her in place.

"Thank you," Maggie murmured, her vision blurred by tears. "Thank you."

"She is American?" one of the men asked. "Do you speak French, Madame?"

"Drink this," a female voice said. "Are you lost?"

Maggie opened her eyes to see a thermos lid with a steaming fluid being held out to her. The woman who held it had a warm smile that seemed to envelop Maggie in a way that all the blankets in the world couldn't. Maggie reached for the cup with trembling hands. It was cocoa mixed with what tasted like rum.

"Where did you come from, Madame?" another of the men asked as he draped a thick blanket over Maggie's shoulders.

"I don't know," Maggie said. "I...I spent the night in a cave."

The sounds and snorts of horror from the four rang in Maggie's ears as she finished the hot drink and felt it infuse and renew her from the inside.

"Where did you come from before that?" one man asked.

Maggie shook her head before answering. She wasn't sure if she should tell them the truth or just get them to bring her to Toulouse. One of the men helped her up from the ground and led her to a large rock all the while chattering that it had been warmed by the sun and would be more comfortable. He was right. Why hadn't she thought of that? It wasn't much but it was warmer than the ground.

Another of the group brought a second blanket to her and another cup of the cocoa rum which she quickly drank down. Slowly she began to feel the cold leave her fingers. She felt an overwhelming mixture of gratitude and awe that her ordeal was over.

"Are you hurt, Madame? Can you feel your toes?" the woman asked as Maggie handed her the empty thermos cup back.

"How long have you been out here?" one of the men asked.

"I'm happy to tell you my story," Maggie said as she looked at their flushed, excited faces. "But first, does anyone have a phone I can borrow?"

## 52

Laurent hobbled over to where his phone lay smashed on the ground. As he bent over to reach for it, he was painfully reminded that someone had stomped on his fingers, breaking at least one. He swore and used his other hand to pick up the broken phone. He tucked it into his jacket, his fingers brushing his wallet as he did. Not even the semblance of a robbery, he noted. That fact reminded him again of how he'd ruined his one chance to save Maggie. To make these bastards tell him where they were holding her.

He staggered out of the alley and onto the sidewalk, his gait unsteady and his movements hindered by the agony that rippled through his battered body. He felt every inch the effects of the powerful blows that had been delivered to his unprotected sides and hips while he lay unconscious. His arms and legs had not been spared either, making every step a test of endurance.

Deep lines of disgust and despair creased his face as he moved toward where he'd left the car. He looked around.

The alley came out on a tertiary street where there were few people to see him.

Why had they let him live? He'd been defenseless. They could easily have murdered him. Perhaps Chevalier had been impressed with Laurent and felt murdering his wife was punishment enough. Laurent's self-loathing pushed up into his throat like a physical obstruction. It was all he could do not to vomit on the street. He'd wasted the one clue that Maggie had left for him —probably at great personal danger to herself. He'd found it as she'd hoped he would and then he'd thrown it away. And now he was no closer to knowing where she was than he'd been before. Worse, the kidnappers would now take special care to make sure she was moved again.

If they didn't just kill her.

## 53

The snow had finally stopped falling, leaving a pale gray sky with the late afternoon sun struggling to cast a gentle, diffused glow over the snow-covered trail. The members of the mountain rescue group moved efficiently around Maggie, their breath visible in the cold air. One rescuer knelt beside her, checking her vitals and speaking in a calm, reassuring tone, while another adjusted the thermal blanket over her shoulders. All of their voices were a reassuring blend of professionalism and genuine concern.

Maggie smiled at them as she pressed the phone to her ear. She waited, listening to the ringing phone on the other end echoing ominously.

One ring. Two rings. Three. With each unanswered tone, Maggie's disbelief and anxiety mounted.

*Where is he?*

"Come on, Laurent, pick up," she whispered, her voice edged with fear.

After what felt like an eternity, the call went to voicemail. She tried again immediately. Maybe she'd dialed his number wrong. She was accustomed to just pushing the button next to Laurent's name. The call rang again and as she listened, Maggie found herself hoping against hope that there was a reason Laurent wasn't answering.

*Why would he not keep his phone charged up?*

But the second time she tried—and then the third—the result was the same—endless ringing, followed by the impersonal beep of his voicemail.

"Laurent? Are you there?" Maggie said on the voicemail. "Well, I can't believe you don't have your phone with you but darling, I escaped! I'm free and with a local mountain rescue team. I'm using their phone. So, call me back, okay? Please, be okay. Now I'm worried. Call me back!"

She ended the call and stared at the phone, willing it to ring back but there was only silence. As she stared at the phone the forest itself seemed to close in on her, the trees whispering with the wind as if sharing her growing worry. The thrill of her escape was now completely overshadowed by a gnawing dread. Had something happened to Laurent?

Maggie's mind raced with possibilities, each one more terrifying than the last. She tried calling a few more times, but each attempt ended in the same frustrating silence. She felt tears prick the corners of her eyes. She took a deep breath and forced herself to think logically. There must be a simple explanation—maybe Laurent was in a meeting, maybe his phone had died, maybe he was somewhere with no signal.

But despite her rationalizations, a cold knot of worry tightened in her stomach. Maggie handed the man his phone back, her hands trembling despite the thermal blanket wrapped around her. And then a thought came to her that she hadn't considered before this moment.

Had Laurent been hurt during the attack when she'd been taken?

"You husband is not answering?" the lead rescuer, Jean asked.

"It just isn't like him, you know?" Maggie said.

He nodded sympathetically.

"I mean, it's true he doesn't always keep his phone with him," Maggie said, "and he's always letting the battery run down but I've been missing for three days! What does it mean that he isn't answering?"

"You have been missing for three days?" Jean asked, his eyes round with surprise.

"I'm exaggerating," Maggie said.

She really didn't want to share the details of what had happened to her with anyone—even perfectly trustworthy looking rescue people.

"There could be a logical explanation for why he isn't answering," the woman rescuer said, her face open and hopeful.

"Sure," Maggie said.

*Like he's in a coma.*

Maggie chewed a nail and thought about calling Grace. But if Laurent had decided not to worry Grace, then perhaps Maggie should hold off calling her just yet. She would call her once she was back in Toulouse.

"I'm sorry, Maggie," Jean said. "I can radio for the police to come collect you, but we have two other sections we're supposed to check while we're up here. Do you feel strong enough to come with us?"

Before Maggie could answer, one of the other rescuers spoke up.

"I can take you back to Toulouse," he said.

Maggie turned to him. He was older than the others,

appearing every bit the seasoned mountain rescue professional with a rugged, stubbled face and piercing green eyes.

"Are you sure?" she asked.

He smiled reassuringly.

"Absolutely. My car is less than a mile's hike from here."

## 54

It took Laurent a full fifteen minutes to make it back to his car and then another twenty to maneuver himself inside and drive back to his bed and breakfast. Aside from his fingers and possibly a couple ribs, nothing else felt broken and he counted himself lucky. He could walk and he had the use of both arms. It could have been so much worse.

He made his way through the door of his lodging, casting an eye to the bed but not allowing himself to give in to the desire to lie down. He stripped off his clothing—they were covered in blood and grease stains and dirt—and then stood under a blistering hot shower, the stream as hot as he could bear it. And the whole time, his head vibrated with the horror of having had the abductors in his hands and letting them get away.

Out of the shower, he dried off and pulled on a clean pair of jeans and a shirt. He knew he didn't have time to indulge in despondency or even self-hatred. Plenty of time for that later. He carefully taped his broken fingers and eased a clean sweater over his broken ribs. He stood in front of the mirror in his room, ignoring the expression of pain and defeat on his face. His face was swollen and discolored from the repeated blows he'd received. Dark circles underscored his exhausted appearance. One eye was partially swollen shut, impairing his vision and adding to a vague sense of disorientation. The harsh light in the room illuminated the bruises on his skin, each one a reminder of his failure.

How could he have been so blind—so willing to give in to his temper—as to imagine the man in the alley was alone? *Two* men had taken Maggie. He should have been ready for two men.

As he gazed at his reflection, he felt the swell of self-loathing rise within him. He wanted to punch the mirror and feel it shatter beneath his fists as if that might punish himself in some small way. But instead, he clenched his fists and inhaled deeply in an attempt to steady himself. He wasn't done yet. For Maggie's sake, as bad as he felt, he couldn't afford to be.

He turned away from the mirror and limped to the door. He didn't know what was next, but he knew sitting and waiting for it wasn't any kind of action plan. He leaned one arm against the door jamb and took in another long breath and let it out slowly.

Step one: replace his phone in case Grace needed to get ahold of him. After that, a plan would come to him.

His head was pounding, as was his side, hip, ribs and broken fingers. He went to Maggie's cosmetic bag to find pain relief, trying not to see evidence of his wife's little habits or detect the subtle scent of her perfume. He punched out three paracetamols from a blister pack in her zippered bag and ate them dry. Then he took in another long breath as if to fortify himself and straightened his shoulders. He left the room, locked the door behind him and stood on the threshold outside for a moment. It was starting to snow again. He wondered where Maggie was and what she was doing. He wondered if the thugs who beat him would punish her for his stupidity. He wiped a shaky hand across his face and turned to where he'd parked his car, getting inside slowly and driving to rue Pargaminières.

*Step one. Buy a new phone.*

He told himself to think no further ahead than his next step. He told himself not to think, not to reflect, not to attempt to analyze anything that had just happened. He'd given into the urge to punish the man, to enjoy the results of his frustrations, and so he'd lost a chance to find her. He gritted his teeth to force the thoughts away. They wouldn't help anyone, especially not Maggie. To come up with a new plan he had to think clearly.

Thirty minutes later, he stepped out of the cell phone store and dropped the packaging for his new phone in a trash receptacle and inserted the SIM card from his broken phone into the new one. As soon as he did, the phone lit up and he saw he had a new voice message from a number he didn't recognize.

The electric stab of excitement that punched him in the gut was visceral and immediate.

And it quickly turned to dread.

A cold river of dread ran through Laurent turning his bowels to ice water. It might be Chevalier who'd reconsidered helping Laurent. Or it might be the kidnappers calling to tell Laurent that he was solely responsible for the fact that they'd returned to where Maggie was and executed her.

Laurent leaned against a brick wall and covered his eyes with his hand, his fingers throbbing in pain, as he tried to muster up the courage to do the hardest, most terrifying thing he'd ever had to do—listen to the voicemail.

## 55

The light had already begun to fade over the snow-covered mountains by the time Maggie and the rescue team member Daniel set off along the narrow trail heading east. It had thankfully stopped snowing and while the light was fading from the sky by inches, the cocoa and rum and sandwiches had fortified Maggie. She felt a warm flutter of hope as she walked ahead of Daniel, setting a quick pace that he was forced to match.

The sooner she got back to Toulouse, the sooner she'd find out if Laurent was okay or if he was lying in a coma somewhere in a local hospital. She desperately needed to know why he hadn't answered his phone—even if that answer was the worst thing that ever happened to her. Each stride forward felt like a silent prayer that Laurent was safe.

The air was still cold and biting at her exposed skin, but Maggie no longer felt it. The book bag she carried was lighter, too. She'd taken out all the food and water from it. At the moment, the documents she'd found in the cabin were more valuable than either of those.

Daniel walked alternately behind her and beside her. An

experienced mountaineer who seemed at ease navigating the rugged terrain, his movements were sure and purposeful. Maggie took comfort in his easy company.

"You must be freezing," he said, giving her a sideways glance and a friendly smile. "It's a good thing we found you when we did."

"You're right," Maggie replied, her breath visible in the cold air. "Running into your group when I did was an answer to prayer, that's for sure."

"I imagine," Daniel said. "So you say you were abducted?"

"It's a long story," Maggie said. "And if you don't mind, I really need all my breath for this walk. I'm not used to the altitude."

"Of course. I'm just relieved you were able to escape."

Maggie thought that a strange way to put it but marked it up to the fact that she was not a native French speaker no matter how fluent she thought she was. She shifted her bag on her shoulder and peered at the trail before her. The trail wound through dense clusters of pine trees, their branches heavy with snow, creating a canopy that muted the sounds of the forest. The last rays of sunlight filtered through the trees, casting long, blue shadows across their path.

"So, what happened?" Daniel asked casually, his tone conversational. "How did you manage to escape?"

Maggie felt a flinch of annoyance that Daniel was clearly not about to respect her desire not to talk about it.

"I basically waited for the right moment," she said.

She shivered, not just from the cold but from the memory of her captivity.

"The guys holding me had left before but never at the same time. They had a sort of crisis so they both left at the same time. When they did, I was able to get away."

Daniel nodded, his face thoughtful.

"That's brave," he said. "Not everyone would have had the courage to do what you did."

"It didn't feel brave at the time," Maggie said, her voice trembling slightly. "I just kept thinking about those WWII pilots who escaped through the Pyrenees. You know the ones I mean? Their stories gave me strength."

Daniel's eyes flickered with interest.

"That's remarkable," he said. "Drawing inspiration from such heroes. It's no wonder you succeeded. Can I help you with your bag? It looks heavy."

"It's not," Maggie said sharply and then gave him an apologetic look. "Sorry. But thank you."

"I just want to make sure you're comfortable," he said. "Especially after everything you've been through."

"It wasn't that bad," Maggie said, wishing he'd stop talking about it.

"Really? That surprises me. Were your captors kind?"

Maggie felt a faint throb of warning. A part of her was wondering why Daniel assumed there was more than one captor.

*Did I mention there were two?*

Another part of her thought what it was an odd thing to ask someone who'd just been traumatized.

She nearly responded, *Yeah, they were great. We've promised to stay in touch.* She bit her tongue. It was going to be hard enough to sanely navigate the aftermath of what had happened to her, but it would be a crime if one of the results of her ordeal was that she found she could no longer trust people who clearly only had the best intentions toward her.

She turned to him and forced herself to smile. But before she could speak, he spoke again.

"I guess that was a stupid question," he said. "Sorry."

"It's okay," she said. "I just want to put the whole thing behind me as fast as possible."

"Of course you do," he said with a smile that never reached his eyes.

# 56

Laurent looked at the blinking voice mail message light. He'd moved to a small café off the main square and ordered a coffee and whisky. The terrace where he was seated was empty of any other diners since the weather was cold with a threat of snow in the offing. Every part of him ached or outright hurt but all he could think of was the ominous blinking light that could intensify his suffering forever—and all he had to do was push a button.

*Is that what you think you deserve? A moment less of torment for all your failures?*

He closed his eyes and pushed the button, holding the phone to his ear.

"*Laurent? Are you there?*"

Laurent's eyes flew open. He felt his heart stutter in sheer astonishment at the sound of Maggie's voice.

"*Well, I can't believe you don't have your phone with you but, darling, I escaped! I'm with a local mountain rescue group. I don't know their name right off but I'm using their phone. So, call me back on this number, all right? I don't know why you're not answering. Please, be okay. Now I'm worried about you. Call me back!"*

Laurent choked back his tears of joy and hurriedly called the number back that Maggie had called from. The call went to voicemail but that didn't matter. She had called two hours ago. Laurent slapped down money for his drink and bolted from the café to race down the block to where he'd parked his car.

She said she was with a mountain rescue group so that meant she was still in the mountains. He jumped in the car and pointed it in the direction of the A64 highway that ran toward the main mountain pass. As he drove, his mind thrumming with elation and disbelief, he continually punched in the number that Maggie had called from. A tiny worm of dread had crept into his jubilation when, thirty minutes after accessing the voicemail, he still hadn't been able to connect with the number that Maggie had called from. He forced himself not to think about that.

*Just keep calling the number. She's alive. That's all you need to know.*

He was nearly to the spot where he'd first met the goat herder when the phone number he was calling finally answered.

"*Secours en Montagne des Pyrénées,*" a man answered.

"My name is Laurent Dernier," Laurent said, his excitement vibrating down into his hands that gripped the steering wheel. "My wife borrowed your phone to call me?"

"Ah, yes, Monsieur Dernier," the man said. "What a story she has to tell!"

"Is she there?" Laurent asked. "Can you put her on the phone?"

"Oh, she left about an hour ago," the man said. "Denise? When did the American leave?"

Laurent felt a heaviness shift through his body.

"Denise said she left with the new guy," the man said.

"What...what new guy?" Laurent barked.

"His name is Daniel. He just showed up. I'd never seen him before. But he had the jacket. That happens sometimes. People join when they—"

"Who is he? He went with Maggie?"

"Well, yes. I think he offered to take her back to Toulouse. I told her it would be later this evening before we would be heading back."

"That makes no sense," Laurent said sharply. "I am her husband. She would've waited for me."

*Not if she thought I wasn't coming. Not if she thought I was dead.*

"Well, I don't really know what—"

"Give me your coordinates," Laurent ordered brusquely.

## 57

Maggie pulled her coat tighter around her. She was now beginning to feel the cold seep through her layers. The mountain trail was narrow and rocky and still winding. The air was filled with the scent of pine and Maggie thought she could hear the distant sound of a rushing stream.

As they continued walking with Maggie sometimes in front of Daniel, sometimes behind him, the sky darkened, and she felt the temperature dropping further. After that, the path began to slope downward, and Maggie had to focus on her footing to avoid slipping on the icy patches.

She moved carefully, telling herself that each step brought her closer to what she was sure was the end of this nightmare. Daniel offered his hand to steady her a couple of times, and each time she felt forced to take it, scolding herself for her ingratitude. Because of her ordeal, she was weaker and less capable, and his support was helpful. She spent long moments watching her steps to avoid falling and wondering why despite Daniel's kindness, there was something in his eyes that made her uncomfortable. It was a flicker of something hidden, a shadow behind his otherwise warm gaze. He glanced back at her with a reassuring smile.

"We're almost there, Maggie. The car is just a bit further down the trail. You must be exhausted."

Maggie forced a smile, her gut churning with unease. She found she was too tired to even answer.

"These mountains can be dangerous," he said. "Especially as it gets darker."

Was that a threat? Or was she starting to imagine monsters behind every bush and rock? As they walked on, Daniel pointed out potential hazards along the path.

"Watch your step here, the ground is uneven," he said.

Maggie nodded, carefully navigating the rocky terrain. "Thanks," she replied tightly.

There was no explanation for why she was feeling uneasy with Daniel. She had to assume her gut instinct was reacting to her recent ordeal. She hoped this didn't mean that going forward she was going to have trouble trusting everyone she met. She glanced at her companion and felt the distrusting feeling slither into her gut more pronounced than ever.

Her gut was telling her in all caps that Daniel wasn't who he was pretending to be. Was she supposed to ignore her gut?

"You know, I've always loved these mountains," he said. "They have a way of making you feel small, but in a good way. They remind you of what really matters."

Maggie nodded, but her mind was racing. Why had Daniel broken away from the group to take her? She tried to remember if she'd seen him talking with the others, but she couldn't recall. Had they treated him as a friend? As a trusted associate?

"I imagine your husband will be happy to see you," Daniel commented.

"I can't get ahold of him," Maggie blurted out.

"What do you mean?"

She stopped to catch her breath and turned to him. "Can I use your phone to try calling him again?"

"I'm sorry, Maggie," he said, smiling coldly. "I don't have a phone."

That was probably not the first warning signal that Maggie had registered since they'd started walking. But it was definitely the one she heard the loudest. How believable was it that someone would be a part of a mountain rescue group and not carry a cellphone?

"Is the reception spotty up here?" she asked innocently.

"*Exactement.*"

*He must know that I know he is lying. He saw me use Jean's phone.*

Maggie's mind whirled in a panic as she tried to think of what she should do. Was he armed? Should she run? He looked strong. And she was weakened by two days being held hostage. Her heart pounded. She would never outrun him.

Besides, where would she run?

## 58

The drive from Toulouse to the rendezvous point with the rescue group would normally have taken ninety minutes but Laurent made it in fifty. He parked his car in a gravel lot as close as he could to the coordinates the team leader gave him and then hiked the last mile up the steep terrain until he found them.

By the time he arrived at the meeting point it was late afternoon. The last light of the afternoon had begun to fade, casting long shadows across the rugged landscape. A cold knot of worry tightened in Laurent's chest. The rescue team was assembled by a stand of evergreen trees, two men and a woman, all clad in bright orange jackets and sturdy boots. Their faces were etched with fatigue, the weight of stress and the importance of their work evident in their eyes. The tallest of the group, clearly the leader, waved to Laurent and he walked in his direction, his footsteps crunching on the mixture of snow and gravel underfoot. Laurent held out his hand.

"Bonjour," he said. "I am Laurent Dernier."

The man took off his glove and they shook hands.

"I am Jean," he said. "You made it here in record time. It's a good ninety minutes to Toulouse."

"I knew a short cut," Laurent said wryly. "When did you last see Maggie?"

"An hour ago. Maybe more?"

Jean turned to the other two, and they nodded.

"She looked fine to us," the woman said. "We wouldn't have let her go if we didn't think she could handle a short hike."

"Who did she go with?" Laurent asked, his hands on his hips, his breathing growing heavier by the minute.

"Like I said on the phone," Jean said. "We didn't know him. Sometimes base camp sends out floaters or volunteers who are trying to earn various badges or accreditation."

Laurent looked at the others. "So none of you knew him?"

They shook their heads.

"Do you know which way they went?"

Jean pointed to a narrow, winding trail that snaked down the mountainside.

"They headed that way, towards the pasture parking. It's actually kind of a dangerous path, especially this late in the day."

Laurent glanced up at the darkening sky, his mind racing.

"Why didn't you all go together?" he asked.

Jean shook his head and blushed darkly.

"That was my fault. At the time, I still wanted to make our next check point. And your wife didn't want to wait."

Laurent didn't know who he was angrier at—Jean for thinking hitting his daily goal was more important than getting a kidnap victim to safety or Maggie for leaving on her own. He turned to Jean.

"Call your man," he said. "What's his name?"

Jean looked helplessly at the other two rescue members.

"I...I don't have a number for him," he admitted.

"I'm sure Daniel will take her safely to Toulouse," the woman offered with a frown.

"How can you be sure if you don't know him?" Laurent asked her.

Just then the radio on the other man began crackling and he turned away to talk on it.

"I mean, he's got to be a good guy," Jean said. "Why else would he give up his free time to walk in the freezing cold to find lost hikers? Not everybody has the stomach for it, you know."

"Where did this Daniel park his car?" Laurent asked.

"He didn't park where the rest of us did," the woman said. "He met us on the trail."

A needle of doubt drilled into Laurent.

"Is that typical?" he asked Jean.

"Well, no, but he probably just didn't know where to park."

"So you don't know exactly where he parked?" Laurent pressed.

"Jean!"

The man who had taken the radio call hurried back to the group.

"Sorry to interrupt," he said, "but we have a distress call from a group of hikers stranded on the far side of the mountain."

Jean looked at Laurent, his face pinched into an apologetic frown.

"I am sorry, but we must prioritize this rescue. Maggie is with a member of our team—"

"Right, yes, fine," Laurent said abruptly. "At least point me in the direction they went."

Jean stepped into the clearing and pointed in a southeasterly direction. Then he dug out a small flashlight and a laminated card which Laurent saw was a map.

"Look, the trail is tricky," Jean said. "And the weather can turn fast. You can reach us on your cell if you need us. But be careful."

Laurent took the items and stuffed them in his jacket.

"Thanks," he said, heading toward the path that Jean had pointed out.

"Good luck," Jean said, as he turned away to begin mobilizing for the new rescue mission.

As Laurent set off down the trail, the last rays of the sun dipped below the horizon, casting the mountains into a deep, foreboding twilight. Laurent's thoughts were a whirlwind of fear and determination. As the minutes ticked by, he moved quickly but cautiously. The path grew steeper and more difficult, as he pressed on. He told himself over and over again that there was every reason to believe that Maggie was fine. This Daniel person would likely give her a ride back to town and all would be well. But Laurent wouldn't completely believe that until he had her in his sights. And better than that, his arms.

The fact that this Daniel fellow didn't appear to be a certified mountaineer could be explained in a number of ways—perhaps he was determined to be a part of the group and had for whatever reason been denied entrance and was just passionate about joining, or perhaps Jean and his team were wrong. Did they really know every member of their organization to be so sure that Daniel wasn't really a member? In any case, whatever the reason, the fact of Daniel's mysterious identity bothered Laurent. It was a burr under his saddle, a fly in the ointment. It was something that didn't fit.

And right now, if something didn't fit, Laurent was going to prepare for the worst.

# 59

The weather had finally made up its mind, Maggie thought. The biting wind now cut straight through her parka bringing tears to her eyes, making it harder to see the path before her. Worse, the last remnants of daylight had faded into a pale twilight obscuring the icy, uneven ground in front of her. But as she and Daniel descended further on the rocky path, the forest began to thin out and Maggie thought she could see glimpses of open sky between the trees.

Suddenly Daniel stopped and pointed to an area roughly fifty yards beneath them.

"There it is," he said. "Just a few minutes now and we'll be there."

Maggie peered through the trees and saw a dark shape that looked like a vehicle at the bottom of a sharp drop. She had spent the last several minutes trying to think what she should do. One thing she knew more than anything was that she had to stay calm. And she needed to keep him believing that she trusted him.

"Great," she said, feigning relief. "I'm really looking forward to getting back to civilization."

"You'll be safe soon. We'll get you warm and fed."

As she approached the narrow opening of the trail that seemed to lead through the thick underbrush toward the lot below, Maggie's unease heightened. It occurred to her that the car was parked in an area that seemed too secluded; it was actually *hidden* from the main trail. Suddenly she realized what it was that was bothering her: what she was looking at wasn't a parking area. It was a hiding spot. Her instincts screamed at her to stop moving, to turn back, to run.

"After you," Daniel said, his voice polite but with an undertone of menace.

Maggie hesitated.

"Actually," she said, taking a step back. "I think I dropped something on the trail. I'll just go back and check."

"Are you kidding?" Daniel said. "I'm sure it's nothing important."

Maggie forced a laugh, trying to keep the tension from her voice.

"No, really, I'll just be a second," she said as she turned and started to walk back up the trail, her heart racing.

Daniel's voice followed close behind her.

"Maggie, it's getting dark," he said calmly with a hint of steel. "What is it you have lost?"

Maggie's stomach lurched. Had she told him her name? She racked her brain to try to remember. The others in the group had referred to her as *Madame*. Suddenly she knew she hadn't told him her name. She looked over her shoulder as he approached from behind and immediately cursed herself for doing it. That gesture was the biggest tell of all that she was no longer comfortable with him. Any second now he'd know she was onto him.

"It's just a sentimental thing," Maggie said breathlessly, still moving up the mountain path. "My watch. It was a gift from my husband."

"You weren't wearing a watch."

"It was in my jacket pocket."

"You can live without it."

"I'm not sure that's for you to decide," Maggie said, hearing her voice break, her fear now evident to anyone with ears.

"Maggie, stop!" Daniel called.

She was several steps away when he shouted. She turned to look at him. Her breath caught in her throat as she saw him leaning against a large rock, his face half-hidden in shadow. But it wasn't his relaxed stance that sent a jolt of terror through her.

It was the gun he held, aimed directly at her.

"I am sorry, Maggie," he said sadly. "I'm afraid we've come to the end of the road."

## 60

Laurent stopped walking for a moment, his breath coming in quick, visible puffs in the cold mountain air. The trail had grown increasingly rugged, with jagged rocks and gnarled roots threatening to trip him with every step. He reached into his pocket and pulled out the map Jean had given him, unfolding it carefully in the beam of his flashlight.

The sun had fully dipped below the horizon now. Only the faintest traces of light clung to the peaks, casting long, ghostly shadows that seemed to move with a life of their own. Laurent strained to hear footsteps ahead of him or snatches of conversation, but everything was blanketed in an eerie silence.

He angled the flashlight to illuminate the laminated map, tracing the lines that marked the trail with a forefinger. The path forked ahead, one route leading upward into the mountains, the other winding down into a dense forest. Laurent assumed it was the latter that Maggie and her companion were headed for. He scanned the map for any distinctive landmarks, his eyes narrowing in concentration.

There was a small clearing marked just beyond the fork in the path, a potential spot where Maggie and Daniel might stop if she was tired. It wasn't far, but the terrain promised to be challenging, especially in the dark.

He squinted at the map with his good eye and saw that the trail that wound down to the forest floor ran parallel to a cliff. He couldn't make out how steep it was or if it changed elevations. He put the map away in disgust. He would just have to move carefully, knowing that a single wrong step could cost him precious time—or take him over the edge.

The guy wouldn't lead her up into the mountain, Laurent reasoned. If he was on the level, he'd take her to his car. If he wasn't, then he'd try to finish her off on the trail. The more Laurent thought about why this man might attempt to disguise who he was, the more he had to believe he was part of the team who'd kidnapped Maggie. He adjusted the beam of his flashlight which cast a narrow but bright path before him. The weight of the unknown pressed heavily on his shoulders, but he knew he couldn't afford to make any more mistakes.

With a determined breath, he chose the path that led towards the clearing and sent up a prayer that he was right. Because one thing he knew, Maggie wouldn't survive another mistake from him.

## 61

The world seemed to tilt and slow down around Maggie at the sight of the gun pointed at her. The cold mountain air suddenly felt suffocating, her breath hitching in her chest. She stared at the gun, its dark barrel gleaming faintly in the light from her flashlight beam, and then up at Daniel's face. Her heart pounded wildly, a deafening drumbeat in her ears. Daniel's expression was no longer kind or reassuring; it was cold and calculating.

"What are you doing?" Maggie managed to whisper, her voice quivering with shock and fear.

"Do you seriously expect me to believe you don't know who I am?" he asked.

He seemed to be studying her with a detached, almost clinical interest. Maggie stared at him in disbelief.

"I have no idea who you are," she said.

"Look, this isn't my fault," he said. "I gave your husband ample opportunity to back off. I wrote him notes, *I kidnapped his wife*, I had my men beat him within an inch of his life and still this is where we are."

Maggie looked at him in confusion and mounting horror.

"Are you seriously trying to tell me you don't know who I am?" he asked.

Maggie's mind raced, trying to make sense of the situation. She knew this couldn't be one of her abductors. The body type was all wrong and he was older. She'd never seen this man before in her life. Her eyes darted around, searching for a possible escape route. The trail was narrow here, hemmed in by dense trees and steep slopes. It was dark, too. If she could get into the woods, she might be able to hide. She felt a cold sweat break out on her skin, her hands trembling uncontrollably.

"I don't have any idea who you are," she said, her voice small and filled with dread.

"I don't believe that," he said, his face flushed with indignation. "My picture is all over Aix. But okay, fine." He stood up and made a mock bow. "I am Mathieu Beaumont. At your service."

Maggie felt her mind juddering with shock at his words. *The Aix politician?*

"You're...you're that guy who's trying to get Laurent to tear down his mini-houses," she said.

"So, you do know who I am."

"You had me abducted?" Maggie asked incredulously. "Why?"

"Because your husband wouldn't listen to reason, that's why. Because sometimes a little warning can relieve everyone of a whole lot of pain down the line."

"You thought you could kidnap me and Laurent would forgive that?" she asked in astonishment. "Do you know my husband at all?"

"He would've fallen in line," Beaumont said firmly.

"Once he knew what I was capable of—once he knew that the axe could fall again at any moment—only perhaps the next time it would be his cute little granddaughter—he would stop fighting me."

"You're a dead man," Maggie said with a helpless shrug. "He will track you down and kill you. I'm not sure he won't kill your whole family and your dog, too."

Beaumont laughed nervously. "I think not."

"Well, then you're an idiot."

He flushed with anger.

"Maybe it's your husband who's the idiot. Maybe he doesn't care that you've been abducted. I did leave a note telling him he needed to back off. If he hasn't, then what does that say about what he feels your life is worth?"

"Did you sign it? The note you left for him. Did you sign it?"

"Am I stupid?"

"My husband was investigating a murder," Maggie said. "There is no doubt in my mind he thought your message was from Antoine's killer."

Beaumont frowned. A troubled look of uncertainty passed across his face.

"Are you suggesting that Laurent might not know it's me doing this?" he asked. "He…but I left him a note!"

"So, you did all of this—" Maggie said in disbelief, waving her hands to encompass the mountains and the two of them standing together, "You risked going to prison—all of it to keep migrants out of Provence? You know that's hopeless, right?"

"It is not hopeless!" he said heatedly. "That's just typical liberal claptrap! If more patriots like myself were to take drastic measures—"

"You mean, like kidnapping people?"

"Look, none of this was supposed to happen, but the men I hired were incompetent."

"What are you even doing in Toulouse?" Maggie asked, knowing now that stalling was her only hope. And even then, she wasn't sure to what possible end.

"I'd had a man keeping an eye on Laurent, hoping to find him put a foot wrong. As soon as he reported that Laurent had left St-Buvard, I had them follow him. The plan was to implicate him in a drug buy here in Toulouse—away from the Aix police who are in Laurent's pocket—in order to discredit him. But when my men told me that you had joined him, I decided to raise the stakes. It was all working perfectly until you escaped. That's when I knew I had to come up and handle it myself."

"So you joined the mountain rescue team?"

"*Joined* is probably not completely accurate," he said with a laugh. "I met up with them on the trail and they assumed by the jacket that I was one of them."

"Well, aren't you clever," Maggie said in spite of her determination not to trigger him.

"Actually, I am very clever. The problem now is that you've seen my face."

"Look, nobody's died," Maggie said. "So far you haven't done anything you can't walk back from."

"That's where you're wrong. If I were to let you go, I'd have to walk back from a career in politics," he said. "People can be amazingly unforgiving about charges of kidnapping. So I am going to need you to step off the path." He waved the gun at her. "Over there. I don't want your body found until the spring thaw. And oh, by the way, my understanding is that your husband is alive, in case you were worried."

Maggie snapped her head up, hungry for whatever he might say, while reminding herself that he could be lying.

"He did a social media campaign to get proof of life for you," Beaumont said. "It worked, too. I had my men take your photo before you escaped. They sent that to him to get him off our backs."

Maggie stared at him in disbelief. Laurent set up a social media campaign? *Laurent?* who never texts? Who still writes checks in long hand? She felt a piercing sadness invade her core. Because none of that mattered now. Not how desperate and audacious Laurent had been to find her and get her back, not anything that Maggie could think of to say or do in this moment to save her own life.

The inescapable fact was that Beaumont needed Maggie dead in order to save his career. This wasn't something she was going to be able to talk him out of. Not after he'd had her abducted. He was right. Alive, she was the end of his political career. The dread in her heart deepened, morphing quickly into a primal fear. She looked around the clearing, trying to see if there was anything in her immediate surroundings—a place to run, a weapon—anything she might be able to use. Her thoughts flashed back again to the WWII pilots who had kept her brave and focused during her escape. She tried concentrating on their courage and resourcefulness. If she was going to survive, she needed to channel both right now.

Beaumont's expression hardened, a flicker of impatience appearing in his eyes.

"I mean it," he said. "Time to move."

As Maggie took a hesitant step forward, her mind was working frantically. She had to find a way to turn the tables. With a gun pointed at her from just a few feet away, the odds were against her, but she could not let fear paralyze her. She took another step and with each step, she imagined the impact of the bullet pointed at her drilling into her. But swirling beneath her terror, a steely resolve had begun to form. Every one of those WWII pilots had done the impossible. So could she. She had to.

The path ahead was dark and full of sharp rocks and steep drops. Maybe that was her chance. She could see the trail narrowed as it wound around a bend. She also saw a cluster of loose rocks precariously piled to her right and nothing beyond that. It was a cliff, a one-wrong-step kind of cliff.

An idea began to form in her mind.

As she approached the bend with Beaumont close behind her, Maggie deliberately made her foot slip as if on a patch of ice. She stumbled, nearly falling. Suddenly she felt Beaumont's hand gripping her arm to steady her. She imagined his focus momentarily shifting from marching her at gunpoint to keeping her from tumbling down the slope.

"Watch your step," he muttered. "I need you further on."

Maggie took in a deep breath as surreptitiously as she could, her heart pounding. This was the moment. She wobbled again, accompanied by a little gasp, and reached down as if to catch herself. Instantly, her fingers snatched up a handful of snow and gravel. In one swift motion, she turned and threw the mixture into Beaumont's face. Beaumont cried out and raised his hands to shield his face.

Maggie sprinted towards the cliff at the same time she heard the gun shot. It was only four steps. And she saw herself taking them in slow motion. Every stride was counted out by the slow thud of her heartbeat as she reached the cliff's edge.

Expecting any second to feel a bullet slam into her back, she launched herself into oblivion.

## 62

The sharp crack of the gun report echoed across the countryside, shattering the peaceful stillness of the mountain. Laurent froze. His heart began to race as he furtively scanned the horizon.

His skin vibrated with fear.

He held his breath and tried to track the direction the shot sounded like it had come from. His fear surged up into his throat nearly choking him as the calculated, objective part of his brain held the explanation that his heart refused to hear.

*He's executed her.*

His legs trembled at the thought as he struggled to stay composed, his mind urging him to remember the direction where the shots had come from. Even if the worst had happened and the man had killed Maggie, Laurent still needed to find him.

And kill him.

Seconds later, he heard a second shot and then a third.

He started to run.

## 63

Maggie hit the slope below, rolling and sliding down the icy incline, turning her world into a blur of snow and rock and pain. The rough surface scraped her skin as she slid, but she made herself go limp to let the momentum of her fall carry her relentlessly downwards.

"Fine with me!" Beaumont screamed from above her. "You'll be just as dead!"

She came to a stop at the base of a dead oak tree, its trunk hollowed and lifeless but a solid anchor. She stayed perfectly still, her body vibrating in pain and adrenalin. She let her breath come more slowly and prayed that she was at least partially hidden by the bushes and shrubbery around her. She lifted her head to look up and saw the dark shadow of Beaumont's silhouette as he peered down, searching for her.

"Damn it!" he shouted, frustration evident in his voice as he fired another shot and then another.

Dirt and chips of tree bark speckled the ground around Maggie as the slugs hit random errant targets. She didn't think he could see her, but she didn't want to move and give him any opportunity.

Above her, she heard Beaumont cursing and wondered for one terrified moment if he would try to come after her. She looked back up at the darkened slope. If motivated, she might be able to climb back up using saplings and rock divots, but there was only one way down and that was the way Maggie had just come.

The hard way.

"Are you dead, Madame? Did you just save me the trouble?" Beaumont taunted.

Hoping that by keeping silent Beaumont might think she was dead and leave, Maggie closed her eyes and felt herself begin to shiver. She figured it was shock. She couldn't move in order to take stock about how badly she'd hurt herself. But she already felt the cold needling into her bones.

Long minutes ticked by, and Maggie heard no more sounds from the top of the cliff. Had he given up? Was he on his way to his car? Ignoring the pain rippling through her body, and with her heart pounding she felt the beginnings of an irresistible urge to get up and go deeper into the forest to try to put as much distance as possible between herself and Beaumont. She gingerly moved off her hip which was throbbing painfully. It would be better to wait until full dark and let the trees provide cover. On the other hand, if she waited until then, she would undoubtedly kill herself trying to walk blind in the woods.

She could only fall off so many rocky cliffs and live. She was probably already pushing her luck. Plus, if she stayed here huddled on the cold hard ground to be sure that Beaumont had truly left the area, she would freeze to death before morning.

As she agonized about what to do, Maggie found herself trying to find to a safe place inside her head that was warm and pain free. She tried thinking of her children and the Allied pilots. She tried imagining Laurent's face again. Especially when he laughed or rolled his eyes over something she said. But it was useless. Everything was useless. Her brain kept serving up an alternate universe—regardless of what Beaumont had taunted her with—a universe where Laurent was dead.

How else to explain why he didn't answer his phone when she'd been missing for three days? Maggie flinched at the thought and shook her head as if to make the thoughts go away. When she did, she felt the world around her begin to spin, slowly at first and then more quickly out of control. She realized then that she was hurt worse than she thought.

She closed her eyes against the spinning vortex and prayed that the end would be quick.

## 64

Laurent skidded to a stop several yards away from the figure on the ledge. He saw the gun first and then the man's face. At first, he couldn't believe who he was seeing but he pushed past his disbelief. He didn't have time for that. The man appeared focused on looking over the cliff allowing Laurent to creep up silently, using the jagged rocks between them as cover.

Beaumont was standing on what looked like the precipice of a cliff. Laurent was bizarrely aware of the sharp scent of pine in the cool air between them when suddenly Beaumont swung around, his gun pointing at the source of whatever noise he'd heard.

"No way!" Beaumont said with a bitter laugh as he pointed the gun at Laurent. "My guys didn't kill you? No bonuses for them this year!"

Laurent quickly stepped into the shadows of the trees that lined the pathway.

"Let's talk, Beaumont," he called.

"Too late for that, my friend," Beaumont said. "I already killed your wife. Shot her through her pretty head."

Laurent felt his stomach clench at the man's words, but he forced himself not to believe them even though he'd heard the gunshots with his own ears. Beaumont would use every weapon in his arsenal to lure Laurent out into the open, and lying about Maggie's safety was always going to be his most powerful. Laurent inched forward.

"Why don't you come out from behind those trees?" Beaumont said. "And let's end this."

Laurent had a clear view of Beaumont on the ledge, which made him think that Maggie must be on the other side of it. From where Laurent stood, he could see the stark contrast between the sharp, jagged edges of the rocks where Beaumont stood and the clear lack of trees on the other side. It must be a long drop, Laurent thought with a sickening realization. Each movement Beaumont made sent small stones skittering over the edge.

It was all Laurent could do not to rush him. In his mind, he saw himself reaching him before Beaumont could fire the gun. But that wasn't likely.

"Throw down the gun, Beaumont," Laurent said. "You can't shoot us all. Or do you intend to murder the members of the rescue group, too? Because of course they saw you. And they'll lead the police right to you."

Beaumont cursed.

"Look, I'll make you a deal, Dernier," Beaumont said. "Come out where I can see you and I'll let your wife live."

Laurent closed his eyes. He knew the man was lying. But he hated the twist of the knife that Beaumont's words carved into his heart. As they were intended to.

"I thought you said she was already dead," Laurent said.

"No, she's alive, but she won't last another night out in the mountains," Beaumont said. "And she's hurt. Show yourself to me and I'll let her live."

In spite of himself, Laurent felt his hopes surging that Maggie might be alive. He steeled himself against Beaumont's words. He couldn't lose focus now. He needed to block out what the bastard was saying to figure a way to—"

"Help!" a small voice called out. "I'm here!"

Laurent burst out from behind the cover of trees in the same instant that Beaumont whirled around at the sound of Maggie's voice. Belatedly, Beaumont snapped his attention back to Laurent, but by then Laurent was on him. Laurent wrapped one hand around the hard metal of Beaumont's gun, his adrenaline surging through his veins, and wrenched it out of the man's grasp. Then he smashed it across Beaumont's face, opening up a wide gash in his nose and dropping the man to his knees.

Laurent twisted in the direction of the cliff where the voice was coming from.

"Maggie!" he shouted.

"Laurent?" she yelled back.

"You bastard!" Beaumont spat blood out as Laurent stood over him, one boot planted squarely on the man's chest. "I'm bleeding!"

Laurent knelt and slapped his hands against Beaumont's jacket until he found the plastic ties that he assumed he would be carrying. Fury built inside him as he thought of why Beaumont had the ties with him. It was all he could do not to stuff them down the man's throat. He flipped Beaumont over onto his stomach and wrenched his arms back behind him, securing them tightly. Beaumont struggled to get to his knees.

"Be reasonable!" Beaumont sputtered, his face ground into the dirt. "I did everything I could to get you to back off! Help! Help! Somebody!"

Laurent finished tying Beaumont by securing his ankles

together and then securing them to his hands. The whole time, Beaumont squawked and swore. Laurent stood up. Just one nudge with his boot and the man would go over the cliff. Bound as he was, he wouldn't survive.

"What's happening up there?" Maggie called, snapping Laurent out of his brief reverie.

He turned to stand at the side of the ledge and look down.

There, he saw the most beautiful sight he would ever see in his life. His gorgeous American wife on her hands and knees, her hair full of sticks and twigs and dirt streaks on her face, was looking up at him and smiling as if she'd never doubted for a minute that he would come.

# 65

Climbing down to get her was never going to be an option.

There was only one way to go and that was up. Grabbing one sapling after another, Maggie hauled herself painstakingly to her feet and found that while she ached everywhere nothing felt broken. Slowly, painfully, she crawled back up the steep cliff, hand over hand, her feet each finding the stone divots, until she was within an arm's reach of Laurent. He pulled her up the rest of the way.

Despite the pain of the scratches and bruises throbbing up and down her hips and legs, Maggie had never felt anything more exquisite than her husband's arms around her. Laurent held her in his arms, her feet not touching the ground, for a long moment, his face buried in her neck as if the very scent of her was the only thing keeping him going.

"I knew you'd come," Maggie murmured into his chest.

He kissed her then and put her on her feet, but her knees gave way, and he picked her up in his arms and carried her to a tree not far from where Beaumont lay trussed and thrashing on his stomach. Automatically, Laurent ran his hands over Maggie's hip and legs, feeling for injuries.

"I'm fine, Laurent," Maggie said looking over to where Beaumont lay. "What's in his mouth?"

"His glove," Laurent said. "He talks too much."

Maggie turned back to Laurent and instantly recoiled. Even in the gloom she could see one side of his face was swollen and discolored.

"What happened to you?" she gasped.

"*Rien*," Laurent said. "Just a little run-in. Are you sure you're alright?"

He gingerly pulled her hair back from her brow to examine a cut that was bleeding.

"Just scratches and bruises," she said, as Laurent folded up a handkerchief to press against her cut. "Did you hear that he was the one responsible for my kidnapping?"

"Yes, he and I were just discussing that," Laurent said, moving her hand to hold the cloth in place on her forehead.

Maggie was astonished that things had happened so quickly. When she heard Beaumont talking to someone, she had no idea it was Laurent. She only knew that her single chance at survival was to alert *whoever* he was talking with to go to the police. Assuming he wasn't talking to one of his thugs.

Laurent patted her leg.

"*Chérie*, I am calling the police now, yes? Are you okay for a minute?"

"Yes, yes," Maggie said as she watched him pull a cellphone that she didn't recognize from his jacket.

He stepped away and made his call to Rousseau and then another one to Jean with the rescue group telling him that he'd found Maggie and giving him their approximate location.

"I can't believe you found me," Maggie said when he came back to her. Tears glistened in her eyes. "How did you ever manage it?"

"It is a long story, *chérie*," Laurent said. He nodded in the direction of Beaumont who was still squirming and twisting his head around. "But why did you go with him?"

"I didn't know who he was," Maggie said with a shrug.

"You never saw him in St-Buvard?" Laurent asked. "Or on any of the flyers in Aix?"

"I never laid eyes on him before today. I just thought he was a nice man giving me a ride into town. But hey! Where were you? I called you hours ago!"

"I know, *chérie*. I lost my phone."

"You are always doing that! I'm going to have to get you a tether!"

Laurent began to laugh then. He laughed so hard that he had to sit down in the snow, and still he laughed. Maggie, however, didn't find the situation at all amusing.

"What's so funny?" she said with a frown. "It was frankly a very bad time for you to misplace your phone!"

"I know, *chérie*. You are right. I will endeavor to do better."

He reached over and pulled her into his lap and kissed her again, his hands large and tenderly cradling her face.

"I can't believe I found you," he said marveling as he stared into her face.

"Well, I never doubted it," Maggie said, kissing him. "How's Amelie? Have you talked to her? She must be flipping out."

"She's fine. Everyone is fine."

Maggie rubbed her arms through her jacket. She ached everywhere and she was cold, too. It would take the police at least an hour to reach them from Toulouse, probably more if they did the speed limit. She closed her eyes and tried to imagine a hot drink. Better, a hot bath.

"What did Rousseau say when you told her you found me?" Maggie asked.

"She was so relieved that she no longer had a kidnapping on her hands," Laurent said, "and that the suspect for the crime was an out of towner—that she cheered."

"If it weren't for you, I'd be dead," Maggie said.

While it was true that she'd escaped Beaumont on her own, Maggie knew that spending another night in the mountains—only this time with no shelter—would've been a death sentence. Laurent shook his head and Maggie thought he was arguing with her.

"I'm serious, Laurent," she said. "Rousseau was never going to find me in time."

"That is my fault, *chérie*," Laurent said. "Every lead I gave her about your abduction was wrong. I assumed your kidnapping had to do with Antoine's death."

"That was a fair assumption," Maggie said, glancing in the direction where Beaumont lay. "Bastard."

"It's possible Beaumont has more men than just the two who abducted you," Laurent said. "Rousseau will find out during her interrogation."

"Why do you think so?" Maggie asked.

She'd only ever seen the same two men during her captivity.

"Because I got a second message delivered to me at the bed and breakfast." He frowned then.

"What are you thinking?" Maggie asked.

"Nothing. It's just that the two notes were so different. Even at the time I wondered…" He shook his head. "Never mind. Now that I know what was really going on, I'm amazed I ever saw the kidnapping and Antoine's murder as connected. Who would imagine that *I* was a threat in my investigations of his murder?"

"Stop it," Maggie said firmly. "That was a natural assumption. I would've made it, too. And besides, it all came right in the end."

"In spite of me," Laurent said.

She watched him as his face became grim and she wondered who it was who had beaten him so badly.

"Just remember," she said. "My kidnapping might be solved, but there's still Antoine's murder to work out. And to that end, I think I may have found something."

She quickly told him about the documents and photographs she'd found. She had the evidence on her but was reluctant to pull them out when they only had a small flashlight that was running low on batteries. There would be plenty of time later to present her evidence. As it was, she could see how shocked Laurent was as she divulged the incontrovertible proof she'd found against Antoine.

"I'm sorry, Laurent, but it looks as if Antoine had not given up his criminal ways after all. These documents prove he was involved in bringing people from third world countries to work in his kitchens for no money."

Laurent studied the ground, a muscle flinching in his jaw.

"If it's any consolation," she said, "it's possible he was having a change of heart. Remember how Marco said Antoine told him to look over his shoulder?"

"Isn't that what every crook naturally does?" Laurent said in disgust.

"He told his *son* to look over his shoulder," Maggie said. "There's a difference."

"You think the syndicate warned Antoine to get back in line or they would harm Marco?"

"It would fit with Antoine's behavior. Can you see the syndicate putting a hit out on Antoine?"

Laurent frowned.

"Not really. It would do them no good to eliminate him. It's not much of a message if you're dead."

"Agreed. So they were probably threatening him that they would hurt Marco, don't you think?"

Laurent ran a hand through his hair.

"I talked to the head of the crime family, and he denies killing Antoine," Laurent said.

"Do crime lords normally tell the truth?"

"Good point," Laurent said. "But neither do they typically bother denying the terrible things they do. Besides, there are other things that make me believe Chevalier is telling the truth."

"For example?"

"Would a hit man bludgeon his victim to death and leave him in the freezer?" Laurent asked. "Antoine was killed with a meat mallet. Wouldn't a professional killer shoot him? Wouldn't a professional have come prepared and brought his own weapon? And finally, if the hired killer did hit Antoine with whatever was at hand, would he have just left the body? Pros like to dispose of the evidence of their work."

Maggie knew that Laurent had a point. Antoine's death still had too many loose ends. There were so many pieces that just didn't fit. From being assaulted from behind with a handy mallet to being left in his own freezer, Antoine's murder didn't feel professional. It felt personal. That realization was a nauseating and debilitating one.

Because it meant that after everything she and Laurent had gone through, they were still just as far from knowing the truth about who killed Antoine as when they'd begun.

## 66

The mountain clearing was bathed in the flickering glow of the campfire that Jean and his group had created. The rescue team had showed up just before the police. It seemed the stranded hikers had found their own way safely down the mountain. The team had quickly set up a small makeshift camp, their bright orange jackets standing out starkly against the dark forest. The scent of pine mingled with the aroma of coffee and hot chocolate, creating a comforting atmosphere amid the tension.

Initially, Laurent had wanted to toss a blanket over Beaumont and immediately get Maggie off the mountain, but she encouraged him to wait for the police. He was in the process of building a fire when Jean and his group showed up and took over. They provided Maggie and Laurent with blankets, coffee, cocoa, whiskey and water. Jean and his group were all properly horrified that Beaumont had impersonated one of them for his own dastardly intentions and nobody felt inclined to untie him to make him more comfortable before the police arrived. Maggie was glad that Laurent had gagged

Beaumont. If his glaring eyes were any indication, he had a lot to say and none of it pleasant.

Laurent stood near the fire, his eyes on Beaumont, who was now securely tied to a sturdy tree trunk. Beaumont's face was a mask of defiance, but Maggie could see the occasional flicker of fear in his eyes. The rescue team members, though busy with their tasks, kept a wary eye on him, too.

It wasn't long before Maggie heard voices and radio cracklings that announced the arrival of the police. Like Laurent, they'd been forced to park their vehicles a mile beneath the clearing and hike the rest of the way up. Five uniformed officers emerged from the trail, their expressions grim but excited. Maggie felt a wave of relief wash over her when she saw them. In the lead was none other than Detective Rousseau, dressed in a dark parka with the Toulouse police insignia emblazoned on front.

Without stopping to talk to anyone, two officers moved immediately to Beaumont, who was visibly struggling against his bonds. They untied him and replaced the plastic ties with a pair of handcuffs. Beaumont glared at Laurent, but said nothing, his defiance now seemingly laced with resignation.

Rousseau spoke briefly to Jean who nodded and who along with his people began to break up camp. Then the detective walked over to where Maggie and Laurent sat on a nearby stump, Maggie with a cup of quickly cooling coffee in her hands.

"I am glad to see you well and in one piece," Rousseau said to her. She turned and barked out an order to one of her men to secure the scene before turning to Laurent.

"Who is he?" she asked, nodding at Beaumont who now, glaring at Laurent, sat with a Mylar blanket over his shoulders.

"His name is Mathieu Beaumont," Laurent said. "He's a minor politician in Aix, running for membership in the *conseil général*."

Rousseau frowned as Beaumont was led away down the path the police had come by. Maggie could see the butterfly bandage that Jean had put on the man's nose. She knew that Rousseau had seen the injury too.

"He's far from his home patch," Rousseau noted.

"I'm happy to answer all your questions," Laurent said. "But I would like to get my wife off the mountain first."

"Of course," Rousseau said. "When we speak, I'd like to ask what you know about Philippe Martin's murder."

Maggie's mouth fell open and she turned to look at Laurent who appeared completely nonplussed.

"I know nothing," he said blandly.

Maggie watched Rousseau examine Laurent's face in the flickering flames of the dying fire. She wondered if she could see what Maggie could—that Laurent was lying. Probably not.

"Well, what we know so far is that it is a homicide," Rousseau said. "We're processing the crime scene now."

"Any suspects?" Maggie asked.

"Early days," Rousseau said, rocking back on her heels with her thumbs shoved confidently into her belt buckle. "Forensics will tell us everything we need to know."

After eliciting promises from both Maggie and Laurent to come to the station to give full statements of what had happened with Beaumont, Rousseau walked over to talk to the officer who was stretching yellow police caution tape around the clearing. Laurent pulled Maggie to her feet.

"Did you know about Martin?" Maggie asked in a low voice as they edged around the perimeter of where Rousseau's men were working.

"I'll tell you when we're alone," he said.

Once comfortably ensconced in Laurent's car with the heater on full blast, Laurent tried to insist that Maggie get checked out at the hospital, but she insisted she was fine and just wanted to get home as soon as possible. After a brief conversation with both Grace and Amelie, Maggie settled back in her seat and reveled in the fact that she was finally safe and warm with Laurent beside her.

"So how did you know about Martin?" she asked.

He sighed. "I went to question him."

"Oh, Laurent, no. You found the body? And then just left?"

"I called it in from a pay phone," he said.

"CCTV?" she asked, a throb of worry in her voice.

"I didn't see any."

"What about cameras in Martin's apartment?"

"*Chérie*, you are not to worry. I was not seen. Okay? Are you hungry?"

Maggie nearly laughed at her husband's natural proclivity for believing that food could solve any problem.

"I need a shower first," she said. "Meanwhile, what have you discovered about Antoine's murder?"

"You do know my hands were tied in that regard, don't you?" Laurent asked, glancing at her.

"Are you seriously using that metaphor with *me*?" Maggie said indignantly. "When you know my hands were *literally* tied for most of the last three days?"

Laurent pulled off the road and disconnected her seat belt and pulled her into his arms. He held her tightly, but Maggie felt the tremors nonetheless. She closed her eyes and let herself sink into his embrace. This was the moment she'd been waiting for, the moment when she was finally and undeniably safe. She felt her emotions well up inside her and finally let go as she began to cry.

As she wept, the only sounds in the car were the occasional passing car and her own sobs muffled by her husband's chest. She knew Laurent wasn't crying. But as tightly as he held her, she also knew he was struggling mightily not to.

## 67

Two hours later, Maggie was showered, dressed in fresh clothes, and sitting in a restaurant on the square. The temperature had continued to drop and the wind had picked up. From her seat by the window, Maggie could see frost forming intricate patterns on the panes. But she was warm and safe. A crackling fireplace was nearby and the scent of dinner on its way made her mouth water.

She and Laurent had both opted for heaping bowls of cassoulet, the region's famous sausage and bean stew, with accompanying bread and salads. Maggie looked over at Laurent who was perusing the wine list. His face looked much worse in the light. One eye was still swollen nearly completely shut and the bruises on his jaw were dark and vivid. Laurent had rewrapped his fingers with clean tape and promised to go to the infirmary before they left town. She had yet to hear how he had gotten his injuries.

As she watched him concentrating on what he considered very important at the moment—selecting just the right wine for their dinner tonight—she found herself marveling that their lives had so quickly fallen back into normalcy after everything that had happened.

"Why don't we do a process of elimination?" Maggie said after Laurent gave his choice of wine to the waiter. "What about Lucas Moreau? Do you think he would kill to become a sous chef at the most famous restaurant in Toulouse?"

"I don't," Laurent said. "Besides which, Rousseau told me that Moreau was out of town that night and he has several people to confirm that."

"That's annoying."

"But there may be reason to consider Remy Durand," Laurent said.

"Oh? What have you found out?"

"His daughter was beaten and raped by Antoine a few years back."

"Good heavens," Maggie said. She felt a tremble of disgust and fury at the thought that this man and Laurent had once been close.

"So that's a motive for Durand," Laurent said. "I don't totally discount Lucas, even with his alibi. I'm told Antoine slept with his girlfriend."

"Okay," Maggie said with a frown. "That's a bit of a stretch for a motive. Although he did end up with his dream job." She shook her head as if making up her mind. "No, because of the assault on his daughter, I think Durand is the stronger candidate."

Just then Laurent's phone rang. He picked it up and looked at the ID on the screen.

"It's Rousseau," he said before answering. "*Allo*?"

"Monsieur Dernier?" Rousseau said. "Is this a good time to talk?"

Maggie scooted closer to Laurent so she could hear the detective's side of the conversation.

"How can I help you, Detective?" Laurent said.

"I wanted to let you know of a few interesting things we discovered at the apartment of Philippe Martin." She paused.

Maggie was familiar with the technique. Many interrogators led off with a statement intended to throw their suspect or interviewee onto the back foot. She nearly smiled. It would take *some* statement to have that effect on Laurent.

"Were you aware that Monsieur Martin was our prime suspect for Monsieur Dubois's murder?" Rousseau asked.

Maggie had to force herself not to snort in derision. It sounded as if Rousseau was trying to prove that her lack of results so far in Antoine's murder investigation was due neither to incompetence nor the fact that she was working for the crime syndicate.

"I would be very interested to hear how you came to that decision," Laurent said.

"Our conclusion, as you put it, was confirmed tonight when we discovered a journal at Monsieur Martin's apartment that revealed he was stalking Monsieur Dubois. We have his written word that he frequently fantasized about killing him."

Maggie frowned and looked at Laurent whose face gave away nothing. Did Philippe Martin kill Antoine?

"As I'm sure you are aware," Rousseau continued, "sometimes the thought for the deed is nearly as effective as the deed."

*Sure*, Maggie thought. *Especially since the deed would get you sent to prison.*

"Anyway," Rousseau said. "I wanted you to know that we are coming to the final stages of our investigation on Antoine Dubois's death and while it's possible we won't have a live candidate to pay for this crime, it will be satisfying at least to know the truth, *non?*"

"Of course," Laurent said.

They disconnected soon after that and Laurent gave Maggie a baleful look.

"Do you think it's true?" she said. "Did Martin...?"

Laurent shook his head.

"*Non.* Philippe Martin did not kill Antoine," he said. "I considered it at one point, but he had no motive. I don't care what he wrote in his journal."

"Okay," Maggie said. "Well, what about the food supplier, Bouchard? From what you said about him, he definitely smells fishy to me. No pun intended."

Laurent had to admit that Bouchard had worked very hard to point him in the direction of the syndicate as Antoine's killer—something Laurent figured the killer *would* do if he was trying to deflect attention from himself.

"There is only a stolen recipe as his motive," he said.

"But isn't that a pretty big deal in culinary circles?" Maggie asked.

Laurent shrugged. Just then the waiter came with their wine and poured. After tasting it, Laurent nodded and the waiter left the bottle.

"And if Antoine was hit with a meat tenderizing hammer doesn't that look like the murder was spontaneous not premeditated?"

"Yes," Laurent said. "Unless the killer hid in the restaurant until after closing in order to confront Antoine."

Hiding in the restaurant *in order to confront Antoine* was pretty much the dictionary definition of the word *premeditated*, Maggie thought.

"But you don't think it was a hit?" she asked.

"*Non.* A professional killer would have brought his own

weapon. Antoine's murder was the work of an amateur. An emotional amateur."

"So it wasn't the syndicate. Then how do you think it happened?"

"I think an argument got started outside the freezer and ended inside the freezer," Laurent said.

Maggie knew when it came to people, Laurent's instincts were usually solid. Just then the waiter brought their cassoulets. Maggie waited until he was gone before speaking again.

"Couldn't that have been Bouchard?"

"*Non*," Laurent said firmly. "The recipe wasn't that important to him. And Jean-Luc said that Antoine paid him for it. It is a red fish."

"A red herring," she said automatically, as she broke through the toasted crust of her cassoulet to release its savory fragrance.

"Okay, then who else is there?"

It occurred to Maggie that if the syndicate didn't kill Antoine, then Detective Rousseau might really believe that Martin killed him. She might be wrong but at least it meant she wasn't in the pocket of the crime syndicate. She was just incompetent.

"Who do you think killed Philippe Martin?" Maggie asked.

"The same person who killed Antoine," Laurent said.

"Really? What makes you say that?"

"It is more believable that it is a single killer than that there are two different murderers running around Toulouse," Laurent said. "It is simply not believable."

"Maybe not," Maggie said. "But neither is it inconceivable."

"Additionally," Laurent said, "Martin sustained a stab wound to the neck."

"Unlike Antoine, you mean," Maggie said.

"*Oui*. But, like Antoine, the attack appeared spontaneous."

"Meaning that both murder weapons were found at the scene," Maggie said. "The meat pounding hammer in the walk-in freezer and the chef's knife in Martin's kitchen."

"*Exactement*," Laurent said.

"Okay," Maggie said as she ripped off a piece of baguette to dip into the savory sauce of her cassoulet. "So we're right back to Remy Durand."

Maggie was reminded again that Antoine had physically assaulted Durand's daughter.

"Your friend was a real prince," she said. "Sorry, Laurent."

"Do not apologize, *chérie*. I do not condone his behavior."

She nodded at his phone on the table.

"Since you've shown yourself to be such a whiz with communications technology, why don't you text Detective Rousseau with our suspicions? I think she's ready to respect your opinion about now."

Laurent pushed his phone across the table to Maggie.

"You do it, *chérie*," he said with a grin. "I think my technological proficiency has hit its limit."

Maggie quickly composed a text to Rousseau on Laurent's phone and sent it. Then she turned to pick up her glass of wine for a toast.

"We did it, my darling," she said. "You found me safe and sound. Beaumont is in custody and we have just solved Antoine's murder. I think we have earned an evening of rest and celebration."

Just then, Laurent's phone dinged to indicate an incoming text.

"Hold that thought," Laurent said as he pulled his reading glasses out of his jacket pocket.

"Is it Rousseau?" Maggie asked as Laurent picked up his phone and put his glasses on. He frowned at the screen. "What did she say?"

Laurent sighed. "Durand has an alibi."

"One that can be broken?" Maggie asked hopefully.

Laurent picked up the phone and read from it.

"He was seen on CCTV shopping the produce market on rue Peyras before, during and after the time of Antoine's murder."

"It's almost like he knew he was going to need an airtight alibi."

Laurent smiled at her.

"Give up, *chérie*. It can't be Durand. We must go back to the drawing board."

"I can't believe this," Maggie said dispiritedly. "If only Antoine had some kind of romantic liaison gone wrong. I mean, beyond all the sleazy assertions on Facebook about his bad behavior."

Laurent turned to look at her and his eyes widened as if with a sudden realization.

"What?" she asked. "Did Antoine have a girlfriend?"

"Better than that," Laurent said picking up his own wine glass and draining it, his face suddenly radiant with inspiration. "He had an unhappy ex-girlfriend."

## 68

As Maggie and Laurent drove through the quiet streets, the atmosphere in the car was tense as each of them was lost in thought about the upcoming confrontation with Claudine. It was after ten o'clock and Maggie could see the snow had begun to fall again. She thought briefly about how she'd nearly had to spend this very night stranded on the side of a mountain and she shivered.

Laurent turned to her.

"You are okay, *chérie*?" he asked.

"I'm fine," she said. "Just glad to be warm and with you."

He placed a hand on her leg.

"I am not taking that miracle for granted," he said.

"It wasn't really a miracle," she said, "since it was you coming out of the trees guns blazing to my rescue."

"I was unarmed."

"My point still stands."

When they turned onto the boulevard that led to Claudine's apartment, both of them noticed a commotion ahead. The street where Philippe Martin lived was set off this main street which was cordoned off with bright yellow police tape fluttering in the cold breeze. Their lights flashing, multiple police vehicles lined the street. Uniformed officers moved with purpose on the street, their expressions grim and focused.

Laurent slowed the car as they approached the scene. Several forensic vans were parked haphazardly, their back doors open. Officers were setting up barriers, redirecting curious onlookers and residents away from the scene.

"What is this?" Maggie whispered.

"It's Philippe Martin's street," Laurent said.

"So this is his crime scene? Kind of a lot of police presence for that, isn't it?"

Laurent leaned forward, peering through the windshield.

"That's interesting," he said.

"What?"

"Those vehicles. They aren't local law enforcement."

"What are you saying?" Maggie asked, a chill running down her spine.

"I think our favorite Toulouse detective lied to us," Laurent said. "Those are French National Police. I don't believe Rousseau found a journal at all."

"Why would national police be investigating a local murder?" Maggie asked.

Laurent turned to give her a wry look.

"They would if Martin was someone other than who we thought he was. I am impressed. I never suspected."

"Suspected what? You're speaking in riddles."

"If Martin was an undercover operative, his murder would elicit this kind of response."

"What, wait," Maggie said. "Are you saying you think Martin might have been an undercover agent?"

"Think about it. Going undercover is all about facades and disguises," Laurent said. "Something our friend was said to have done often."

"But I thought that phone call at dinner was Rousseau trying to hang Antoine's murder on Martin," Maggie said in confusion.

"Clearly it was her just trying to throw us off the scent," Laurent said as he drove by the group of police vehicles.

Maggie looked at the activity in front of the apartment building. The vehicles were black SUVs with darkened windows. Although she didn't see any overt weaponry, she got the general impression of an American SWAT team. Or perhaps the French version of the FBI?

"So all that about Martin being humiliated by Antoine and hating him…?" she said, shaking her head in confusion. "All that was just a cover?"

"There is no other answer for why a van full of national counterterrorism agents would be involved in investigating Martin's murder," Laurent said.

"Why was he undercover? Who was he investigating, do you think?" Maggie asked.

"The syndicate, I imagine," Laurent said. "Now that I think about it, it is possible that Antoine was working with Martin."

Maggie felt her head whirling in her effort to grasp and process this new theory.

"Can you get Rousseau to confirm any of this?" she asked.

Laurent snorted in answer which Maggie took to be a negative.

"When I found Martin's body, I saw something in the apartment," Laurent said. "But I didn't have a chance to look at it closely."

Maggie looked at him in surprise. "What was it?"

"At the time, I thought it was broken glass of some kind, perhaps caused in the struggle that ended with Martin's murder, but now that I think back, what I saw could have been broken crystals."

"Is the distinction important?"

"It is, yes, *chérie*. Because Antoine's girlfriend is into New Age practices. She has dozens of crystals at her apartment."

They drove on, leaving the chaotic scene behind, but for Maggie the weight of its implications went with them. The street grew quieter as they approached Claudine's apartment, but the image of the cordoned-off street and the palpable tension of Martin's murder scene lingered in her mind, adding another layer of urgency and unease to their mission tonight.

"So you think Claudine killed Martin, too?" Maggie asked. "But why?"

"We will have to ask her, *non*?"

"I mean, the crystal—if that's what you saw—is definitely helpful for placing Claudine at the scene of Martin's murder," Maggie said, thinking hard. "But it doesn't give us a motive and it doesn't get us any closer to knowing why she killed Antoine. Are we just grasping at straws?"

"*Au contraire, chérie*," Laurent said. "Claudine and Martin knew each other. He was a steady customer at *L'Étoile Gourmande*—"

"In disguise, you said."

"Sometimes, yes. But Claudine told me she always knew it was him regardless of his attempt at concealment."

Laurent parked on the street and turned off the car.

"Okay, but Philippe Martin aside," Maggie said, "now we're right back to the question of who killed Antoine? Because while I get that Antoine was a royal jerk, I have to say that getting dumped is a pretty weak motive for murder—I mean, all romance and mystery novels aside."

"There might be another piece to Claudine's motive," Laurent said ominously.

Something had been niggling in the back of Laurent's brain as soon as he had started thinking that Claudine might have a bigger reason for killing Antoine.

It had to do with the little figurine he'd spotted in her apartment that first day he visited her. The one he couldn't get out of his mind. Maggie looked at him expectantly.

"Well?" she prompted.

"What if she was pregnant?" he asked.

# 69

Maggie was astonished by Laurent's suggestion. "You think Claudine might be pregnant?" she asked.

"It fits with what I saw in her apartment the day I interviewed her," Laurent said.

As he spoke, he found himself remembering the lullaby music playing in the background in her apartment. But more than anything, it had been the ceramic figurine of the mother and baby that had lingered in his subconscious like a whisper of something from his own childhood. At the time, he thought that perhaps he'd seen a similar figurine on the shelf of his Aunt Delphine, the woman who'd raised him. It was for that reason that he'd dismissed it as unimportant.

"If she's pregnant, do you think Antoine knew?" Maggie asked.

Laurent grimaced but he didn't answer.

"Is that why he broke up with her?" she asked.

She turned to stare out the windshield quickly filling

with snowflakes as the ramifications of this new thought gelled in her mind.

"Well, one thing is for sure," she said softly. "That definitely makes for a great motive for murder."

There was no point second guessing. They'd come here to ask difficult questions and get answers. They both got out of the car and walked quickly to Claudine's building. The snow fluttered down and dusted their shoulders as they hurried inside. Within moments they were standing outside Claudine's apartment. Laurent gave Maggie a reassuring nod before he knocked on the door. From inside, Maggie could hear soft, ethereal music playing. They didn't have to wait long. Claudine answered the door, greeting them both with a serene smile, her long, flowing dress and beaded jewelry in sync with the surroundings of her apartment décor which was an artful reflection of her new age sensibilities. And under all of it was the faint, cloying scent of incense.

"Monsieur Dernier?" Claudine said, looking from Maggie to Laurent in confusion but still keeping a smile on her face.

Maggie stepped inside the apartment without waiting for an invitation.

The living room was a vision of colors and textures. Silk scarves draped over antique furniture and dreamcatchers hung from the ceiling, swaying gently. And yes, crystals were everywhere. They were of various sizes and colors arranged meticulously on the coffee table and the bookshelves.

"*Bonsoir*, Claudine," Laurent said, his tone polite but firm. "We need to talk to you about Antoine."

Maggie turned to see Claudine's smile falter slightly, but she maintained her composure.

"But of course," she said. "Will you come in have some tea?"

Maggie took a deep breath and faced the young woman.

"As you know," she said, "Laurent and I have been looking into Antoine's death. There are so many things that don't add up."

Claudine's eyes flickered with something unreadable, but she gestured for them to sit on the plush, colorful cushions scattered around the living room.

"I'm afraid I fear Antoine had many enemies," she said.

Her hand went to her belly, confirming to Maggie that the girl was likely indeed pregnant.

Laurent walked into the living room but stopped in front of a stuffed rabbit positioned on the bookshelf. It was positioned on its haunches with its ears straight out from its head.

"What is it, Laurent?" Maggie asked.

Laurent turned to Claudine.

"You left one of these on my doorstep a few days ago," he said.

Claudine looked at her hands, her cheek flushing.

"Don't be ridiculous, Monsieur," she said, huffing. "I believe that animals who have passed on to the greater universe can serve as a powerful doorway to deeper spiritual realms. Their energy and spirit linger to provide a... unique...connection to the mysteries we all search for."

"Even when you slit their throat first?" Laurent asked wryly.

Maggie turned to look at Claudine and saw the truth of what she'd done written across her face.

"I don't know what you're talking about," Claudine said hotly.

"I have asked the police to analyze the note you left with

the dead rabbit," Laurent said. "I have no doubt that it will soon be revealed to have been written by you. Threatening someone with death is a felony in France."

Claudine's eyes flitted around the room in a panic.

"It wasn't a threat, Monsieur. It was…I'm honoring the soul of an ancient…"

"Just stop it," Maggie said as she came over to where Claudine stood. "There was no honoring of any souls going on. You were trying to get Laurent to stop investigating Antoine's death."

"But why would I do that?" Claudine asked, her eyes darting from Maggie to Laurent. She bit her lip. "Everyone knows the crime syndicate put a hit out on him."

"Nobody believes that," Maggie said firmly.

"There were too many personal elements involved in Antoine's death for it to be a professional hit," Laurent said. "The way he was assaulted, the fact that he was left in his own freezer… it all points to someone who knew him well and who was not used to killing."

A flash of anxiety crossed Claudine's face, but she quickly regained her composure.

"You cannot possibly think I killed him," she said, her voice level. "Why would I?"

Maggie leaned forward, her voice insistent.

"I wonder when the kitchen staff is questioned if they'll say they heard arguments between you and Antoine."

"They'll never testify," Claudine said, shaking her head.

"If you're counting on them being too afraid of being deported then you don't know the whole story," Maggie said. "They're not illegal immigrants, they are trafficked people. And they'll happily tell what they know—what they overheard—in order to be released from their bondage at L'Étoile Gourmande and reunited with their families."

Claudine's hands trembled as she clutched a crystal pendant around her neck.

"I loved Antoine. I would never hurt him."

Laurent exchanged a quick glance with Maggie.

"Antione was killed in a place only a few people had access to," he said.

"What about Lucas Moreau?" Claudine said quickly. "He hated Antoine!"

"He did," Laurent said. "But I understand he has an iron-clad alibi for the time in question. And before you suggest Remy Durand, so does he."

Claudine began to shake her hands in agitation as she looked around her apartment as if looking for a way out.

"At this moment," Maggie said, "the police are matching your DNA to the DNA found in the freezer where Antoine was killed."

"They'll never!" she said, tears welling in her eyes.

"But they will," Laurent said gently. "They've already gotten a warrant for the hospital to test your blood from your last pregnancy checkup."

Of course this was all lies, Maggie thought as she watched Claudine's face. But it would happen for real soon enough. Claudine collapsed onto the couch, her hands covering her face as her tears started up in earnest.

"I didn't mean for it to happen," she whispered, her voice breaking. "I just wanted to talk to him. But we started arguing and things got out of hand. I... I don't even know how it happened."

Maggie's heart ached as she watched Claudine crumble. She wanted to reach out to the young woman, but she knew she needed to let her talk.

"He was going to leave me," Claudine said. "And the baby! He said he needed something different. I tried to make him see, but he wouldn't listen. It was an accident, I swear."

Maggie knew that the way the killing blow had been delivered it could not possibly have been an accident. An act of passion? Sure. Impulse? Probably. Deliberately done? Without doubt.

"Accident or not," Laurent said, his voice soft but resolute, "Antoine's death needs to be accounted for. We need to hear you say it."

Claudine nodded, tears streaming down her face.

"I did it," she said. "I'm sorry. I was sorry immediately after."

"And Philippe Martin?" he asked.

Claudine looked at him and the devastation was plain on her face.

"What else could I do?" she asked. "He was watching the back of the restaurant when I came out that night. I didn't see him at first, but he sent me a note saying he'd seen me."

"Blackmail?" Maggie asked, although she knew it couldn't possibly be. Not if Martin truly was a police agent.

"I don't know," Claudine said, shaking her head. "I think he just wanted to talk."

"How did you kill him?" Laurent asked.

"I didn't mean to," she said tearfully.

"So how did it happen?" Laurent asked again.

She slumped on the couch, her chin trembling.

"I...I went to his apartment. I think he tried to pretend he didn't understand what I was doing at Antoine's restaurant that night. I didn't know what game he was playing. He wasn't being honest with me! So I...I don't know why I did it."

"What happened?" Laurent pressed.

Maggie gave him a frustrated look.

*Can't we leave this to the police?*

But Laurent wouldn't take no for an answer.

"He went to the kitchen to make tea," she said miserably. "He knew I liked tea. I went with him to help and when he turned his back, I grabbed a knife out of the knife block and stabbed him in the neck. I wiped off the handle and left it on the floor next to him."

Maggie winced at her cold-blooded recitation. Up until this moment, she had been feeling sorry for Claudine. But it was hard to feel that way after hearing how coldly she had dispensed with Philippe Martin.

"You need to come with us, Claudine," Laurent said. "It will look better for you if you give yourself up."

"What difference does that make now?" Claudine said as she picked at the hem of her sleeve, tears rolling down her cheeks. "If you don't tell the cops, they'll never figure it out!"

"We will tell them," Laurent said sternly. "And it matters for the babe you carry. Every minute you can buy yourself out of prison matters for the child's sake."

Claudine touched her belly with both hands and nodded again, her sobs eventually subsiding into quiet whimpers. The weight of her actions and the impending consequences seemed to settle over the room like a heavy fog. Maggie realized as she watched Claudine, her shoulders hunched in defeat, that even though the truth at last had been brought to light, Maggie didn't feel one bit better than when she and Laurent had been clueless as to who killed Antoine—a man who'd caused havoc and anguish every step of his miserable life.

And clearly wasn't finished yet.

## 70

The next morning, Maggie awoke before Laurent. The morning light filtered through the lace curtains of their bedroom, casting a soft glow onto the bed. Maggie watched him sleep on his back with one arm thrown across his face. She was astonished that he still slept. In all their years together, he was always the first one up. Usually, he'd already walked the vineyard and certainly he'd already made coffee. Half the time, the cup was sitting steaming hot on the nightstand waiting for her.

She put a hand on his arm and watched his eyelids flutter open. She knew it was testimony to the intense anxiety he'd been under in the last few days that he could still be so exhausted.

"You are awake," he murmured, and closed his eyes again.

"I am," Maggie said. "But there's no rush. We've got all morning."

"I'm up," he said although he made no move to get up.

Maggie smiled and leaned over and kissed him. It had been a long night at the police station last night when they'd showed up with Claudine in tow. After hearing what Claudine had to say, Detective Rousseau reacted as if France had just won the World Cup and within moments was taking credit not only for apprehending Maggie's three kidnappers—the two men who'd held her captive had been rounded up at a popular bar in town—but also for collaring Antoine Dubois and Phillippe Martin's murderer.

Claudine had been solemn if hardly dry-eyed as she waited to be processed. Maggie had no doubt that the woman would confess fully to everything. Because she'd been the hostess at *L'Étoile Gourmande*, Claudine naturally had access to all parts of the restaurant. She'd waited patiently that night for Laurent and Antoine to finish their lengthy catch-up in Antoine's office, and then, after Laurent left, she followed Antoine into the kitchen where she insisted they talk about her situation.

It quickly became clear to Claudine that Antoine had no intention of accepting responsibility for the baby—regardless of how many paternity tests Claudine might legally require him to take. When he brushed her off and went into the freezer to pull out a tenderloin fillet for the next day's dinner service, Claudine followed him and, in a moment of frustration, picked up the meat hammer on the shelf and slammed it into the back of his head.

Once she'd seen what she'd done, she slipped out of the back-alley door of the restaurant, sure that nobody had seen her. And if it hadn't been for the fact that Philippe Martin had been surveilling the place at that time of morning, she would've been right.

By the time Maggie and Laurent gave their statements of the events on the mountain—all of which was confirmed by Jean and the other members of the mountain rescue group—it was very late. They'd had gotten back to the bed and breakfast in time to collapse exhausted into bed.

Soon enough, Maggie prodded Laurent out of bed and into the shower. She was eager to return home and had already had two phone conversations with Amelie. After dressing quietly and packing, she and Laurent checked out and thanked their gracious hosts for their patience for the odd comings and goings of their stay. Once Laurent put their luggage in the car, he and Maggie walked the short distance to a nearby café, its facade adorned with a wrought iron balcony and blooming geraniums in its many window boxes for their breakfast.

They took seats by the window inside the café, where Maggie watched as the town slowly came to life. From here she could see the Pont Neuf bridge and the Gothic spires of the Basilica of Saint-Sernin. The waitress brought them a classic Continental breakfast: flaky croissants, buttery *pain au chocolat,* and *café au lait.* They ate in comfortable silence, Maggie savoring each bite. A part of her wondered if she would ever take a simple cup of coffee for granted again. But she knew, in time, the relief and wonder would wear off. At one point, Laurent reached across the table to touch her hand. For a moment, she would swear he did it as if to prove to himself she was really there.

Once they'd finished breakfast, they made their way back to the Toulouse police station. After making their formal statements last night, they'd agreed to return this morning to go over them and sign them. The station's cold stone exterior stood in stark contrast to the cozy charm of their breakfast café. Its bustling interior reminded Maggie once more of the horror of what she'd just lived through.

An officer greeted them as they entered the station and led them to a small room where they read over and signed their statements. The room was plain, with a large metal table and two chairs, the walls covered with official notices and maps. Maggie was surprised not to see Detective Rousseau this morning, but she imagined she had been up late the night before getting all the details from Claudine for both Antoine and Philippe Martin's deaths.

As soon as Maggie and Laurent had handed the signed documents back to the officer, they exchanged a look of mutual relief. Was it truly over? And all the loose ends really tied up? As they left, the officer at the front desk cheerily encouraged them to come to Toulouse in the springtime for the next big culinary festival called *Toulouse á Table*. Maggie gripped Laurent's hand tightly in lieu of answering.

Once out on the street, Laurent pulled out his phone and called Antoine's son, Marco, who answered immediately.

"I'm in Toulouse," Marco said. "Where are you? Can you meet me at the restaurant?"

No need to ask which restaurant.

"We are near," Laurent said. "See you in five minutes."

Maggie frowned. "Who was—?"

"Marco," Laurent said. "He is in town."

They turned and headed down the street toward the main square which they crossed. There in front of *L'Étoile Gourmande* was a young man in a tailored suit and sunglasses. He wore his dark hair short. He recognized them immediately and walked over to greet them, shaking Laurent's hand first and then Maggie's.

"I feel like a handshake is lame compared to what I owe you," Marco said.

Laurent felt a stirring of emotion at the sight of the young man. Marco was the spitting image of his father at this age. He looked exactly like the friend whom Laurent had spent so many years with.

"I am surprised to see you here," Laurent said.

"I didn't plan on coming. But I know Papa would want to be buried in France. I felt I had to be here. Thank you for finding out what happened to him."

"So you know?" Maggie couldn't help but ask.

It was surprising to her that Rousseau—so slack in every other respect—had already contacted next of kin to apprise them that the case was solved. On the other hand, she imagined the detective had been eager to take her victory lap.

"You mean that he was killed by a jealous girlfriend?" Marco said. "Yeah. The detective told me. I guess in a way, the old man would've preferred to go out that way, you know?"

Maggie glanced at Laurent. It wasn't the whole truth, but it was close enough to give a grieving son closure over the loss of his father.

"You know you have a half sibling that will be born soon?" Laurent asked.

Maggie couldn't help but smile. There was no way Laurent was going to let that fact go by. He was not going to let the baby enter the world with no family at all. Not if he could help it. Frankly, Maggie was a little surprised he didn't have plans for *them* to adopt the baby.

"I do," Marco said. "I'm not married myself, but I already told the detective that I'll use my inheritance to help raise the kid for as long as Claudine is...you know, in prison."

Maggie was so touched by Marco's statement that she felt tears stinging her eyes.

"I mean to talk to her, too," Marco said. "And let her know she's not alone."

Maggie wouldn't be surprised if Marco didn't actually

help fund Claudine's defense. And why not? Antoine was a scoundrel and past helping. But the people he'd hurt and left behind—Claudine, Marco and the unborn baby—they might still have a decent life in spite of him.

"Are you having lunch here today?" Laurent asked as he indicated the front of *L'Étoile Gourmande*.

Marco turned to look at the restaurant with its gaily striped awning and picturesque dormer windows.

"I was thinking about it," he said. "But it's closed for some reason."

Maggie knew that the reason *L'Étoile Gourmande* was closed—along with half a dozen other restaurants in Toulouse, including Remy Durand's *Café du Midi*—was due to the information she'd given to the counterterrorism agents last night about the human trafficking ring she'd discovered in the cabin in the mountains. She prayed that the poor people caught up in that would be aided in finding a new life, but she was relatively sure it wouldn't be in France. As far as punishing the guilty party, that was out of her hands. If Rousseau really was in the pocket of Chevalier's crime syndicate, she would likely work to mitigate his culpability. Maggie was under no illusion that human trafficking would cease to exist in the area. It would simply go on hiatus until all the attention died down.

"Besides," Marco said. "I already know from all the online press that it's a great place to eat. And I know my father loved it more than any of the people in his life."

Maggie was surprised to hear how self-aware Marco was. He knew the score but somehow without all the debilitating bitterness that often came with it. She didn't know who raised this young man, but whoever it was had done a commendable job.

"I guess I just wanted to see it," he said.

He held out his hand again to shake with both of them and to thank them again for everything they'd done to help him learn the truth about what had happened and to move on from there. After that, he turned and walked on down the sidewalk.

"Ready to go home?" Maggie asked.

Laurent turned to her and slipped his arm around her waist.

"*Bien sûr, chérie,*" he said. "*Toujours.*"

## 71

The early autumn evening wrapped itself around Domaine St-Buvard, the crisp air carrying with it the faint scent of fallen leaves and woodsmoke. Laurent had set up a fire pit in the back garden which now sent sparks dancing into the twilight. The flames cast a golden glow over the gathering, creating a circle of warmth amidst the encroaching chill of the night. Grace, Amelie, Philippe, Danielle, and Maggie, all bundled in soft blankets, sat comfortably around the fire pit in a collection of mismatched rockers, woven chairs and Adirondack chairs,.

Grace leaned back, her face illuminated by the flickering flames, a contented smile spread across her lips as she cradled a steaming mug of Laurent's famous hot cider. Amelie sat cross-legged on a large, plush cushion beside Philippe, both toasting marshmallows on long sticks with the three dogs stood eagerly nearby in hope of any fallen morsels. The sweet smell of melting sugar mingled with the smoky aroma of the fire.

Maggie had already filled Grace and Danielle in on the details of her experience in the Pyrenees and would say no more about it while the children were nearby. She looked up as Laurent came in from the house, his form silhouetted in the French doors, his hands holding two more mugs of cider. The bruises on his face had faded but he still wore a splint on one of his broken fingers. She caught his eye and although he smiled at her, as usual, it was difficult to determine his exact mood or thoughts.

"So tell us about Monsieur Beaumont," Danielle said, leaning toward the fire, her thin shoulders covered in a thick cardigan.

Maggie knew that Philippe and Amelie would not strain to hear details about a politician and sure enough, the two children began giggling and talking between themselves.

"He's being held in detention in Toulouse for arraignment," Maggie said, her eye on Amelie just in case she became interested.

"He really idnapped-kay you?" Grace said.

Philippe and Amelie both turned to look at her.

"I think even in Pig Latin," Laurent said, "that is clearly understandable."

Grace laughed.

"Well, what else can I use? Both our kids are bilingual. I can hardly speak French over their heads."

"I know what that means, Mami!" Amelie crowed to Maggie. "Aunt Grace said *kidnapped!*"

"Clever girl," Laurent said to her. "Reward yourself by going in and getting more napkins."

Amelie jumped up and ran toward the house.

"Only Laurent can convince Amelie that a chore is some kind of reward," Maggie said.

"Back to the kidnapping," Danielle said. "Quickly, while Amelie is gone. How did the politician think kidnapping Maggie would persuade Laurent?"

Laurent snorted as if he too was bewildered by the man's logic.

"Well, he was desperate," Maggie said. "And he truly believed he had the power to pull it off."

"Delusional," Grace said.

"Completely," Maggie said.

It had been three weeks since Beaumont had been charged with kidnapping and attempted murder and since then the barrier to the influx of undocumented migrants in their area seemed to have abated. For now. Like so many other places in France and around the world, there was no easy or long-lasting answer to the problem of terrified people running from war-torn homelands. Even so, Maggie had encouraged Laurent to take the whole situation as a warning and so he was in the process of taking steps through legal assistance and reaching out to the community for the support he needed to ensure the continued existence of the mini-houses as well as the work that the monks at *l'Abbaye de Sainte-Trinité* were doing as well.

Laurent sat beside Maggie, his arm draped casually around her shoulders. The two of them exchanged quiet smiles, their connection palpable even in silence. He leaned forward to poke at the fire with a long stick, sending a shower of sparks skyward as Amelie came running back to the group. Above them, the sky deepened from twilight to a star-speckled canvas, the cool breeze rustling the leaves of the nearby trees. In this moment, it occurred to Maggie that, surrounded by friends and loved ones, the fire pit was more than just a source of warmth; it was the heart of their gathering, a beacon of togetherness in the crisp autumn air.

Later that evening after Amelie was in bed and their guests had left, Laurent let the dogs out one last time and came back into the house to help Maggie with the dishes.

She could tell that something had been on his mind all evening and she'd argued with herself on and off about asking him. As usual, she'd hoped he would come to her in his own time. Aside from that, she had something she wanted to talk with him about, too.

"I was wrong about Antoine," Laurent finally said as he sat at the kitchen bar.

"In what way?" Maggie asked as she wiped down the counter.

"I think," Laurent said, "that because we were so close when we worked the Côte d'Azur, when we went our separate ways, I thought he would leave behind the life we had shared."

"The criminal life, you mean," Maggie said. "Like you did."

Laurent smiled.

"Yes, *chérie*. Like I did. And when I heard that he'd become a famous chef with a world-famous *brasserie*, of course I believed that we had both, miraculously, turned away from the deeds of our past and created new lives. We were both miracles."

Maggie knew exactly what Laurent meant. For him, that life of fleecing tourists had been more like a stage in his life or even a perversion of his natural personality. It was the result of having fallen in with a certain crowd—Maggie instantly thought of Roger Bentley—and wanting the easy money. That, combined with Roger's avuncular manner and sense of adventure had given Laurent something he'd never had before: acceptance and fatherly affection. But when the opportunity came for him to turn away from that life and explore a different way to live, Laurent had done it, if not easily—because Maggie still remembered several minor incidents in their time together—then at least eventually.

Now Laurent was realizing that he'd been assuming that that time had been an anomaly for Antoine too. And it had instead been a natural byproduct of who the man was: opportunistic and soulless.

"He was a good friend for the time you were together," Maggie offered weakly.

Laurent turned to her and smiled.

"He wasn't the man I thought he was," he said.

"Well, he wasn't you," Maggie said. "He definitely wasn't you."

"You always make me sound omnipotent," he said. "After all these years? After all I've done?"

"Must be something to it, then," she said with a shrug.

He got up from the counter and pulled her into his arms and kissed her.

"It isn't me, *chérie*," he said. "It's you."

"Oh, silly," Maggie said, blushing as she felt Laurent's arms tighten.

"It's true," he said. "I am the man I am because of you."

After that, he kissed her deeply and Maggie felt that special moment when her worries and trials all seemed to melt away. When he pulled back and looked into her eyes, he smiled.

"Oh, by the way," he said as he nuzzled her neck, "I should warn you that you might be getting a call from Roger Bedard."

## 72

The sun had long set over the fields of grapes when Laurent and Maggie finally found their bed. Laurent took his habitual night shower while Maggie moisturized her elbows and knees. She checked her phone to see if there were any messages from any of the children. They were all on US time and often forgot and called in the middle of the night or just much later than Maggie usually stayed up. There was nothing.

It had been a wonderful evening with loving friends and to Maggie it felt like an underscoring of all the good things she had to be grateful for in her life. Especially after her ordeal in the mountains. When Laurent came out of the shower, toweling his hair dry and pulling on boxers and a tee—his usual sleepwear—Maggie knew she needed to break her longstanding rule of trying to wait him out. If she knew her husband, he would keep his worries and self-doubts to himself until he solved what they both knew was essentially an unsolvable dilemma. It was time for Maggie to speak.

"I think Philippe is old enough now to help you start the pruning in the vineyard," she said.

Laurent looked at her with surprise. In all the years they'd been together she had never yet remotely suggested anything having to do with the vineyard.

"He needs a project," she said diplomatically, attempting to make it sound as if it was for Philippe's sake. "Grace would appreciate it."

"What is going on, *chérie*?" Laurent said as he got into bed.

"Don't you have pruning you do this time of year?" she asked. "Or what about that root protection thing you do?"

"Maggie?" Laurent asked, raising a cocked eyebrow and clearly not about to be manipulated.

"Can I ask you what was wrong with this year's harvest?" Maggie asked. "And please don't tell me we got record yields or bigger grapes or some such thing. If you make me explain what I mean, I'll be cross."

Laurent looked at her for a moment as if making up his mind and then he sighed and turned and leaned against the pillow.

"I don't know what was wrong with it," he replied.

"Only that something was," Maggie said.

He shrugged helplessly.

"I find myself caring....less than I did," he said.

That surprised Maggie. Laurent had always been so proud of the awards and accolades for the high-quality wine he produced year after year.

"And more about...?" she prompted.

"*Je ne sais pas*," he said. *I don't know.*

"I don't believe that."

He ran a hand over his face.

"I suppose, I care more about the people who need the work," he said.

Maggie's eyes widened although she'd been halfway to believing this was the problem even before he said it. But now, she saw another opening she hadn't seen before. An opening that made Beaumont's tirade against him all the more galling. And for Laurent, all the more revealing.

"You spent more time focusing on making sure your pickers were taken care of," Maggie ventured, "than you did pruning and watering the grapes."

He didn't answer.

"And yet you are still unhappy," she said.

He turned to look at her.

"My passion for Domaine St-Buvard is inviolate," he said. "And my commitment to produce the best wine I can."

"Nobody is suggesting otherwise," Maggie said. "Only that it's possibly not enough anymore."

He looked at her for a moment as if making up his mind about something and then he nodded. It was just as Maggie had guessed. Laurent's passion for winemaking was still there, but it wasn't enough to fulfill him anymore. He longed for something more, something beyond the vines and bottles. She had seen the changes in him over the last few harvests. He used to pour his heart and soul into the wine he produced, taking great pride in every single bottle. But now, his focus had shifted.

"Why does it upset you?" Maggie asked. "We all change. It's what makes life interesting."

Laurent snorted. "So American."

"And proud of it," Maggie said pointedly. "You could take a few tips from us."

Laurent rearranged his pillow and then turned toward her in bed.

"What is on your mind, *cherie*?" he asked.

"Always you, dearest," Maggie said. "Did you ever think that maybe you might be interested in politics?"

Laurent groaned and turned away.

"I didn't notice you had drunk so much tonight," he said.

"I'm not drunk," Maggie said wryly. "I'm fishing."

"Fishing?" Laurent said with a frown. "Another American idiom?"

"I'm pretty sure the French have one just like it. By the way, I talked to Luc today."

Laurent had been looking at the book he'd picked up from his bedside table but now he turned to look at Maggie.

"You never mentioned he called," he said.

"No, because *I* called *him*. We had a long talk."

"All is well?" Laurent asked with a frown.

"All is wonderful. I asked him when he was coming home."

"Thanksgiving, yes?"

"Yep," Maggie said. "Not to complicate things, especially if you're about to go into local politics—"

"Maggie…" Laurent said wagging a forefinger at her.

"But he said he and Charlotte are wrapping up their lives in Napa so that they can come home …for good."

Maggie watched the transformation in Laurent's face. His eyes widened and a smile spread across his face.

"Luc is coming back to run the vineyard?" he asked, almost breathlessly—as if barely daring to hope that Maggie might say yes.

"He is, my darling," Maggie said as she kissed him on the cheek. "But not just to run the vineyard. He and Charlotte seem to think Domaine St-Buvard would be the perfect place for their baby to grow up."

∽

To follow more of Maggie's adventures and sleuthing be sure and check out *Murder in Metz, Book 26 of the Maggie Newberry Mysteries.*

## LAURENT'S RECIPE FOR RACLETTE

Raclette is a winter dish often found in most brasseries in the French Alps. The dish originated in the Middle Ages when cow herders would carry into the pastures cheese which they would then warm by the campfire at night and scrape onto bread.

The word "raclette" comes from the French verb "racler" which means "to scrape" and the cheese is named after the way it is served.

Laurent makes his raclette in the traditional manner by heating the cheese until bubbling on a special kind of grill and then scraping it onto small potatoes served with charcuterie or cold cuts, along with condiments such as cornichons and pickled onions.

Note that you don't have to purchase a raclette grill to enjoy this cozy Alpine meal, since slices of raclette cheese can be simply heated on a griddle. This recipe serves 4.

You'll need:
- 1.5 lbs of raclette cheese
- 20 small, firm new potatoes—skin on

- A selection of *charcuterie*, at least 3 thin slices per person: your choice of parma ham or prosciutto, salami, bresaola or other local cured meats

Be sure to prepare all foods before frying the raclette cheese!

1. Boil the potatoes with skins on. Serve in a bowl on the table.

2. Fry thinly sliced cheese for 1 to 2 minutes on a non-stick griddle until the cheese bubbles and creates air pockets. Serve over potatoes on everyone's plates.

3. Serve with a green salad and plenty of crusty bread along with cornichons and pickled onions

*Bon Appetit!*

# ABOUT THE AUTHOR

*USA TODAY* Bestselling Author Susan Kiernan-Lewis is the author of *The Maggie Newberry Mysteries,* the post-apocalyptic thriller series *The Irish End Games, The Mia Kazmaroff Mysteries, The Stranded in Provence Mysteries, The Claire Baskerville Mysteries,* and *The Savannah Time Travel Mysteries.*

Visit www.susankiernanlewis.com or follow Author Susan Kiernan-Lewis on Facebook.

Printed in Great Britain
by Amazon